MASERATI

A LOVE WORTH FINDING

I0618141

TSHEPISO MADIHLABA

First Published 2024 by Tshepiso Madihlaba
Copyright © 2024 Tshepiso Madihlaba

ISBN 978-0-7961-0683-4 (Print)
ISBN 978-0-7961-0684-1 (eBook)

Cover and interior crafted with love by the team at
www.myebook.online

Acknowledgements

This book is dedicated to family, friends and everyone who has encouraged me not only to keep writing, but to share my stories with the world.

A special thanks goes to my two children, who have been and continue to be my greatest teachers in life – they serve as mirrors, reflecting my strengths and shortcomings. As I encourage them to explore their full potential, I am equally called to explore my passions to the fullest.

To my late mother, Sanita Madihlaba, I hope I continue to make you proud.

Chapter One

Maserati had been standing in front of the mirror for what seemed like eternity, straightening the creases on her skirt for the umpteenth time. Slowly and meticulously applying the MAC matte red lipstick, she examined the results with uncertainty. The results looked so clichéd; she quickly wiped it off and settled for the natural lip balm.

'Perfect, Maserati!'

She preferred her face with no or very little make-up. It reminded her of her grandmother's natural beauty.

I can't believe I am actually going through with this, Maserati thought, still standing in front of the mirror, preparing to go out shopping for the first time in almost a year. She seemed to have gained her former glow back. She instinctively touched her cheeks as if to feel the warmth of the glow. She mastered a sheepish smile, and then an even bigger one.

It had been almost a year since that fateful day when her life had come tumbling down – when she discovered that the love of her life, her fiancé, and the man she was intending to spend the rest of her life with had betrayed her.

Tshepo…

Her mind wandered to that moment, and she could see it as

clear as day. Tshepo embracing another woman. And learning there had been many more, and the realisation that she had not known this man as she thought she did.

She recalled the hell she had gone through in the last few months. The pain was deep and unbearable, and for the first time she understood why they called it a heartbreak. She had felt her heart break into a million little pieces and for the longest time felt like it would never heal.

But now, here she was, almost a year later and that sad feeling that used to envelope her heart and thoughts was all but gone. All Maserati felt was a sense of anticipation for what lay ahead. Her new life without that... that man! She finished getting dressed and left for Hyde Park Mall, home to some of the most high-end fashion retailers in Africa.

The day was so bright, the leaves seemed greener than she had seen in a while, and birds were chirping away, melodies so sweet. It was a beautiful day.

She walked with a renewed sense of confidence. The first shop she entered was her favourite shoe shop. The smell and sight of beautiful shoes was enough to bring a warm glow to her face.

Maserati hated most shopping and did not find it therapeutic at all like many other people did. But boy oh boy, her shoe-finding excursions were always such guilt-free, heart-flutter-inducing occasions.

Shoes and books were her easiest purchase without a doubt.

Maserati always deceived herself into thinking that her love for shoes had reached a peak, at least that was the pep talk she tried to give herself on a weekly basis. But nothing ever prepared her for the rush and tingle she felt in a shoe haven.

Her business trips took her to some of the most exotic cities in the world: Paris, Barcelona, Milan, New York and Dubai. And there were always several pairs of shoes by Zanotti, Buscemi or Louboutin that had her name on them. But of course, she was a sensible girl and knew where to draw the line.

Well, if she could find a marker she would certainly draw the line.

This was the reason God would probably never let Maserati win the lottery.

Every time she made her way to the mall, Maserati said a little prayer.

'God grant me inner strength, self-restraint, and the serenity to know that a pair of those Zanottis is a down-payment for my retirement and school fees for my future babies. Grant me the strength to not be seduced by the whispers of the latest spring collection, the strength to go past my favourite shoe shops and to ignore the sales lady that tells me my legs look sexy in those killer slingbacks. She is doing the devil's work. I pray this knowing that I'm only human with a weakness for these works of art. Amen.'

'Why do you love shoes so much, Maserati?' her mom constantly asked every time she visited her daughter's home and was amazed at her walk-in shoe closet that resembled a mini showroom.

'Mama, stop investigating my shoe closet and asking me such rhetorical questions.'

But seriously though, why do we women love shoes so much? This certainly was not a rhetorical question. This question begged and deserved investigation by Harvard-educated researchers.

For most women, this love of shoes does not extend to any old form. When women say they love shoes, they actually mean they love high-heeled shoes. Skyscrapers heels; ankle, knee, and lower back arthritis-inducing high heels that required one to keep their chiropractor's number on speed dial. Women speak in inches when they meet their heart flutter-inducing pair.

Maserati did not even recall when she started her love affair with shoes.

She always said, 'I must have been born with it.'

It did not help matters that she and her best friend, Mantwa shared this common affliction. Shopping with Mantwa was inviting trouble from a mile away.

For a scientist like Maserati, empiric evidence always strengthened an argument. And so, she spent many hours looking for the evidence she needed to put a stop to being interrogated for her love of shoes. And of course, the internet is a willing participant in providing proof for anything under the sun.

Maserati was chuffed to find credible evidence in the form of research conducted to investigate the motivation for women wearing high heels. Men and women alike found women in heels more attractive, more confident, and sexier compared to those in flats.

This evidence was enough for Maserati and Mantwa to take their case to the highest court in the land and be exonerated of their shoe-loving crime. Who can argue with clear evidence that showed, unequivocally, that there was no such thing as an excessive love of shoes?

Case closed.

Maserati tried various styles of shoes, prancing around the shop, checking her silhouette in the mirror. She had forgotten how much fun shoe shopping was.

'You should take the black pumps,' a deep velvet voice said from behind. Maserati did not need to turn around. She could see in the mirror who the voice belonged to.

Tall, caramel and handsome with beautiful brown eyes. What a warm inviting stare, Maserati thought, surprised at her reaction. She smiled sheepishly. And blushed profusely.

'I'm Ben,' the velvety voice said, extending his arm for a handshake.

'Maserati.'

'My favourite car in the world. Classy. Elegant. I see the resemblance.'

This could have been a déjà vu moment, but Ben's beautiful brown eyes reassured her otherwise.

'You'd make any shoe in this store look good, but you should definitely consider taking those. They are absolutely gorgeous on you.' He did not back away from the recommendation.

Was he flirting? Maserati couldn't tell – she felt like she'd lost touch with the dating scene.

Come to think of it, she hardly had any dating experience given that Tshepo was her first serious long-term relationship. Unless you counted one high school sweetheart and two boyfriends and a fling at university before Tshepo as experience!

She certainly was short on the boyfriend quota if the current dating trends were to be believed. You apparently haven't lived until you've had a couple of heartbreaks and left a trail of broken hearts along the way, as well. Nowadays, people can see each other for months or years and still consider themselves as just passing time, despite throwing in endearments like 'My Person' in the mix, causing a great deal of confusion for all involved. The dating scene is a minefield.

'You seem to be unsure of which pair to take. The black looks good on you. But then again, so does the red. In fact, I doubt there's any shoe in this store that would not look good on you.'

Classic flirting 101. Even a nun would not have missed that one!

'Thank you. I'm just browsing.' Such lies, Maserati. She felt her nose grow inches. Pinocchio.

'Sure you are.' He smiled. 'Well, enjoy the rest of your shopping, I mean, browsing, Maserati.'

And off he went. With each step he merged further into the crowd, disappearing, taking with him this glorious moment like it didn't just happen.

Wow! So, they don't even ask for your number these days? Maserati thought, baffled that the guy who was seemingly hitting on her mere seconds ago, had just left with not so much as a request for her number or an invitation for coffee – the ultimate code word for other activities unrelated to drinking coffee.

Oh, girl. You must have lost your mojo, she thought. *Good thing your shoe mojo is still alive.*

Letting out a hearty laugh, she continued trying on more shoes, and left with four pairs, including the black and red pumps that Ben had recommended.

She couldn't forget those brown eyes though.

Chapter Two

One year earlier…

Maserati had been walking on cloud nine ever since Tshepo, her university sweetheart, proposed on her birthday while they were on a romantic getaway in Barcelona, Spain. Sure, they had discussed a future together, but still the proposal came as a complete, beautiful surprise. Her heart was almost bursting at the seams with the joy and love she felt at the thought of finally becoming Mrs Tshepo Mabilo. Maserati Mabilo… or perhaps double-barrelled – Maserati Mojapelo-Mabilo.

She scribbled and practiced her new name all day at work.

Listening to Metro FM on Sundays or Tbose's shows on Kaya FM suddenly took on a whole new meaning. It was as if each playlist was a personal love letter from her sweetheart. She listened to the romantic music and was always humming the tunes.

Her best friends, Mantwa and Khutso called her nauseatingly happy.

'Dear, we get it. You are going to be Mrs Mabilo,' Mantwa would tease her friend.

'Oh my gosh, I am so happy. Tshepo is the most kind-hearted, caring, and considerate human being I have ever known. He treats me like a queen, and we'll be together for the rest of our lives.' Maserati could not believe her luck in finding her soulmate.

Maserati and Tshepo had met while in their last year of university. She was in her final year of medical school, close to becoming a doctor and he was completing his Master's degree in Business Administration. A chance meeting at the library on a cold Saturday morning five years ago was the beginning of their whirlwind romance. She had been at the library researching for her assignment and she and Tshepo were the last to leave. They bumped into each other at the door. Tshepo was so charming, a true gentleman as he held the door open for her, smiling a big, warm, welcoming smile.

'Hi, my name is Tshepo. And you are?'

'Maserati,' she replied.

'Like the car? They don't come any classier, just like you!'

Maserati giggled and blushed at the comparison.

'So, what brings you to the library on such a cold Saturday morning when everyone is sleeping late today?' His voice had such gentleness, a sweetness she hadn't expected. As she answered he listened attentively, never taking his eyes off her face.

'I know a quaint little Tapas restaurant around the corner, the food is absolutely amazing. It's like my own little piece of Spain. Care to join me? I would be honoured if you could.' That smile again.

Maserati couldn't resist and agreed to join him.

As they walked to the restaurant, he offered his jacket as it was getting quite chilly. *Chivalry is not dead*, Maserati thought. They found a cosy corner table next to the fireplace. Maserati was amazed at how easily their conversation flowed. Tshepo was confident with a great sense of humour. They spoke about everything from their childhoods to their dreams for the future, their ideas so similar, so aligned. They hadn't noticed time passing by; it was as if the clock had stopped, and it was just the two of them in the entire world.

They became inseparable after that.

And then the worst happened.

She and Tshepo had been planning a small intimate celebratory dinner for their engagement with a few close friends. Everything seemed to be going wrong that fateful day. She should have known it would end in disaster.

First she broke a sentimental vase she had received from her future mother-in-law, and it was cold, rainy, and gloomy, ruining the prospects of hosting the dinner outdoors by the pool area. Tshepo had texted her letting her know he would be a few minutes late but in time to help set up for their guests. She still had a few last-minute grocery items to pick up before she headed home, but her local liquor store did not have their favourite bubbly.

Maserati drove frantically to a neighbouring shopping centre. As she looked for a convenient parking spot, her eyes caught a familiar sight – that warm welcoming smile. *I know that smile*, she thought. *But why is my Tshepo holding and kissing another woman?*

Confused and dazed, she found a parking spot, her chest heaving and tight from anxious anticipation. She approached the familiar figure. Tshepo hadn't noticed Maserati park and walk towards him and was still in an embrace with someone else.

'Tshepo?' her voice whispered, betraying her emotion.

'Tshepo!' she repeated.

Tshepo, startled, pushed the woman away from him. 'It's not what it looks like, baby.'

Everything that happened afterwards was a blur.

Chapter Three

It felt good to be at her favourite café in 4th Avenue, Parkhurst, Johannesburg, after months of not visiting, while surviving the debacle that was… that idiot Tshepo.

Maserati Mojapelo loved the solitude of frequenting coffee shops and cafés with a good book. While she enjoyed lively company, it was these solitary excursions that revived her spirits. Her love for coffee shops was not inspired by any sort of ambition or delusion of being a coffee connoisseur. Whether her coffee was of the arabica or robusta variety did not matter much, as long as it made good cappuccino, good *hot* cappuccino to be precise.

Maserati loved the ambience found at many coffee shops, whether it was the popular franchises or the quaint little no-name ones. Her love affair with coffee shops began while she was still studying Medicine at the University of Cape Town. She had discovered a quaint little place in Observatory, where she visited most Friday afternoons, to just curl up on their cosy couches with a book in hand.

The coffee shop owner was a delightful old English lady, who served her endless cuppas or hot ham and pea soup on those chilly Cape Town days. It was heaven. She introduced her friend

Tebogo to this place, and occasionally they would both go, each with a good book in hand and just get lost in the magical world of the written word.

Gradually the lone coffee shop escapades became not just about reading or catching up on her work reports, while sipping hot caffeinated beverages, but also more about watching people go about their day. Aah, people-watching, such a favourite pastime. You need not be a behaviourist nor a social scientist to be fascinated by people going about their days, wondering what their lives are all about, what makes them tick, and what challenges they are currently facing and yet are able to put on a brave face and interact with the world. Interactions between people, and between people and their environments are fascinating to observe.

Maserati found people-watching such a meditative experience. She found it had a calming and almost spiritual effect on her. Tebogo once asked her about these lone coffee shop escapades and she said, 'I guess it's the subconscious realisation that we are all human, going through similar situations and experiences and trying our best to navigate life. While our private lives may be filled with joyous experiences mixed with unimaginable turmoil, we put on our public facade and navigate the world. It leaves me feeling grateful for my life, that I am alive, drawing breath and able to appreciate the beauty of life and its complexities.'

The distant intrusion and assumptions about strangers' lives was a meditative experience because it was always an opportunity for some reflective solitude. Maserati felt that it softly forced her to go internally, to review her life and be one with the Universe.

Maserati chuckled to herself every time she went all philosophical on reasons to drink coffee. But Maserati loved to marvel at the lady pushing a trolley full of groceries, the couple holding hands and in love, or the couple having a passive-aggressive interaction. She smiled internally at the teens and twenty-something-year olds walking with confidence, despite their limited life experiences. The busyness of all the people criss-crossing before her reminded her that behind each and every one of these strangers before her, was the One who created them. What secret did each individual hold? What was God's purpose for all of them? Had they realised that purpose? Were they unfolding into that purpose?

At the end of each visit to a coffee shop, she left with a renewed sense of optimism, hope and gratitude for life. And those were the benefits of being this lone coffee shop observer, observing life through the movements of God's beautiful people.

She loved Parkhurst. The suburb was quaint, with narrow streets lined with lush trees providing a small town, but lively, ambience. Fourth Avenue in particular, was lined with many bustling sidewalk cafés, filled with an eclectic mix of young and old, hip and trendy; the arty-farty types and all types in between. It reminded her of Paris sidewalk cafés. For a Johannesburg suburb, it was worlds apart from the mall-ridden northern suburbs of the city and provided the perfect escape from the fast pace of the city.

Today it felt even more welcoming than her past visits.

Lovemore, her regular waiter had managed to find her a central table on the sidewalk, giving her a perfect view of the bustling avenue where she could engage in her favourite pastime of people-watching. Bliss!

'You look well,' said Lovemore, handing her the menu. 'I haven't seen you here in a while.' He hoped he wasn't being intrusive. His tip depended on his being a great waiter, knowing when to offer commentary and when to be discreet.

'I've been hibernating,' she smiled. She had become a bit fond of Lovemore. Had it been another waiter, she would have given him that icy, dismissive look that had earned her the nickname of 'Diva' by her friends.

'Well, you chose the perfect day to come out of hibernation. Anything to drink? Or the usual?'

'I am afraid my hibernation has not done away with my predictability. The usual, yes. Exactly how I like it. You haven't forgotten, right?'

Lovemore chuckled. 'Boiling hot cappuccino coming up.'

'Absolutely.'

With that, Lovemore disappeared inside the café to get her order.

Maserati preferred her cappuccino boiling hot. No, make that scalding hot! She felt there should be the risk of landing in the burns intensive care unit at the local hospital when she took the first sip of her cappuccino. How was that being a demanding difficult customer? If one was going to spend three hours at their favourite coffee shop reading a riveting best-seller, one should not be inconvenienced by coffee going cold in the middle of a fascinating storyline. Thrillers are best served hot! The general guidelines for making cappuccino may suggest the ideal milk temperature to be between 60 and 70 °C, a whole 40 °C below boiling point, but who in their right mind drinks lukewarm coffee anyway? Shouldn't one just rather order a can of Coke, if one is interested in a cold dose of caffeine?

At one of her neighbourhood mall coffee shops she frequented, this order of a scalding hot cappuccino was first received with some confusion.

Maserati just could not understand the confusion around her request for a boiling hot cappuccino with an aggressive steam coming from the cup. This order was met mid-sentence, by frozen looks from the waiters, trying hard to decipher her description.

'Excuse me, Ma'am?'

'Yes, you heard correctly,' Maserati retorted.

Needless to say, many an order never met her standard and was always returned. On several occasions, the intervention of the shop manager was necessary.

'Ma'am, there seems to be some confusion with your order. We have flat white cappuccino, double espresso cappuccino, caffè latte… Umm, we do not have the one you want on the menu. Did you want any of the ones I listed?'

Now she was the one with the frozen look.

Really? Who needs a Harvard degree to know what boiling temperature is?

I should purchase a thermometer to help them out, she thought, rolling her eyes with irritation.

Then one day a miracle happened. A young enthusiastic waiter took Maserati's 'strange' order like a champion. And ten minutes later she saw a sight to behold, her waiter carefully walking towards her, with a steadiness and precision surpassing even the most skilled neurosurgeon, balancing the tray that held the cup with her cappuccino, the steam from the cup flowing merrily above. This was a big moment. She could have done a triple cartwheel right there in the middle of the coffee shop! This waiter was a clear example of an employee with initiative. Or maybe it was the barista. This was an important milestone that needed acknowledgement. Maserati had wasted no time in calling the manager to commend their first successful delivery of her order and the waiter was handsomely rewarded with a generous tip.

But these successes did not usually last. One day, she was tricked. Her order came through. At first glance it had the right appearance – steam was flowing from the cup. But these trying-to-be-clever waiters had only steamed the cup; it was so hot that a sip left the top layers of the epidermis from her lips on the rim. But alas, the coffee was lukewarm!

Jesus Christ! she murmured under her breath, followed by many other expletives unbefitting a good girl such as herself.

What was so difficult about making a HOT beverage!

Chapter Four

'Hello my lovies. How are you? What ya'll doing on such a blissful Saturday? Guess where I am?' Maserati sent a text to her friends on their WhatsApp group.

Khutso was the first to respond. 'Hi dear. Obviously, Parkhurst. The excitement in your text gives it away. LOL. I'm glad you're out and about.'

Mantwa's reply came shortly afterwards. 'Ah, dear! You did not tell me you were going out; I would have come with. Are you at Rockets? I could do with some serious cocktails and music.' Mantwa was always up for fun. She and Maserati shared a common love for all kinds of dining experiences. Shoes and dining were big items in their monthly budgets. The women regularly met up at Rockets, the trendy restaurant on 4th Avenue known for its similarly trendy crowd and a vibrant buzzy atmosphere.

'No dear. I am at Café Bean having a solo escapade. It is a good day for meditation.'

Khuto's message pinged next. 'I love your profile picture. You are glowing, dear. It is so good to see you look so happy. I missed that sparkle in your eyes.'

Maserati's WhatsApp profile picture was a selfie she had

taken a few days ago. She had felt radiant and happy. Of course, a little filter always added some oomph to selfies, but her radiance was clearly obvious.

Signs of a girl at peace, Maserati thought, as she took another glance at the picture.

'Thank you dear, I feel alive.'

'Hello stranger.'

His voice and presence were commanding.

It suddenly felt like a dark cloud was hovering above, threatening to spoil this beautiful day. Maserati had been dreading this inevitable moment for months. As vast as the city of Johannesburg felt, it was equally such a small world. She was bound to run into him at some point. They had loved the same spots in any case. She was just not expecting to run into him so soon. Oh well, so much for feeling alive.

She raised her eyes from her phone screen, to meet his. Gosh, those eyes. My God, those piercing eyes.

She appraised him quickly.

Damn, he looked good – as if he'd stepped straight from the pages of GQ magazine. Some people were truly in the front line when God dished out good looks and charm. He had it all, in abundance. And he knew it! Today was no different. Casual and yet so elegant in Tom Ford jeans and a white shirt, unbuttoned to just below his collarbone, exposing just the right amount of a ripped chest. Tshepo was not blessed with height but he made up for it with his toned muscles and excellent dress sense. Giuseppe Zanotti white sneakers completed the look. Even under the cover of the jeans, you could not miss his Denzel Washington-esque bowed legs, thanks to his soccer-playing days. The man was yummy…

'Mabi……uhm, Tshepo,' she tripped over his name, as she almost blurted 'Mabilo.' She had endearingly called him by his surname throughout their relationship. He had always loved it. It was a sign of her love for him but mostly, for Tshepo, it signified respect. He had loved that about her.

'What are you doing here?' She scolded herself mentally as soon as the words left her mouth. *What a ridiculous question to ask!* Of course, he was allowed to go anywhere and be anywhere. She had no exclusive access rights to Parkhurst or Johannesburg or the Gauteng province for that matter. Tshepo could damn well go wherever he pleases.

He must have taken the question as an invitation to join her, because he was pulling the empty chair, and just like that there he was sitting centimetres from her.

God, he smelled so good. The bold, masculine scent of Tom Ford Noir lingered between them. She met his eyes, and quickly looked away. She could feel herself blush like a little unsure schoolgirl who's just met her crush. She hated that feeling. No, she hated that he still had an effect on her.

Damn it.

He confidently fixed his gaze on her face and smiled. Lord, those shimmering white teeth, and his smile framed his face so perfectly. The bigger the smile got, the more the glimmer in his eyes made him even sexier than she remembered. How can one person be blessed with all these perfect features?

'What are you grinning about?' It made Maserati feel better to reduce that beautiful smile to a grin.

'You, and your beautifully peculiar ways,' he answered, still smiling.

'My peculiar ways?'

'Yeah,' he laughed. 'I was sitting inside reading the paper when I heard a peculiar order that only one person in the whole city can make. Lovemore was giving stern orders to the barista to make sure the cappuccino was boiling hot. He must have said it twice for emphasis. I knew it had to be you. Who else could it be?' Tshepo continued, laughing jokingly.

'But how is my coffee preference strange? Huh?' Maserati rolled her eyes.

'It's cute. That's one of the things I love… uhm… loved about you.' Tshepo was tripping over his words unsure whether expressing in present or past tense was appropriate. 'I have always found your assertiveness one of the sexiest things about you.'

They locked eyes. His smile was replaced with a serious look on his face.

She looked away, blushing against her will.

'Well, you weren't thinking about your love for my peculiar ways when you had your tongue deep in that skank's throat!' She surprised herself when she realised she had blurted the words out loud. She shifted in her chair, convinced that she now resembled a perfect deep red beetroot, the likes you find only at Woolworths.

After a few awkward moments, Tshepo broke the silence.

'How are you doing? How's work? Are you still travelling frequently?'

Oh God, this is going to be a long dreary afternoon after all, Maserati thought, irritated and disappointed at the disruption of what was supposed to be an afternoon of blissful and peaceful solitude.

Again, Tshepo Mabilo had managed to spoil yet another wonderful thing in her life.

Chapter Five

Despite her best attempts to put that day behind her, her mind took her back to that traumatic moment in the carpark…

'Tshepo…?' her voice whispered, betraying her emotion.

Tshepo, startled, pushed the woman away from him.

'It's not what it looks like, baby!'

Everything that took place afterwards happened so quickly it was all a blur. She vaguely recalled hurling her entire body at the woman. Fake hair was pulled, faces were scratched; though not hers. Balls may have been kicked, and enough swear words were hurled to make a sailor sound like a preschooler in the cursing curriculum.

Maserati got in her car and drove off with such speed, she nearly knocked Tshepo as he tried to stop her from driving away. She wailed uncontrollably, the sound even surprising her. As tears and snot streamed down her face, a sharp pain was ripping her chest apart.

My heart is breaking into tiny pieces! she thought. She could not recall feeling pain so deep even when her beloved grandmother passed, and that had been a lot of pain. Was this what they meant by heartbreak?

Maserati broke every traffic law possible as she zoomed down William Nicol to their home in Dainfern Golf Estate, a home they just barely bought together a few months earlier. She made it to the driveway, leaving the car door open as she ran inside the house. As she made her way up the stairs, she caught sight of the dining room table, all decked out ready for the engagement party that night.

The party! The damn party. In barely three hours people would start arriving. How was she supposed to welcome guests in such a state?

'God, why me?' she wailed. 'God, what did I do to deserve this? Why are you punishing me? Why is Tshepo doing this to us? Why God? Why?'

She collapsed on the stairway, hardly having the energy to make it to the bedroom. The cold marble tiles against her skin were nothing compared to how she felt inside – cold and dead. Something inside her was dying a slow painful death.

As she lay distorted against the sharp contours of the staircase, the physical pain paled in comparison to the piercing pain she felt in her spirit, in the depths of her soul.

Beep... Beep...

Beep... Beep... Beep

Messages from Mantwa and Khutso came flooding in.

'Hi dear. Tshepo says you got sick, and the party is cancelled. Are you okay? Should I come over?'

'OMG dear. What happened? Tshepo says you suddenly fell sick with cramps, and you were at the hospital, and that the party is off? Are you alright?'

Then more messages from other worried guests.

'Hey. Tshepo says the party is off. Something about you rushing off to casualty for a consultation with a doctor. Call me back.'

Beep, beep...

She switched her phone off.

Chapter Six

'Fuck, fuck, fuck!'

Tshepo shouted at no one in particular, realising the hot mess he found himself in. His fiancé, the woman he planned to marry, the woman he had declared undying love to, had just caught him red-handed in another woman's arms. A woman he had been seeing for just under a year.

'Tshepo, what the hell is going on?' asked Pam, who had just realised she was a third wheel in a love story she did know existed. She was only a side-chick! She, Pam, a beautiful actress in a popular television soapie, had just had her weave rearranged by some screaming woman in the parking lot of one of the busiest shopping centres in her suburb. How had she not known about this woman before in their year-long love affair?

'You fucking bastard! Asshole! Was that your wife?' Pam was wagging a very angry finger in Tshepo's face. 'Leave me alone! Never ever contact me again, you swine!' Pam stomped to her car in anger, also almost hitting Tshepo as she sped off.

Tshepo was gripped by fear, aware that a few spectators had noticed the commotion since it started. He hoped that no one had recorded the saga on their phones for social media. Black Twitter is savage. And he had a reputation to uphold, as a COO of an Economic Development parastatal, touted as the next MEC of the same department in the Gauteng province, the economic hub of the country. It was important for Tshepo to project a clean reputation and he had worked so hard to do just that.

That feeling of fear was replaced by a fleeting sinister feeling of power, as the realisation that two of the most beautiful women in Joburg had just had a fight over him. It was fleeting but it invoked a powerful sense of being The Man! And he liked it.

And then shame overcame him. Tshepo had vowed to never be the stereotype of Black men in his father's day; the men who treated their women as less than equal, not worthy of respect and dignity.

Tshepo got in his car, unsure of whether to drive home, where he assumed Maserati would be or whether to go to a friend's house. Then he remembered the dinner party. He certainly didn't want to see friends and explain this mishap. Instead, he sent a mass email to all their friends.

'Hello all, the dinner party is cancelled. Maserati is not well. Don't worry she will be fine. I am taking her to see a doctor. Will follow up with updates. Sorry for the inconvenience.'

Then he switched off his phone and drove the whole night, aimlessly towards nowhere.

'I am not that man. I cannot be that man.'

As the shame became overwhelming, Tshepo began to weep.

Chapter Seven

'Life is going to be different when I'm older.'
'I'll have everything I want.'
'I'm going to be different.'

This had been Tshepo's mantra for as long he remembered, from childhood.

Tshepo had lived a childhood filled with shame; the shame of having a drunk for a father, the shame of having a mother ridiculed by her marriage, a woman who for all intents and purposes was a single mother in marriage. What else would one call being married to an irresponsible person like his father? What did she ever see in him?

He had felt shame for being a child that had never had something new. Every child deserves to have one new thing in their life that's intended for them and them only. But Tshepo and his three siblings, his older brother, and younger sister and brother, had a different experience. Due to their father's irresponsible drunk behaviour, squandering his teacher's salary on gambling, drinking, and women, his mother had the unfair sole responsibility of bearing all the financial burden of the household and childcare needs. To do this on a teacher's salary was a tall order for his mom.

So, nothing they ever had was new.

Toys and clothes were hand-me-downs from cousins who had scored the lottery by having responsible fathers.

Tshepo's mother hustled on the side to make ends meet. She made and sold curtains, she was network marketer for Tupperware and Forever Living products, and anything her hands could make, she made and sold.

The kids joined in on the hustle, selling sweets, ice popsicles, and anything kids fancied and could afford at their schools. When his older brother matriculated, there was not enough money for university. So, he hustled his way through a Marketing Diploma at an affordable Technical College, by continuing to sell his mother's goods and other things that college students fancied. It was a struggle, but he leveraged his strength in sales and marketing to get through, and eventually found a job in the marketing department of a telecommunications company.

Tshepo yearned for a life of ease. His childhood was marked by scarcity, and he dreamed of a life of plenty. He was blessed with brains between his ears. The boy was book-smart. A teacher recognised his intelligence and helped him apply to a private school that offered limited scholarships for underprivileged kids with potential. He got in and never looked back. He smelled the abundance awaiting him in the future. And it smelled so sweet!

He passed his matric with flying colours and got a bursary to study for a degree in Civil Engineering, from the renowned University of Cape Town. When he graduated, he was fortunate enough to find work at a big private construction company in Johannesburg. A mentor advised him to go for an MBA as he held business ambitions bigger than his current job. Again, Lady Luck was on his side as he secured a scholarship for a full-time MBA programme back at his alma mater.

It was in his last year of the MBA programme, that a chance meeting let him to the love of his life, Maserati Mojapelo. She was in her final year of medical school. The future indeed started to not only taste sweet, but it looked rosy too. He, Tshepo Mabilo, who had grown up struggling on the verge of poverty, was completing a prestigious degree, and was one day going to marry a doctor.

The life of abundance was materialising right before his eyes.

But there was something sinister always trailing, always close, threatening this dream of abundance. No matter how much Tshepo gained and achieved, it always felt like what he had was never enough. He loved the thrilling feeling he got every time he bought something new. But as soon as the feeling wore off, he started craving something newer.

When he bought his first car, a luxury Mercedes-Benz sedan, it took less than six months before he bought another car, a two-seater Audi convertible. His closet overflowed with clothes and shoes. And not just any old clothes and shoes, but designer wear. Tshepo Mabilo was not that little boy in second-hand clothes anymore.

And there was that little hidden problem of the women. His father had mistresses. And it wasn't like his father even tried to be discreet. He had shamed his mother constantly with one incident after another. One time a man found him in bed with his wife and beat him to a pulp. Tshepo's mother was called to take him to hospital.

Tshepo had vowed that he would never be like his father. Never. Ever.

But then he came to know the thrill of a woman's affection. He could not get enough of it. And he reasoned that no one needed to know. He was not harming anyone. And he would stop when he wanted to. Easily. He was not like his father, who lacked self-control.

Maserati did not need to know about all this.

When he met Maserati, he was in a two-month relationship with Rebone. But it was already a fading relationship.

Tshepo loved the thrill of meeting someone for the first time; the courting, and charming the women and watching them

25

respond to him with awe and interest. One of the things a skilful salesperson masters is the ability to be charming, and to let people in. Working his mother's side hustle jobs as a child, knowing that their well-being depended on it, had helped him cultivate this extreme easy charm. It didn't hurt that he was so damn good-looking, dressed well, drove the best, and lived well. He had all the trappings that some women looked for.

His lifestyle and work provided the perfect support for this little secret. There were so many business trips, which provided a perfect alibi.

No one needed to know.

No one needed to be hurt.

When he and Maserati started planning a life together, she had started noticing his excessive love of things.

'Mabilo, I thought I loved shoes but you mister, take the cake. What is this obsession you have with clothes and shoes? And the cars?'

Poor thing didn't know about his love for women too. Tshepo had done a great job early on their relationship to gain her trust and prove his commitment and love for her.

A week after Maserati upgraded from a Corsa Lite to a BMW sedan, Tshepo went and bought a Jeep SUV on impulse, bringing his car tally to a total of four cars; probably two extras he didn't need to have. Maserati remembered having a fleeting feeling that it felt competitive, that Tshepo could not stand her having a new thing, and hence the new Jeep. Maserati was wary of conflict and never wanted to start drama. So, when she questioned the financial wisdom of buying yet another car instead of focusing on investing in a property portfolio as they had planned for their marriage, he had blown a fuse, overreacted, and told Maserati that he held an MBA and therefore had a better understanding of financial matters than she did. She let the issue rest.

But this constant need for the thrill of newness had started worrying him.

He was also getting overwhelmed with managing all the

women in his life. Ever since he started university, he'd always had two to three women at the same time. He would try to end one relationship when he met someone new, but it would only last for a short time. Certainly, when he met Maserati, he wanted to completely stop. And he *had* managed to stop for the first year of their relationship, winning her complete trust and devotion. But it felt like he was giving up that abundance he'd always wanted in his childhood.

Tshepo had not realised abundance was not only a numerical measurement. One could have abundance from one single, but full, experience.

When he was alone in deep thoughts, he wondered how much of his childhood scarcity mentality had impacted him. If he was honest, it had impacted him greatly and he needed to work on finding ways to resolve it. But he never allowed himself to think about it in any real and honest depth. Instead, he let it run his life by acquiring new things he didn't really need.

When Maserati caught him in that parking lot with Pam, he knew he should have put a stop to the other women.

But the fear of not having enough was more overwhelming.

Chapter Eight

Maserati squinted from the sharp assault of the bright sunlight through the window. Her left side was sore, and she felt as stiff as a board. Her eyes felt like she had gone toe to toe with Floyd Mayweather in a ten-round boxing match.

'Where am I?' Her voice was faint and hoarse from her dry and sore throat. She was disoriented. As she was still trying to get her bearings, she got startled by the turn of a key and squeak, coming from downstairs in the direction of the kitchen.

She started to get up.

'Ouch…' She slumped back down on the stairs. Her head was heavy and pounding, her temples throbbing like a pulse of a million volts had just shot through her body.

Tshepo walked in and found Maserati still hunched on the stairway. He approached slowly looking dishevelled and tired; his eyes bloodshot from a night of crying.

What would this motherfucker be crying about? she thought angrily. *He was not the one betrayed. He has no business coming in here looking like a sorry victim.*

'Rati… Baby…' Tshepo sat down slowly next to Maserati. 'Baby, I am sorry. I am really really sorry. Please Rati, my love. Let me explain. Please.'

And right on cue, the floodgates opened. She did not think she had any more tears left but clearly her high school Biology teacher was right when he said the body's composition is over sixty percent water. She buried her face in her hands, face down on the top of the stairway and wailed, a wail that came from the depths of her soul. It made no sense to feel such pain and still be alive.

Tshepo reached out his hand and touched her right shoulder. He moved his hand down her upper arm and gently pulled Maserati towards him. She wanted to fight him but had no more fight left in her. He kept pulling her gently towards him and he cradled her face into his chest, stroking her hair while he rocked her back and forth, in an attempt to ease her pain like a mother comforting a tiny infant.

'Rati… Baby… Please don't cry, don't cry. I'm sorry I hurt you. I love you. Please don't cry.' It was all he could manage.

His big arms enveloped her like a timid helpless puppy, as she lay sobbing against his chest, which strangely still felt like the safe refuge she had come to know. In Tshepo's arms she had felt at home. When the world was raging and she was exhausted from all the daily stressors, she always looked forward to the stillness and peace that came with lying in his muscled arms that provided the security she needed from the demanding world.

And here she was again, in the arms of the man who had just brought such indescribable pain, feeling her resistance giving way to feelings of security. She smelled the deep familiar musk of his skin, and her body went limp as she surrendered to his comforting strokes against her back and those soft reassuring kisses on her forehead.

'Baby…' Now his voice assumed a gentle tone she had not expected.

'Baby…' A soft, kind tone.

'Baby, I really am sorry…' A soft, kind… and sexy tone.

He lifted her chin, He and kissed away the tears flowing down her cheeks with the gentle touch of his lips.

Maserati felt an unparalleled surging need for the reassurance of his love. She needed him to protect her from this pain. She looked up at him and he met her gaze with a stare of remorse.

She kissed him, slowly, softly, and then her kisses turned into rushed surge of emotions. She kissed him everywhere on his face, as if not getting enough. She whimpered as her mouth devoured his lips, and her grip on his shoulders tightened.

'Make love to me,' she said, in between kisses and breathing. 'Please make love to me.'

Tshepo was turned on by Maserati's vulnerability, but he hesitated slightly, making sure she meant it.

'I need you. I need you inside me… Mabilo, hold me, kiss me,' she begged, as she ripped open his shirt. Tshepo responded with a passionate longing kiss and in one swoop, picked her up in his arms as he led them from the cold staircase to the inviting ambience of their main bedroom.

He sprawled her on the large, luxurious king-sized bed and explored her body with his tongue and caresses, as they experienced a passion that was primal in its rawness. He unbuckled his belt with expertise as he let his pants fall to the floor, before pulling her flimsy La Senza black panties aside, and her bent legs slightly apart as he worked his way down to her nether regions.

She arched her back as his mouth met her lower lips and arched even further as his soft warm tongue separated them to circle and explore her warm bean. Tshepo enjoyed nothing more than hearing those soft moans and watching his woman relax and surrender to his love.

'Aahhh…mmm….' Maserati arched her back even further as she received every stroke of his expert tongue, holding the back of his head to increase his vantage point to the holy grail.

Then she pulled his face up towards her as she reached down and felt the hardness between his legs. She guided him towards her and he slowly entered her warm moist haven. She let out a soft cry as she shed a tear, overwhelmed by the intense connection she felt for him with each deep pleasurable thrust. They made love in a way they had never done before. She felt connected to his being and his spirit, more than just physically intertwined. As they both reached climax, Tshepo held her tenderly. 'I will never let you go, my love.'

And they both fell into a deep sleep as they lay wrapped in each other's arms on the massive bed, oblivious to the world outside, and its troubles.

Chapter Nine

'Ouch!' Maserati touched the temporal sides of her brick-heavy head.

'Hmmm… ouch, ouch,' she murmured, her eyes still closed as she pulled herself up to a sitting position, propped up against her pillows. She tried to open her engorged eyes, but they were stuck closed due to all the crying. She eventually pried them open, and quickly regretted that decision.

'Where's the light even coming from?' She cupped her hand over her forehead to create a protective shield for her eyes.

When her eyes finally opened, she noticed the clothes next to the bed. Tshepo's jeans and belt were on the floor, but no Tshepo in sight. The memories of the day before came flooding in. She instantly put her hands over her heart and felt that constricting feeling again in her chest, and began gasping for air. Her chest was heaving and felt like it was closing tight.

I can't breathe!

Through her rising panic she heard clinking sounds coming from downstairs. And music. And more clackity clanks. As the waft of coffee drifted into the room, she realised that Tshepo must be downstairs.

Take a deep breath, Rati, she thought, taking in the comforting aroma of her favourite brew, followed by a forceful exhalation that seemed to expel a fraction of the panic she felt earlier. Her body began to relax. Another deep breath in and out, and she felt herself growing calmer. It really is true what they say about the magic of breath.

'Many of us die because we do not breathe.' She remembered a spiritual teacher say this on one of Oprah's shows.

As she was appreciating this wisdom about breath, Tshepo appeared through the door, carrying a tray laden with bounty, deserving to be featured in the Food & Wine magazine. Cooking had always been one his superpowers, and one of the many reasons she fell so deeply in love with him.

Maserati had a deceivingly fit and petite figure for a girl who could eat anyone under the table. This amused her. She remembered in university when she joined in the diet craze with some of her friends. That delusional act lasted only but a miserable week and the thought of continuing to deprive herself of bread was as torturous as pouring salt to an open wound.

A beautiful dining experience was one of Maserati's self-care routines. Tshepo had certainly provided her with many such beautiful experiences. He had fed her dreams with his words and through his cooking, he not only nurtured her body but had nurtured their relationship.

Some of their best time together was spent in the kitchen exploring his culinary skills or eating out, whether at Michelin star restaurants or right through to a local township's *shisa nyama* joint.

That, and his lovemaking! She cracked a smile as the racy thought ran through her mind.

'That smile could only mean you approve.' Tshepo mistook her naughty smile as a stamp of approval for the lovely spread he was presenting in front of her.

'I believe the lady might be hungry. We have here a medley of your favourite berries and yoghurt, followed by a choice of eggs Benedict with salmon and chives, hollandaise sauce on the side just the way you like, with herbed mushrooms in basil pesto and wild rocket. Freshly squeezed orange juice for a healthy dose of vitamin C, and a hot boiling cappuccino to finish it off.' Tshepo spoke with his greatest impression of those buttoned-up waiters who believe their tips are tied to how they enunciate the menu items.

Okay, I love to eat, but damn! The man did not need to serve a meal fit for a small army, she thought, as she assessed the bounty, wondering where to begin.

'You outdid yourself yet again, Mabilo,' she said with a chuckle. The use of her endearment term for him was not lost on Tshepo. It was as if yesterday had never happened. He was secretly pleased, and confident that there was a chance to mend things.

'I am pleased the lady approves.'

He extended the tray's legs and placed it over her thighs and helped her prop up so she could sit in comfort while devouring her meal. He moved to the foot of the bed and sat directly across her and watched her eat as he had done so many times before.

He had dated real prima donnas before when it came to food – the type that would count the calories in water. That experience had almost killed his love for cooking, until this beautiful creature walked into his life. Her passion for food was so refreshing, and she had no qualms about eating, unlike so many of the body-conscious women he knew. This was one of her sexiest qualities.

His cooking felt like a love letter to her.

'Hmmmm, this is so good.' Maserati had all but forgotten the few minutes earlier when her breath seemed to be escaping her lungs. Her tastebuds celebrated with every hearty bite of the smoked salmon.

'I swear this is one of the best breakfasts I've had from you. How can it be so delicious?' she asked, taking another bite and licking her fingers.

Tshepo's response to what he knew was a rhetorical question, was to smile that big alluring smile, and continue to watch her with glee.

'Aren't you going to eat?' she asked. Not that she was truly concerned as she was able to wolf down the entire breakfast by herself.

'I wasn't too hungry, plus I nibbled on some when I was prepping for you. Besides, these are all your favourite dishes. I prefer my breakfast a little greasy.' He laughed, nervously. What he wanted to really say was she was all that mattered at this moment, and he couldn't care less about his own nutrition.

He sipped on his warm coffee and glanced at her over the edge of the coffee mug. He was still pretty much aware of the elephant in the room, while she on the other hand seemed oblivious to it.

'Why you insist on drinking warm coffee is the greatest unsolved mystery to me,' she teased.

He broke out in a roar of laughter, and laughter being infectious, Maserati laughed too, attempting to join the broken pieces of what had been their perfect union. To the outside uninitiated world, there was nothing funny about lukewarm coffee, but their laughter was anchored in the sacred knowledge of a life shared over many years. They laughed until their ribs hurt, Maserati's merry tears flowing down her cheeks, wiping away the stains of the sad tears she had cried only a day before.

'Oh, my gosh…' she snorted adorably as she tried to stop and catch her breath. 'Oh. My. Gosh.'

Breakfast no longer mattered in that magical moment of laughter.

In unspoken unison, Tshepo picked up the tray and placed it aside as Maserati reached towards him. She was in charge. Within minutes, they were skin to skin. Tshepo steadied himself on the bed as Maserati straddled him, aiming for his magic stick.

And she began to ride.

Unlike the bull at the rodeo, Tshepo wasn't trying to buck off the rider. He grasped her around her waist, guiding her up and down that gliding stick. As her breasts bounced with the flow of the motion, he kissed them and took her nipples in his mouth, one after the other, he flicked them with the tip of his tongue, as she let out soft moans.

She reached for his mouth and kissed him. She lifted her derriere just so, and his thrusts responded.

'Baby…' she murmured, gazing into his eyes, and in that moment felt the surge shoot down her spine.

'Aahhhh…'

And her body spasmed with conflicted joy as he erupted.

Chapter Ten

M aserati woke up two hours later, hungry. The breakfast bounty was now sitting cold by the bedside, but she devoured it, for no one likes a hangry woman, Maserati admitted to herself. She looked over at Tshepo sleeping peacefully.

The room smelled like sex. And looked like turmoil.

The turmoil they had both chosen to gloss over with two days of passion.

But the things left unsaid must be said eventually.

She looked for her phone which had remained switched off for the past two days. Her friends must be worried. As her phone switched on, the beeping sound was relentless.

A hundred missed calls, and fifty messages.

Oh my gosh, these girls are so dramatic, Maserati thought, lacking the energy to go through them all. But that was the kind of friendship she had had with her girls. She would have probably not only called and left messages if one her friends was in her position, she would have broken down walls to get to her.

Ten of those missed calls were from her mom this morning, probably wanting feedback on how the engagement dinner party went. She was so excited for Maserati and Tshepo.

'We are coming over,' read a message from Mantwa, sent at 13h30. It was 14h00.

Oh boy, they are probably close by, Maserati thought. She would have preferred to see them once she was calm and had her story together about what had happened two nights ago.

She got out of bed and got downstairs so she could have some privacy as she called Mantwa.

'Hi dear. Are you okay? We are on our way,' said Mantwa on the end of the line.

'Hi dear. I am alright. I just can't explain right now but I am okay. Where are you?'

'I was just about to leave. Khutso asked that I should pick her up too.'

'Oh, good, you haven't left? There's no need to come now.'

'What? Why, don't you want to see us? What's going on Rati? This is so unlike you. I have been worried sick. Tshepo's phone is off. None of his friends have heard from him since the night that was supposed to be your engagement party. Your mother called me this morning looking for you and asking about the party. What's going on?' Mantwa was now convinced something was wrong and that it was necessary to come over to make sure for herself that Maserati was okay.

'Dear, trust me please. I am okay. I appreciate your concern, and I will call Mama.'

But Mantwa continued to question Maserati, and finally she had no choice but to spill the beans on what had transpired.

'What?!' Mantwa was hissing. And this was the reason Maserati would have preferred to tell them face to face while calm, to tone down the anger she knew her friends would feel towards Tshepo. She too wasn't sure of the way forward.

'That bastard. How can he do this to you? Over some low-grade actress. I thought he was different.'

Maserati had realised only later why that woman in the parking lot seemed familiar. She was in some soapie on one of those low-budget channels.

Mantwa had always believed that all men cheat. She reckoned the difference between good men and bad men was that good men were never reckless – they respected their wives by making sure their affairs were conducted underground; never to be discovered. Any man who is found out, according to Mantwa's logic, is careless, stupid, and disrespectful.

'Don't come over now,' pleaded Maserati. 'I need to sort this out and I will call you. Please let Khutso know I am okay. I will call Mama.'

Maserati was not looking forward to calling her mother. She would have many questions about the engagement party that never happened. And she didn't feel like lying to her mother but at the same time she didn't want to worry her by telling her exactly what happened. Her mother loved Tshepo. In her eyes, Tshepo was an angel, and could do no wrong.

Tshepo had that effect on the elders in her family. He was always so respectful. And of course, they were happy that she had landed herself a nice and humble COO. Tshepo always came bearing gifts including expensive mature brandy for her uncles whenever there was an event at her home.

But she couldn't avoid the call indefinitely. She took a breath and called her mom.

'Maserati, are you okay? I've been calling since yesterday. How did the party go? Where is Tshepo? Oh, my child, I am so happy for both of you. Tshepo is such a good boy, my child. Soon there will be little grandchildren running around. I can't wait my child. I am so proud of you both.'

Mothers! And their non-stop projection over our lives.

'Mama. Tshepo is fine. Uhm… the party, the party, well we had to postpone it because I think I ate something bad and ended up with food poisoning.' She was now lying to her mother to cover up for him. Her mother was just too excited to notice anything.

'Oh my nana, that's terrible. Are you okay? Why didn't you

tell me? So, when do you plan to have the party? Next weekend?'

Jesus.

'Uhm… we have to check everyone's schedule, but we will let you know. Mama, I must go. Someone is at the door. I just wanted to let you know I am okay. I'll call you soon.'

With that Maserati hung up. She felt bad for lying to her mother about something so serious. She was just not ready to deal with her mother's disappointment once she found out the truth. It would devastate her.

Beep… beep. Another message, but it wasn't her phone.

Tshepo's phone was lying on the kitchen island. He must have left it when he was making breakfast earlier.

Beep. Beep.

And then Maserati did what she never thought she would do in her life – go through her partner's phone. Thirty minutes later she wished that she hadn't. Not only did she find intimate messages between Tshepo and the actress, but she found that there were two other women that Tshepo had been seeing. Pam had messaged, pleading for them to work it out, that she forgave him, and she didn't want to throw away their year-long relationship. Another young woman, no older than twenty-one, had sent provocative pictures, suggesting that this wasn't the first time they had exchanged photos. Maserati scrolled through the picture gallery and found pictures of Tshepo with other women – some on vacation, some in hotel rooms, and some very compromising.

Breathe, Rati, breathe…

'Aaahhh….' she screamed and threw the phone against the wall, breaking the screen to smithereens.

Why is this happening to me? Maserati slid to the ground, crying softly, with no tears this time. There was nothing left. She felt defeated, confused, and numb.

Who have I been sleeping with all this time?

Chapter Eleven

Tshepo woke up to an empty right side of the bed and figured that Maserati must have gone downstairs as the tray of food was also gone. He put his pants on and started walking down the stairs. Midway, he could feel the energy of the house had shifted. He was not walking towards the Maserati he had spent the last day and half making love to. He was walking towards the hurt and disappointed Maserati who had found him mid-embrace with Pam at the parking lot.

He tensed up and realised he was inappropriately dressed for the impending conversation. He walked back upstairs, not only to put on his shirt, but also his armour for what was to be a very hard conversation that could end it all.

Should I tell the whole truth? A sinister thought wandered through his brain.

'Tell the truth,' his white angel nudged him.

'Are you sure you want to do that?' his dark angel countered.

'Tell only what's necessary,' was the resolution he took as he walked back downstairs.

He was wrong. He was not walking towards a disappointed Maserati, but to an impending World War 3.

Maserati was lying on the floor, curled up in a foetal position,

41

her eyes blank. Tshepo's heart sank. Spotting what used to be his phone, scattered in pieces all over the kitchen floor, he did not need to guess why Maserati looked like that. He had been found out. Completely.

He knelt cautiously beside Maserati, slowly reached out and touched her shoulder gently. She did not respond. And she did not move. Her eyes were open though, and she was breathing silently, so he was sure she was alive even though her eyes lacked the spark that was present mere hours before.

After what felt like hours, she finally spoke, still curled up on the floor.

'How many women were there?'

Tshepo's dark angel took over.

'Baby, let me explain.'

'Tshepo, how many women were there?!' she asked fiercely.

'You are the only woman in my life, the only one that matters. The only one that has always mattered. The one I want to spend the rest of my life with. The one I want to build a family with. These women were nothing. They were just floozies. Baby, you know this job comes with traps. And like a fool, I fell for it. But I promise you, these women meant nothing to me, I love only you baby. Rati, Rati, you are my world.'

Her eyes were fixed on him. Watching the corners of his mouth twitch as he was speaking and his eyes flicker around the room, unable to maintain eye contact with her as he lied.

She gave him another chance to redeem himself.

'Tell the truth, Tshepo. And maybe we could still salvage this.'

Tshepo reckoned that admitting to the truth would be signing his death order. He would take a chance with the dark side.

'Baby, I am telling the truth.' His mouth twitched multiple times.

In that instant, Maserati knew he wasn't about to tell the truth. With a sudden burst of energy she ran upstairs, furiously packed a bag and stormed back down.

As she headed out of the door, she turned to the dejected Tshepo, still standing in the kitchen.

'Tshepo, this is over.'

Driving away, she texted Mantwa. 'I'm coming over and need a place to stay.'

Her mind whirled as she drove. Discovering that Tshepo had been having multiple affairs during their relationship was the worst thing she had ever experienced.

How could the love of her life, her soulmate, betray her like this?

How did she miss the signs?

Was she not enough?

Did he not love her?

Did he EVER love her?

Was the engagement all a lie?

How can one break trust so easily?

The questions came at her, fast and furious.

Chapter Twelve

The next few weeks were hell.

All those soft ballads and romantic music on the radio took on a different, sad meaning. Each verse, each melody, pierced her heart, and left it even heavier. Why had all these music stations changed their playlists to such sombre, heartbreak songs? Toni Braxton and Babyface filled every minute of every hour on every single one of these stations. Why is the universe turning on her, reminding her of her pain? Tears flowed in abundance. All she wanted was the pain to stop.

'Why does it hurt so bad, why do I feel so sad?' sang Whitney Houston, taking a turn to drop her spirits even further.

Her family and friends were worried about her and her well-being, all offering unsolicited and well-meaning advice on what she should do.

'My friend, hear him out, arrange a sit-down and talk. Perhaps you could understand where he came from. You don't just throw away five years with someone,' said Khutso, forever seeing the good in people and always on a mission for reconciliation.

Khutso was invested in the Maserati/Tshepo fairytale. She was the kind of woman, whose bookshelf was filled with books on how to become an obedient, submissive wife, and backward Stepford Wife type books. Bless her heart. Maserati loved her innocent, naive and non-cynical approach to matters of the heart. She'd been with her husband Lesetja Malema, an Investment Banker, for close to ten years. Lesetja was one of only two men she'd ever been with. And she was content.

'Dear, you know how men are,' said Tebogo, the peacemaker, adding her two cents to the mix. 'He was probably feeling anxious about being tied down; this was just an ego-stroking exercise. That man loves you. You can't throw away all your years together without at least trying. Go for counselling if you must.'

Mantwa on the other had spewed fire, angry at seeing how hurt her friend was.

'That piece of shit. Men don't know a good thing when they see one, when they have one. Running around with mere skanks! I would have run them both over with the car. I swear I would be in jail right now!'

Maserati eventually just blocked everyone out. She immersed herself in work and avoided any form of social interaction with anyone for weeks. She just needed the space to process what had happened.

The thought of Tshepo would send Maserati straight back to depression, hurt, anger and confusion. She still believed in the Tshepo and Maserati dream. A dream she had imagined and fantasised about for so many years before.

Maserati had never failed at anything in her life. She would come out of this a winner. She and Tshepo were going to make it.

A couple of weeks in, she considered giving him a second chance. She was willing to make things work if Tshepo agreed to be honest and faithful going forward. Like her friends Khutso and Tebogo said, no one throws away a long-term relationship without trying to make things work.

Maserati and Tshepo had had similar childhood back-grounds. They came from homes where infidelity had caused confusion and created lasting childhood wounds. They had both witnessed their mothers being disrespected by the men in their lives. They had laid awake many nights sharing dreams and promises of a life completely different from those of their parents.

And for the most part, Tshepo had been nothing but a gentleman and a great partner during their five-year relationship. He was friendly, approached everyone with a genuine smile and a ready joke. He was kind and welcoming, and generous with gifts to her family. He respected elders and made sure the elders in their lives were cared for, financially and otherwise. He was thoughtful. Maserati's mother completely adored him.

Although not a teetotaller, he had an aversion to excessive alcohol. He had seen what alcohol did to his father and had vowed not to be anything like him. Here and there, when out for dinner or hanging with friends he would have no more than a glass of fine whisky. And he understood the mileage one could get from Maserati's uncles by presenting them with aged whiskies and brandies.

So of course, Maserati's uncles loved him to eternity and laughed at all his corny jokes at family gatherings.

How do you throw all that history away?

Maserati eventually reached out to him and offered forgiveness on condition that they would work on better and honest communication going forward; that no topic or issue was too big or taboo enough for discussion. Maserati was convinced that Tshepo's behaviour stemmed from his childhood traumas and if they could just tackle the source, they would be well on their way to mending Tshepo. And their relationship. She had suggested counselling to which Tshepo was hesitant. However, he had promised to read up on books dealing with the subject of childhood wounds and how to heal them. He even put aside some time to watch Oprah's Soul Sundays together. He seemed open to talking.

One big condition that Maserati had stated in no unclear terms: NO MORE OTHER WOMEN! Tshepo had apologised and insisted the women meant nothing and some had trapped him due to his status. There was even suggestions of witchcraft being at play. Anything really, to get out of a messy situation. He started leaving his two phones lying around, unlocked. He began to take phone calls in front of her or as loudly as possible – anything to reassure her that he was done with other women.

But when he wasn't in the room, or while he was sleeping, she would go through them, including checking all his social media private messages, just to make sure.

She just could not shake off the mistrust. She was turning into a woman she did not recognise –calling him randomly during the day, to potentially catch him in a compromising situation, she 'coincidentally' dropped into same venues where he said he was having meetings, she offered to go places with him, places that in the past she would avoid like a bad rash. She searched jacket inner pockets for receipts.

Rati even began stalking some of the women on social media, scanning the photos with a magnifying glass, for any signs of him in the background. Once or twice she had even called the actress and warned her to leave her man alone. Her days had become filled with obsessive thoughts about his whereabouts at any given moment. She had become less focused at work. She felt really pathetic.

But a leopard that likes its spots, never changes them.

Maserati had not noticed the third phone that never made it out from his car, concealed in the glove compartment. And had not realised that the three-day lekgotla had in fact only been a two-day conference. She also had not noticed that the official text messages that came from DDG, with hidden codes for secret love meetings, came from the very married, but nevertheless always ready to mingle, Deputy Director General, Stella Serobe.

Maserati's worst fear was becoming 'one of those women': the weak ones, the desperate ones, the unempowered, the dependent and overly reliant on men ones. Just like her mother who had stayed with a philanderer. She had judged her mother her entire life and had despised her father to this day for the embarrassment he had caused the family. Maserati had never thought of herself as one of those women. And yet here she was, turning into a shadow of herself because she loved Tshepo.

She had never failed at anything and she wasn't about to start. And she was certainly not giving her father the satisfaction of knowing she too had been cheated on. She had made it clear in one of their arguments that she would never fall for anyone like him. Tshepo wasn't like him. He was kind. And willing to work on this relationship.

Things were taking a toll on her mental and physical well-being. She was not eating or sleeping well, and it was beginning to show through her progressive weight loss.

———

'Dear, I think you should see a therapist,' Tebogo suggested to Maserati over one of their brunches at the Irene Country Club in Pretoria. It was a perfect Sunday midmorning, with the luscious jacaranda trees providing the perfect purple background suited for the ensuing conversation on healing.

'I don't need a massage at this point, dear.' Maserati knew what her friend was suggesting, but the thought of seeing a therapist would mean she had failed as the self-assured, self-determining, and self-actualising super-shero she had assumed herself to be and more importantly, the super-shero that everyone had come to expect.

Her life was supposed to be perfect. How was she supposed to be perfect seated on a shrink's couch like a failure?

As a doctor, she knew better. She knew the value of a good session with a therapist on mental well-being.

'You know what I mean!' Tebo was not budging.

'We should really debunk the stigma around therapy as Black

people. And most certainly we should debunk the myth of the Strong Black Woman. We think its progressive but we are more damaged by the expectations that we should brush off our deep hurt like water off our backs. You need to see a therapist to help you get unstuck on this issue.' Tebo, who a couple of years ago had gone through the trauma of infidelity herself, spoke with some wisdom. They had gone through couples and individual therapy, and it must have worked, as they were still together working on their marriage.

'I find that meeting with my church cell group helps me deal with my challenges,' said Khutso, who had been trying to get Maserati to attend Higher Anointing, a charismatic church that had just taken off amongst the Black middle class in the Waterfall and Midrand areas. And many a testimony of these higher anointings had been shared on social media – husbands, wealth, and all manner of favours have apparently been found at the church.

'Please, not church…' Mantwa tipped her head backwards, visibly rolled her eyes and sipped on her mimosa, not even trying to hide her legendary scepticism over churches. She and Khutso had never seen eye to eye when it came to church. It wasn't that she didn't believe in God, she just didn't believe in these charismatic churches especially as many of them had been accused of fooling the gullible masses with promises of miracles galore offered at a nominal cost. Usually in acquiring material wealth, which proved to be elusive.

Maserati and Tebogo giggled, for they knew this was an argument best left to the two of them. The safest position on the matter was to be neutral. The truth was that both had valid points for and against the charismatic church.

'No church is perfect. Unlike the orthodox churches, like the Roman Catholic, Higher Anointing has never claimed to be perfect. It is a home for imperfect people seeking redemption.' There was no denying Khutso's passion for the church.

'Just because there was a scandal with that church in

Mabopane with that stupid Pastor… no, he does not even deserve to be called pastor. That charlatan, who made his congregants drink petrol as a test of their faith. Those are the stories that mess it up for all the good churches. Most churches are out here doing good for their communities. Sure, there are problems like in every organisation. But that's why we need God.'

'Preach, dear, preach.' Maserati lifted her hands in the air as if ready to go into praise in support of Khutso. Although, Khutso could not tell whether she was teasing or genuine in her gesture. Maserati was happy to fuel the fire of this unwinnable conversation, in part to deflect from the topic of her needing to see a therapist.

To the outside world, Khutso appeared as the meekest amongst this group of women. Her traditional outlook on life, family and politics contrasted with the feminist energy of the other three. She was the kind of daughter-in-law their grandmothers would approve of as the perfect makoti. Her views on marriage and family were on the subservient side, a Proverbs 31 woman, as church folk would say. But Khutso's strength lay in her convictions. She owned every choice she made in the conduct of her life, marriage, and family life.

This was the beauty and dynamism of their friendship. Each person brought a different perspective to the table, which served not only the collective friendship but each other as individuals.

The group needed the softness of Khutso, just as it needed Mantwa's ferocity, Tebogo's balanced view, and Maserati's constant seeking.

Chapter Thirteen

Maserati sat uncomfortably on the couch. This certainly was not the chaise that she usually saw on those TV show depictions of the therapists' rooms, always with a chaise for the patients to lie down on as they told their deepest, darkest secrets free from the gaze of the therapist. No, there was no lying down with your back to the therapist in here. There she was shifting in this ghastly beige sofa, facing the intrusive stare of Dr Mosibudi, sitting stoically upright, notepad and pen in hand ready to scribble down the details of her sorry love life.

Lord help me, thought Maserati, shifting again, making peace with the fact that there was no position comfortable enough to bare one's soul to a strange woman who, with her luck, just happened to resemble Iyanla Vanzant. What were the odds! Iyanla was known for being brutally honest with people to help them bring healing to their habitual life dysfunctions.

'Call a thing a thing, boo-boo!' Maserati remembered Iyanla in one of her famous TV shows, chastising a young lady who had spiralled out of control from seeking affection and love in one abusive relationship after another, instead of dealing with the real truth: the trauma of being abandoned by her father when she was two years old.

'So, what brings you here on my couch, Dr Mojapelo?' Dr Mosibudi's voice was expectedly assured, albeit an octave higher than Iyanla's.

'Maserati. Please call me Maserati, Doc.' Maserati smiled for she understood the title etiquette that Dr Mosibudi was employing. It was common in the health profession to acknowledge your colleague's pedigree accordingly.

Dr Mosibudi did not repeat the question. Correct titles or not, the question remained.

'Uhm….'

Girl, you better stop with the shifting, jeez. Get a grip, thought Maserati. She was already feeling the heat, and this was only question number one.

'Uhm.. Where do I start?'

'Start anywhere. Start where you are comfortable.'

Maserati took a deep breath. Breath is life. As she exhaled, the words flowed.

'Heartbreak. I am here because my heart is broken, and I cannot seem to stop it from bleeding. From hurting. I am stuck in this vicious cycle. I feel like I should know better, I should know the right thing to do and just… just do it, damn it! I want the hurt to stop. I am stuck and I want clarity. I want to move on. Move on from this madness. Move on from this pain. Move on from this man. I am better than this. I deserve better than this.'

She had not realised her eyes were closed. As she opened them, she saw Dr Mosibudi scribble on her notepad, one word. One word. After pouring her heart out like that, and the woman scribbles one word!

Am I even at the right therapist? Maserati started wondering again if this was a good idea. At the same time, she felt a lightness in her spirit.

'Why is your heart broken?' Dr Mosibudi asked, staring her square in the eyes.

Okay, Rati, it is time for you to call a thing a thing, boo-boo.

Maserati had been consumed with looking for reasons why

this had happened. The more she had sought answers from Tshepo, the more dissatisfied she was with any of his responses. She looked for answers in women's magazines; *True Love, Cosmopolitan, Fair Lady,* and the ever-popular *Oprah*. Every month these rags ran articles on men cheating, clearly an epidemic of Mount Everest proportions. Article titles ranged from 'Why I stayed', 'He Cheated Twice, and I took Him Back', 'My Self-Respect, Why I Left a Cheating Loser', and on and on.

The reasons women stated for staying were as varied as the reasons stated for leaving. Women stayed to preserve families, for financial security, and the need to succeed at all costs. And love. Women left to preserve families, their self-respect, out of shame. And love.

None of these could provide her with a clear singular answer to her inner conflict: stay or leave?

Stay, because she loved Tshepo and they had a good life, with great dreams for the future, a future filled with love, eternal happiness, wealth, travel, and babies. Leave, because of the broken trust, and Tshepo's actions of total disregard and disrespect for her.

This inner conflict truly surprised and pained Maserati. She, who had always been clear on her position on cheating spouses. 'I would leave in a flash,' she'd always said, never a doubt in that assertion. She never understood women who stayed in seemingly abusive, unloving relationships. And cheating was a stepping stone to other forms of abuse in her books.

As a young child, she had watched her mother stay in a relationship that was past its expiry date. It was common knowledge that her father had had an affair with a neighbouring woman when her mother had gone back to her mother's place on maternity leave. The thought of her father frolicking with the woman next door, while her mother was recovering and nursing a newborn, their newborn, invoked a lingering loathing for her father. The image she'd had of a loving relationship between her parents was forever tainted.

When her mother returned from the three months away, a well-meaning neighbour had brought the indiscretion to her attention. It may have been discussed in hushed tones, but there was no sweeping the neighbourhood gossip under the rugs. Maserati's mom was beautiful, elegant with perfect features. You would not believe she had just popped out a baby three months prior. And she had been raised to revere education; she was a professional nurse with two specialties.

And yet her father chose to fornicate with an unsightly, out-of-shape woman, whose greatest achievement was a bought matric certificate, and a lowly career as a corrupt traffic officer, notorious for accepting bribes and issuing unmerited drivers' licences to desperate and often unroadworthy drivers. How does one leave a decent, dignified bed to lie in bed with a snake?

Maserati could never really hide her disdain towards her father. And this only worsened when it became clear that her mother would not leave him. She was too young to question her mother's decision to stay. Did her mother even decide? To her mind, it was a foregone conclusion, that her mom would pack up with her two kids and leave.

She knew her mother was deeply hurt by this whole thing, and greatly embarrassed by the gossip. Maserati recalled that she did not walk as tall as she used to, around the neighbourhood, that she did not appear to be the self-assured woman she had known her to be, at church, at work, at funerals or any gathering where people displayed their dignity and standing in the community. Her smile seemed faint. The only time it lit up was when she was playing with Rati and her younger sister. There was no mistaking that her clothes had become looser than before. Where was that sparkle?

Meanwhile, her dad seemed to walk their neighbourhood unbothered, unchanged, and in fact probably envied by other men in her neighbourhood. It was common knowledge that all fathers kept side pieces. The difference, it seemed was that the side piece should ideally not be from the same neighbourhood.

So, her father's audacity to step out of those unspoken boundaries and be blatant with an ugly neighbour must have cemented his manhood tenfold. To Maserati, he appeared cocky, while her mother seemed to be shrinking from her former glory.

She did not recall that there ever was an apology from her dad to her mom. And certainly, none to her. By inflicting this hurt on her mother, he had also hurt her. Ms. Corrupt Traffic Officer, with her brazen lack of respect and forgetting her place as the side piece, was shunned by the women of the community. She was not to be trusted around their husbands, so they stopped inviting her to any kind of gathering. Isolated from her community, she one day upped and left and settled in another zone of the township, never to be seen again.

One day Maserati looked up, and mom and dad had fallen back into their usual routine, as Mr and Mrs Mojapelo. All forgiven and forgotten.

'Why do you think your mother stayed?' Dr Mosibudi asked, and this time her notepad was full of scribbled notes.

'I don't know.'

'In your opinion, what do you think made her stay?'

'I guess, she loved him. I do not know. Maybe us, children. I would hate for her to have decided to stay because of us. She was smart, a professional and had supportive parents and siblings. She would have been okay on her own.' Maserati was convinced her mom probably stayed because of her and her sister.

'Did you ever ask your mother why she stayed?' Dr Mosibudi probed further.

Maserati burst out laughing. How could Dr Mosibudi ask such a silly question. Does she not know better? No Black child dares ask their parents such grown-up questions, unless one is asking to be smacked upside their heads.

'Ask her? No, I never did. I could not. It would have been disrespectful as a child to ask my parent such a question. Plus, I didn't want to create discomfort for her.'

'I think your conflict about staying or leaving your partner arises from your mother's experience.' Maserati was not sure if Dr Mosibudi was telling or asking her. She offered silence.

Dr Mosibudi continued, 'Here is a woman that you look up to, smart, beautiful, educated, independent, and who made smart life choices. And yet when she suffered one of the greatest betrayals by someone who was meant to honour her, in your opinion, the choice she made was in complete contrast to your gut reaction. And for the first time you questioned her choice. But part of you felt that since she was smart and you trusted her judgement, there might be a fitting reason for her choosing to stay. For all of it to make sense to you, there had to be a good reason, right? But you never asked her. You never got to know why. You lay judgement at both her staying and for not knowing her reasons. That is conflict, right there.'

This was a mic drop if there ever was one!

Maserati left Dr Mosibudi's office very clear on what she needed to do.

Go home to her mom.

Chapter Fourteen

I t was a conversation twenty years overdue.
'Hello, Mama. How are you? How is Papa?' Maserati
tried her best to sound normal. Her mom could always tell when
something was wrong, just from the tone of her voice. Since this
debacle with Tshepo, she had phoned her mom less and less,
instead preferring to rather send texts, because completely foregoing their daily communication would have send the biggest
signal to her parents that something was indeed amiss with their
daughter.

'Hello Rati. It is so good to hear from you. How is my
favourite son-in-law?' To Mrs Mojapelo the wedding was just a
mere formality. In her mind, Tshepo was already part of the
family.

Ignoring the last question, Rati replied, 'I am fine Mama, as I
said yesterday in my text. I wanted to see if you will be home
this weekend. I was thinking of coming over for a short visit.'

'Of course, we'd love to see you. Papa has some trip planned
with Mr Nchabeleng; you remember him from Papa's university
days? But he will be so happy to hear you are coming. I'm sure
your dad can cancel the trip.'

'No, Mama. Papa does not need to cancel the trip. In fact, it was mainly you I wanted to see.'

'Rati, is everything fine, my child?'

'Yes, Mama. Yes, everything is fine. It is just a short visit, and I wouldn't want Papa to change his plans at such short notice. Plus, if I remember, Mr Nchabeleng holds grudges.'

Her mother burst out laughing. Maserati loved to hear her mother laugh. She remembered a time when her mother had seldom laughed.

'You remember? That man has a temperament of a middle-school girl at that time of the month.'

They both burst out laughing thinking about the fragile ego of Papa's best friend. It was arranged. Maserati would drive up to Polokwane on Saturday morning.

———

'Hi dear. Want to come on a road trip this Saturday?' Maserati texted Mantwa. She did not feel like driving the nearly 400-kilo-metre drive by herself. Her friend was always a fun road-trip-ping companion. And they had such deep conversations that reminded her why they had been friends for over fifteen years. Plus, her mother loved Mantwa.

They packed a selection of road trip goodies. The plan was to not make any unnecessary stops.

'Dear, what is this visit about?' Mantwa had tried not to be inquisitive the whole week. But she knew it probably had to do with Maserati's sessions with Dr Mosibudi.

'I just need answers from Mama about why she stayed with Papa after what he did to her. I was so sure even at that young age, that she was going to leave him. Dear, it was awful. The looks and gossip from neighbours. But she stayed. I didn't get it then and still don't.'

'Our parents are from a generation where you turn a blind

eye to these things. But I think your mother's choice to stay was hers. You may not like it, but you have to respect it. I see how you get impatient with her sometimes, and I want to punch you in the face. She is your mother.'

'I know, dear. I don't mean to disrespect her. But I feel like she let me and Malebo down by choosing to stay. What sort of example did she set for us, her daughters?'

'I hear you. But our parents are human beings first before they are parents. We can't carry their mistakes forever into our adulthood. You have to forgive and accept them just as they are. Your mother loves you and your father too.'

'Hmmm.' Maserati had a hard time believing the last part about her father. Most of their adult relationship had been filled with conflict. For the most part, Maserati chose to ignore him and would rather inform her mother of anything significant in her life. What her mother did with that information, well, that was none of her business.

Maserati's mother was already standing by the gate when they pulled through. She did this every time Maserati or Malebo came home. Showering them with hugs and kisses, she carried their bags into the house. Maserati's mother was proud of the women her children had turned out to be. And a little showing off to their neighbours was warranted.

Even though Maserati had told her mother not to fuss over this short visit, it had fallen on deaf ears. Her mother had cooked up a storm. All the hearty meals that Maserati loved; chicken curry, steamed bread, and her mother's famous oxtail, the recipe for which she had claimed with pride. Her father was always left speechless after that magnificent meal. To think he had risked losing everything with a woman who resembled the back end of a cow.

'Mama, I told you not to overwork yourself.'

'Speak for yourself. I want to eat all of this food, Mama.' Mantwa was sucking up.

'Thank you Mantwa. You know your friend has no gratitude.'

'I am right here, people. Right here.'

Her mother loved fussing over her when she visited. She never wanted Maserati to lift a finger. And Maserati did not mind being looked after. It made her feel like a child again. Her mother's little ten-year-old daughter.

'Your garden is flourishing,' she said, admiringly. Mama had started a small garden to keep herself busy and it was yielding tomatoes, spinach, green peppers, carrots, lemons, and oranges.

'All these veggies in the meals came from the garden,' replied Mama. 'And your father, bless his heart, he's been so helpful. He looks after it and waters it for me when I am away at church conferences.'

The way she spoke of her husband, with love and tenderness, baffled Rati. Her friend Tebo's husband had cheated but Maserati had never felt so disillusioned about him as she did about her own father. When you have high expectations of someone, their transgressions carry much more significance. She had high expectations of her dad. He was supposed to be a spotless hero, one who could do no wrong.

There was no better time to discuss the elephant that had brought her home.

'Speaking of Papa…'

'Hmmm?' Mama assumed a defensive posture. She'd been down this judgemental road with Rati before. The child needed to learn to accept her decision once and for all.

'What about Papa?'

Mantwa shot Maserati a look that said, 'Respect your mother.'

'I never told you the full story of why the engagement party was called off,' Rati began. There had been some vague explanation about sickness, bad weather, and rescheduling.

'Hmmm.'

'Well, the truth Mama, is that I found out that Tshepo cheated with many women during our relationship. And I was so angry.

So angry, Mama. And disappointed. I just thought he was different. Different from… other men.' They both knew who the comparison referred to.

'I thought we wanted the same things, the same future. So, I have been trying to give him a second chance. Because I didn't want to throw away our five years together. But the trust is gone. I don't like who I have become with him, Mama. But you, after Papa… you stayed. How were you able to stay when the trust was broken?'

She had dreaded this part of the conversation because she didn't want to cross the respect boundaries. It was taboo for children to ask their parents these questions, but for the sake of her healing, she needed to ask. She had held on to this all her life. Maybe if she understood, then maybe she would have a different perspective on the issue.

Mama reached out to her hands and held them as she spoke.

'Rati, my child. I am no fool. I suspected something serious had happened. But I wanted to hear from you. I am really sorry to hear about these things that Tshepo did. But men, men cheat, my child. It does not make it okay, but they do. It's like somehow their brains have not been wired to resist temptation, like women can. You see Papa's best friend, Mr Nchabeleng? That man is a slice of dark chocolate cake, I would like to eat. But I am sticking to my diet consisting of only your father, my child.'

Whoa, whoa, what just happened?!

Maserati's mouth was agape with shock. Her very own mother, the chair of the women's club at church, the respectable lady who spoke at all the neighbourhood funerals, was talking about lusting over her husband's best friend?

What did she call him… 'A slice of dark chocolate cake!'

Who was this imposter posing as her mother?

Mantwa was on the floor, dying with laughter. She hadn't meant to, but her mother had also shared similar stories about stolen moments. Parents are indeed human beings first before they are parents.

'Yes, your father cheating with that imbecile of a woman hurt me deeply. I was disappointed and embarrassed. But I loved him. Love is a game only fools play, my child. Sometimes you are a fool in love to win in love. I had faith in the life we were yet to build. Then there was you and your little sister. I knew he loved you and that you were his greatest achievement. So, I stayed.'

'You could still have loved him from a distance, Mama. And having children should not be a reason to stay.'

'I could have. But that was not the choice I made, Rati. I stayed and decided to work on my marriage. Your father still wanted to be married to me. You know he is not a lovey-dovey person. But I told him what needed to happen for this marriage to mend. I worked on myself. And he slowly just followed suit. Your father was remorseful.'

'Remorseful? C'mon Mama.'

'Watch it, Rati.'

'Sorry, Mama. I never once saw him as sorry. He walked around here full of pride.'

'That was your young, skewed perception. Your father was remorseful. He had embarrassed himself. He lost self-respect mostly because the kids at school used to tease you about the traffic cop woman.'

'But he never apologised. Not to me.'

'Not in words. You know our generation; we think respect only goes in one direction. He tried in his actions. But you rejected his efforts at every turn.'

'He *should* have apologised, Mama. He should have come to me now as an adult if he couldn't do it when I was a child. He and I have had so many arguments about this and not once has he said he was sorry. He just keeps insisting that people are not perfect, which feels like an excuse to me.'

'You are both stubborn, Rati.'

'So, you stayed, and trusted him again? Did he never do it again?'

'It took time to rebuild the trust. It was the little actions from him. Do I think he never did it again? I don't know, I don't think so. But one can never say with one hundred percent certainty. And it is not for me to say. It is for him to say. All I know is, I worked on my marriage, and I am happy. We have our ups and downs, like every marriage, but I am happy to grow old with your father. Rati, your father is right. No human being is perfect, and that goes for you, too.'

Maserati loved perfection. A perfect world was a safe world.

'Love and life are about choosing. Every single day you make choices that will bring you fulfilment in the long run,' said Mama.

'That is true, Ma,' Mantwa agreed.

'My question to you is, what do you want to do about Tshepo? What will make you happy?'

'I don't know Mama. I am trying to give him a second chance, but the trust is gone, and I sense that the other women are still around. I just feel unappreciated and taken advantage of.'

Warm tears trickled down Maserati's face. She never cried in front of her parents. Never. She'd always felt the need to protect her mother from distress, and as for her father, she'd never wanted him to see her vulnerable.

'Aaw, Rati. It's okay, Mmapelo.' Mother Hen was all over her child, soothing the hurt away.

'You must do what's best for you, my child. Do you want this relationship with Tshepo? If the answer is yes, what will it take to make it work? What sort of relationship do you want? What is his take on faithfulness? These are the things you must both sit down and talk about. If you are both willing and want it to work, it can.

'But if you don't think you can move past this, then don't force yourself into it. Choose what will make you happy, Rati. It is okay to do so. And you don't have to be held hostage by the choice you make today, if you realise tomorrow that the choice is not working anymore.

'Every single day we make choices and decisions. But, with that comes accountability and responsibility.'

For so long, Maserati had held a view of her mother as a weakling, a woman who chose to stay with a man out of tradition rather than love. But her mother, the smart independent woman she was, had made her choice with full autonomy. She followed her heart and did not allow herself to be held hostage by 'what would people think' syndrome, even if those people were her children. Her mother had hoped that she had raised her girls to not necessarily follow her same actions, but to rather be empowered women with their own life paths.

Maserati had carried a grudge and fought a battle that her mother had long let go. The lesson she had failed to see all these years was that she had the right to make choices suitable for her. Some of her choices regarding Tshepo had been driven by her need to not end up with someone like her dad. She had expressed her insecurities early on in their relationship, but Tshepo had been wonderful, reassuring and proving his love for her over and over again. With time, he had gained her complete trust.

Tshepo was perfect. He was not her father.

She missed all the signs when the affairs started just within a year of their relationship.

She needed to release herself from the bondage of perfection and the lifelong grudge against her father. This would free her to have clarity about what needed to happen with her relationship with Tshepo.

On their return to Johannesburg, the following day, she was very clear on what she had to do.

Despite his promises and attempts to make amends, this last month with him had left her insecure, suspicious, distracted and anxious. It needed to end.

She gave back the engagement ring despite his inauthentic

pleas for forgiveness, and the endless calls, flowers, and What-sApp texts. She blocked him on all her social media and asked the security at her residential estate and workplace to return any courier services coming to drop gifts for her.

It was time for a new chapter.

Chapter Fifteen

'Your boiling hot cappuccino, ma'am,' said Lovemore, returning with her coffee, interrupting her thoughts, and bringing her to the present.

The tension between her and Tshepo was so thick you could cut it with a knife.

'Thank you. I am actually ready to order my food.' Not even the unwelcome presence of Tshepo was going to spoil her appetite. There are a couple of things that Maserati loved in the world – shoes, books, and food. In that order.

'Okay, what would you like to have?' Lovemore asked, with paper and pen in hand, trying his best to ignore the obvious lingering discomfort between the two.

'I will have the creamy chicken livers with penne.'

'And you sir?' Lovemore asked, hardly looking in the direction of Tshepo, clearly choosing Maserati's side in this conflict he knew nothing of. Although Tshepo sensed this frostiness, he ordered a light salad with a glass of sparkling water.

'Still a health freak, I see,' said Maserati, making a mental observation.

'You are also a creature of habit, Rati.'

Feigning ignorance. 'What do you mean?'

'I could have won a million-dollar bet that that's what you were going to order. You hardly ever vary your order every time we…. every time you came here.'

He teased her and he knew she didn't like it. She looked beautiful when she got mad. *Her eye-rolling deserved its own meme*, he thought as he burst out laughing.

'Gosh, it's really good to see you, Rati. Really.'

'Maserati,' she retorted.

'Huh?!'

'Please call me Maserati.' He had no right to call her by nicknames that signified a special time between them. He forfeited that right the day he could not keep his hands to himself, and betrayed her trust in the worst way possible, on the eve of an important milestone in their relationship.

'I am sorry, Ra… My apologies, Maserati.' Awkward silence.

Right on cue, Lovemore was yet again the hero of the day as he returned with their food order and broke that awkward silence. He placed their plates in front of them and could sense that palpable tension. In this battle, he had chosen sides without being asked, and would have tackled Tshepo to the ground, had Maserati asked.

As a waiter for many years, he had witnessed many a couple's quarrels. The telltale signs ranged from clenched jaws, hushed tones, heads tilted in the effort to prevent a river of tears from free-fall, touchy hands being slapped away, to any of the non-verbal cues under the sun that screamed lovers' tiff. And as the discerning person he was – something that set him apart from his fellow waiters – his discretion and non-intrusion had been rewarded with generous tips by his patrons.

He flashed Maserati an empathetic look. 'Before I leave you momentarily to enjoy your food, is there anything else I could get you? A bottle of still water perhaps for the table, and a glass of Coke, with a smidgen of ice and lemon slices for you, my lady?' Lovemore had studied Maserati's habits and passed summa cum laude.

'You know me so well, Lovemore. Yes, please.' Maserati smiled at her favourite waiter in the whole wide world.

'Very well, then. Please enjoy your meals.' And he expertly excused himself to give them space to resolve whatever it was these two needed to resolve.

They ate in silence. She was not about to make it easy for him.

After what felt like eternity, Tshepo spoke.

'I'm sorry for what I did, for what I put you through, Maserati. I've wanted to tell you this in person for a while. And when I saw you sitting here, I knew this was my chance to offer my apology to you. I know this may be a little too late, and these words may never erase the pain you felt. I let you down in ways that even I am surprised by. I let myself down. I broke the sacred trust you placed in me and placed in all the dreams and life we were building together.'

The ice was thawing.

Hold it together, girl, Maserati thought, keeping her gaze downward, avoiding any eye contact lest her eyes betrayed her.

'You deserved none of it, Rati, none of it. All you ever gave me was love. Unmerited love and respect, you gave without reservation. With you, I could envision a future. You inspired me to work hard, to focus all my energies into a path of success that I wanted to build for us and our future family. And just as we were succeeding, I went and sabotaged it all. And I now know that this is a consequence of a childhood faulty belief that I do not deserve good things in life.

'And it killed and continues to kill me inside that through this false belief that I am not deserving of all that is good, I went and created chaos in our perfect life, and I am the source of your pain and disappointment. You were everything, no, you are everything I want in a life partner, and I messed it all up in a moment of stupidity. A moment I will regret for the rest of my life. And I will spend the rest of my life making it up to you. If you allow me….'

Tshepo trailed off, realising he had said quite a lot more than he had planned to. But this was a one-time shot and he could not let it pass by, as Maserati had refused to take his calls over the last six months. It was now or never.

'Rati, I am truly, truly sorry.'

These were the words she had longed to hear all this time. And just like that, the ice melted, and she could feel the sting in her eyes. No, no, she was not going to cry in front of him. No, she was never going to give him that satisfaction.

She abruptly stood up, reached out into her purse for a wad of cash which she dropped on the table before she dashed off without a word, softly sprinting to her car. Tshepo knew better not to run after her. He knew she needed to get away from him and he had no business intruding into that space. But for a moment before Maserati dashed off, they locked eyes for a split second. He had gotten through to her. And she knew that they both knew.

And so, he sat back down, confident that their journey was about to resume.

Tshepo gestured to Lovemore for the bill. He paid by card.

'The lady left a tip for you,' Tshepo said, as he made his way out of the restaurant towards his car. Lovemore counted the cash with no doubt that the lady would indeed be generous, but a R400 tip was more than the total bill had come to, and way too generous even for his favourite patron.

But who was he to refuse such a gift?

Well, maybe they did resolve their quarrel after all, thought Lovemore. That was the only conclusion he could come to, as he happily cleared the table.

In the safety of her car, the tears Maserati had buried deep inside her, welled up and came pouring out. It was as if the whole year had led up to this point. Maserati had imagined his apology over and over in her mind during the last year, down to picturing what he would be wearing and where they would be when he offered the epic apology. But hearing these words from

Tshepo today confirmed just how much she had really wanted to hear him say how terribly sorry he was. And what happened ten minutes ago, opened her up. And when they locked eyes, she could tell he knew that he had managed to soften her heart. The door was open for the next step.

Maserati started her car, revved it up as she joined the road, heading off home. Knowing she was going to call him.

Not as soon as she got home.

But eventually.

Chapter Sixteen

Tshepo's swag was undeniable.

But it was in another gear when he walked towards his car because he was looking forward to the call, he knew he would receive from Maserati later that night. His ancestors must have been working overtime that day because he had secretly been frequenting Maserati's favourite hangout spots for the last couple of months hoping to bump into her. Although she was never big on the Joburg's social scene, it was as if she had completely disappeared from its face. At some point he had given up and even stopped stalking her friends' hangout places as well. He would see her friends from a distance, but Maserati was never in sight.

But today was the beginning of the beginning. No wonder his swag was a bit perky.

Denzel Washington is the sexiest man of all time. That Denzel walk is the walk of a man who knows he is the man. A man who's got balls. Do you think that dip in his walk is just for nothing? No. That walk is because he constantly feels the friction of his balls against his thighs. It's his constant reminder that he is *the man*! That smile is a smile of a knowing man.

Denzel's walk had nothing on Tshepo's at that moment. He

walked like a man whose road had been paved with gold and all he had to do was walk right in and take up his rightful place in his lady's life.

As he got into his car, his phone rang.

He didn't have to look to see who the caller was. He knew as soon as he noted the time. 5:15 pm. It was Busi.

His current girlfriend. Of three months.

Busi was driving back from out of town and Tshepo was meant to meet her at her place as soon she got in. But she was the furthest thing on his mind. Other priorities were occupying his mind.

But Tshepo was a gentleman through and through and would never ignore a lady's call.

'Busi, babe. Are you home already?'

'Hey, babe. I'm almost home. I missed you. Are you on your way here?'

Busi had imagined the reception she would get from her lover during the whole three-hour drive home. That man was a beast in bed! Theirs was a physical union often confused as a relationship and the confusion was always on Busi's side. Though she wasn't totally to blame. Tshepo was suave.

'I am glad you got here safely. I bet your mom was over the moon that you dropped by.'

'She was, babe. But she was so disappointed that you hadn't joined me. The whole family is looking forward to meeting you and…'

Realising she was going to keep talking all the way home, Tshepo interrupted, 'Babe. Something urgent has come up. The MEC has called a meeting with the CEO and me. It sounds like the organisation is not happy with some of the recent contracts and he must brief the Premier first thing in the morning. I hate it when these guys do this, some of us have lives, you know, and beautiful women to come home to.'

He had learned over the years to leverage the power of name dropping and his important work to get into and out of situations as he deemed necessary. And this was a necessary situation to get out of. He was not missing Maserati's call for any reason. But he knew the power of keeping the door always slightly ajar. You never know when you need to get back in.

'If I could take you with I would, but you just had a long trip, and it would be unfair of me to ask you to wait for me for a meeting that might drag on. Let me make it up to you during the week. Will you let me do that, my Cherrie?' That charm was his Achilles heel.

'My Cherrie' got her every time. Tshepo could do no wrong. His power and affiliation to the top political brass in the province was why she was attracted to him. She imagined that her understanding would pay off big time one day when Tshepo assumed an even more powerful position than he currently held.

In the three months they had been together, they had wined and dined with some of Gauteng's top politicians and business-people. It was a circle she had longed to be part of as she saw the benefits some of her friends were reaping as side pieces for the political and business elite of Gauteng. If Tshepo had an urgent business matter with the MEC, her role was to not be in the way.

'Babe, I understand. I know you would be with me if you didn't have to go. I'll be waiting even if it ends late.'

'You are the best, my Cherrie. Let me know when you are safely in the house, okay. I'll speak to you later.'

He is so caring, Busi thought, as she made a turn into her small townhouse complex to her home she shared with a friend.

'One day soon, I will not be sharing a home with anyone but my man.'

Tshepo got home, made his way to the study and got comfortable. He had been eagerly anticipating a call from Maserati since he left Parkhurst. He just knew she was going to call. He got himself comfortable with a glass of 25-year-old Macallan. A call from Maserati, the love of his life, was a special occasion.

The universe would decide otherwise.

———

An hour had passed since Maserati got home, when she took out her phone contemplating what she would say when she called him. She started to dial the number that she had come to know as well as her own identification number. She had called this number a million times since they met years ago.

0-8-3-5-5-3-0-6-6-6

And stared at the phone screen.

How come she never noticed that his phone number ended in 666? Wasn't that supposed to be the devil's number? What other signs had she ignored in the past?

Maserati put the phone aside, left it on silent mode, took a long bubble bath, got into bed, and fell asleep.

This chapter was closed!

Back home, Tshepo kept glancing at his phone. Three hours later, still no call, at least not from Maserati. But Busi sent a text.

'How's the meeting going?'

'The meeting just ended. Can you be here in 20 minutes?' Tshepo needed somewhere to offload all this pent-up energy in his nether regions.

Busi had hardly set her foot in the door when Tshepo pounced on her like a predator hungry for prey. He ripped off her underwear and had her right there in the hallway. And ten minutes later he was zipping up his pants and walking towards the study to down the glass of the expensive whisky he had poured earlier in anticipation of a celebratory call. Busi misinterpreted this whole act to mean she had been on his mind the whole time in his meeting with the MEC.

He was wondering what happened to Maserati. And was slightly irritated that he'd been wrong about her calling him.

A month passed, then two, then three and he stopped counting.

The call never came.

Chapter Seventeen

During that time, Maserati kept her head down, focusing on her work as an Associate Medical Director for Tobbas, a multinational pharmaceutical company.

Her job required attending a lot of national and international business and scientific conferences. Many times her company hosted advisory boards on strategies to tackle some of the world's pressing health issues with key stakeholders from academia, government, and non-governmental organisations. She found her job really gratifying, making an impact on a global scale.

Maserati loved interacting with leaders in the various fields of medicine, and this meant that she and the team were usually quite busy at these conferences.

One of the key conferences usually attended was the International Infectious Diseases Conference (IIDC), and that year it was being held in South Africa for the first time. Cape Town was the perfect venue for Rati, providing her the opportunity to interact with colleagues from her alma mater, the University of Cape Town. The IIDC attracted thousands of delegates from all over the world, and this year a large contingent from Africa also attended. Not only would she have to host the delegates her company had invited at their advisory board, but she would also have to host her colleagues including her senior leadership from their Chicago headquarters.

The various organisations were invited to a gala dinner by the Ministry of Health. These events provided an ideal opportunity for networking and she was able to introduce her colleagues and seniors to the team at the Ministry of Health. They had a ten-seater table in the gala dinner venue. It was amazing to watch Maserati work a room which is why people never believed her when she told them she was an introvert. But when she had got this job, she had quickly learned the art of small talk as a pathway to her success. While she tired easily around too many people, she was willing to relegate her shyness to the back seat when necessary.

Maserati wore a three-piece black David Tlale pantsuit with a tie. A very bold, masculine, no-nonsense look, which was equally sexy. This look screamed, 'I mean business.'

The theme of the meeting was 'Together, Revitalising Public Health.'

On the agenda was a keynote address 'Transforming Public Health for The Future' by a Dr Bušang Emanuel Nkosi. His biography was line after line of accomplishments.

Maserati skimmed over Dr Nkosi's biography: Studied Medicine at UCT, Health Systems and Public Health Specialist from Johns Hopkins, did a stint in Geneva at the World Health Organisation, where he continues in an advisory capacity, Consultant at the Bill & Melinda Gates Foundation, on the board of RAIN Foundation, CEO at LeMa Health Innovations, etc.

Jesus, when does this guy sleep? Maserati was always sceptical of biographies that read like they came straight out of the Egotistical Manual of Boasting.

And there he was.

Even seated several metres away from the stage, she instantly recognised those brown eyes. She could not say what was so special about them but even today, watching him take up his position in front of the podium readying himself to give his keynote address, his eyes felt grounding to her. As he started to speak, his voice boomed through the speakers with clarity and authority. This was a man whose confidence was in unlimited supply. He commanded the room.

Instinctively, Maserati looked around her and indeed everyone was mesmerised, including the Ministry of Health folks who often believed themselves to be more important than everyone else in the room. She glanced at her colleagues from Chicago, and the Vice President of International Enterprises, James Gaines was gesturing to her, asking if she knew who that was. Gaines always maintained a level of objective equal assessment, and was hardly ever impressed by anything or anyone. But Dr Bušang Emanuel Nkosi was clearly not everyone.

Gaines whispered, 'Do you think we can meet him afterwards?'

Of course, she wanted to meet him again, but not for the same reasons as Gaines. Hers were very personal reasons of intrigue.

He had lied about his name when they first met at the shoe store.

Ben! Hmph... why in this new age of digital connectedness, would people lie about their names? Maserati wondered, eager for an opportunity to interrogate him.

Ben, Bušang, whatever his name was, argued that the world was in the digital age and health care systems, particularly in developing nations, must quickly evolve and adapt, and take advantage of benefits of digital tools and technologies to bring healthcare to people wherever they are including those in very remote and rural areas, which are seldom beneficiaries to the country's fortunes. His arguments were strongly supported by robust evidence as shown by graph after graph of compelling data generated by the work that his group was doing in advocating for digital healthcare solutions in Africa.

'The future is digital. And the future is in fact here, now. The right to health and healthcare is a right enshrined and protected by our constitution. And a healthcare system that is not willing to move into the digital era is a system that does not hold the best interests of its citizens.'

He looked in the direction of the Minister of Health, and the challenge was as clear as day.

'Telehealth and telemedicine are going to be the great equaliser – where being poor, or being from an under-serviced rural or informal settlement, will no longer be a reason nor a barrier to receiving good quality care.'

He concluded his presentation with a powerful call to action.

'If health is a state of complete physical, mental and social well-being and not merely the absence of disease or infirmity, and public health is the art and science of preventing disease, prolonging life and promoting health through the organised efforts of society, then digital health solutions are going to be the bridge to assuring just and equitable distribution of those efforts for all citizens of this country.'

The audience erupted in applause that quickly became a standing ovation.

And for a brief second, Maserati watched him get slightly uncomfortable, clearly humbled by the enthusiasm of the crowd.

Hmm. That's interesting.

Many accomplished men revel in adoration and ululation.

But at the same time, Ben knew that he had succeeded in conveying a powerful message for the audience, most of whom were people of influence and were responsible for health policies that could either benefit or harm. His presentation was a direct challenge to them to employ all available tools to make sure Health to All was not just a catchy slogan, but a reality for all people including the marginalised.

Chapter Eighteen

A fter the presentations and formalities were over, people started mingling.

Ben made a beeline for Maserati. He had seen her as she entered the gala hall. You could not miss her; such was her striking beauty. Of course, all the men and women noticed her too though she seemed completely unaware of the attention she drew as she entered the hall.

Ben was surprised to see her there. He could not forget the first time he had seen her at that shoe boutique in Hyde Park. He had boldly walked up to her, surprising even himself, as he was usually quite measured in these matters. But he could not help himself. He had encouraged her to choose two stunning pairs of shoes, but quickly felt he had intruded on her space – for some women shopping was retail therapy, a moment to not be interrupted by unwanted favours from men. He did not want to come across as a prick with no boundaries, so just as quickly as he had commented on the shoes, he had made an exit and walked off trying very hard to not look back. But he had regretted that decision for months. And here she was, he could not believe his lucky stars. And this time, he wasn't letting the chance slip.

As he was heading towards her, she seemed to have the same idea.

She got to him first.

'Dr Bušang Nkosi.'

'Maserati,' he remembered.

And he did not miss the accusatory tone as she said his name.

'Fancy meeting you again.'

'Have we met? I don't believe we have.' Her eyes seemed to challenge him.

'As I recall, I met a man named Ben a couple of months ago. You must be his twin because the similarity is uncanny.'

'Touché. Let me reintroduce myself. My name is Bušang…'

Maserati interrupted, '… so you go around just lying about who you are?'

Just then Dr Jay Lamola, a member of the delegation from the Ministry of Health, walked over to them, smiling at Rati. 'Dr Mojapelo, I see you have met our superstar here.'

He reached out to Ben for a handshake.

'Dr Bušang Emmanuel Nkosi! That was some goddamn speech you gave there, as always, Chief, and your challenge did not go unnoticed. In fact, we plan to set up an inter-ministerial task force between Health, Industry & Technology, and other important stakeholders. The Minister would love to consult with you, of course. I'll ask my people to reach out to your people, so we can make this thing happen.'

Dr Lamola was one of those. If name dropping was a sport, he would be an Olympic gold winner.

It was how he had emphasised the name Bušang Emmanuel Nkosi that the lightbulb finally switched on for Maserati.

Ahhhh, it's an acronym, she thought, embarrassed that she had called him a liar. Who goes by an acronym anyway? Why couldn't he have just introduced himself by his real name that day? Bušang had a much more regal sound it. Ben was just so basic.

Thank God, Lamola had an attention span of a goldfish, and

he was soon off to another important stakeholder, the CEO of the biggest distribution companies all the way from India. The man was a limelight hogger.

'Phew, I didn't think he was ever going to leave us alone.' Ben said, turning his attention back to her. Not that he had paid Lamola any attention anyway, the whole time he was going on and on, Ben's eyes were on Maserati. For a second, she had looked as though she was blushing. Ben wondered what that was about because he would bet his last dollar that her blush had not been induced by anything Lamola had said.

'So, I owe you an apology,' she said uncomfortably. 'I thought you lied about your name.'

'Oh that. Well, before we were rudely interrupted, I was about to fully introduce myself…'

'I got it. Ben is an acronym for your full names.'

'Indeed.'

'I like Bušang.' She hadn't meant for it to come as a whisper. Her cheeks felt warm.

'Me too.' That smile again. And those brown eyes.

His eyes reminded her of the colour of the soil, igniting a feel of rootedness. They felt safe. Maserati could not quite get why his eyes would invoke such a feeling. What happened to just admiring men for their muscles?

He stood a towering 1,9 metres; his presence quite assured. At 1,6 metres, she literally had to look up to him.

'So, Dr Mojapelo.' Maserati hadn't told him her surname, but that motormouth Lamola had greeted her as such.

'So, are you also with the Ministry of Health? What brings you to the IIDC?'

'No, fortunately not with the ministry.' They both cracked up laughing.

'I'm with Tobbas,' she said, pointing to a sign that indicated the company's credentials.

'Ah you work for the 'other side',' Ben teased.

The pharma industry had an unfair reputation and there was

a long-held joke in the medical field that working for pharma was akin to selling out. But Maserati had come to know first-hand, the value that the industry brought to healthcare.

'Hahaha. Yes, I work for the other side. So that was an amazing speech that you gave there. Your assessment of the future of medicine is really apt. For many years, quality health-care seemed inaccessible to many. Technology may very well be the equaliser.'

'Thank you.'

And more shoptalk followed as Gaines and four of his global colleagues joined them. They had stepped out briefly to take an urgent call from headquarters, and now they were back, ready to mingle and network with the crowd. James had been impressed earlier by Ben's speech.

'Dr En-cosy,' Gaines enunciated carefully, extending his hand. 'That was some speech there.'

Maserati shifted gears to work mode.

'Let me introduce you. This is James Gaines, the VP of International Enterprises. And he is here with our team for the conference.'

'James, this is Dr Ben... Bušang Nkosi.' His biography escaped her, and she wasn't about to tell her co-workers how she had met him at a shoe store.

'I couldn't agree with you more, good sir,' said Gaines. 'The future of medicine is digital. And our company has been leading some innovative work around this subject, exploring how digi-talising our services can bring more medicines and improve the lives of all people around the world. In fact, we have been looking at partnering with experts such as yourself, to formulate our global digital health strategies.'

After the shoptalk and exchange of business cards and promises for follow-up meetings, Gaines and the global team called it a night. Maserati walked them out, confirmed the following day's itinerary and bid them goodnight.

Maserati returned to find him surrounded by more people, but he swiftly excused himself.

'So, it looks like most people have left.' Ben looked around the room.

'Yes. But for some of us, the night is still young.'

'It is?'

'Yes. A couple of us are heading out to a spot in Green Point for drinks and some music. You should come,' Maserati dared him. She wasn't sure if he was the type to go dancing, but there was only one way to find out.

It was refreshing that after a taxing day, delegates found some time to wind down in an informal setting with colleagues.

'I'd love to.' Ben would agree to anything at this point to spend more time with her, get to know her a bit more. However, he wasn't sure a rowdy loud dancing spot was an ideal place to get to know someone. He couldn't be more wrong. Maserati loved dancing. At the very least, he was going to learn that about her.

That and her love for shoes.

Chapter Nineteen

The cab dropped Rati and two of her colleagues, Lungi and Pearl, just outside Havana in Green Point. The place was buzzing with many of the delegates, both local and international. This was always the fun part of these conferences; it was good for people to network outside the work formalities. This offered an opportunity to introduce the international visitors to some of the best local scenes, music, and cuisine. Other things happened, but that wasn't the focus.

They had all changed from their business attire into suitable looks for a night on the town. Maserati wore a white fitted shirt, with skinny jeans and a pair of Louboutin Pigalles in nude, a classy balance between a party and work look. Networking did not stop at the conference hall.

'Time to let our hair down, girls!' Lungi had a wild edge about her. Maserati always had to remind her to reign it in. They still represented a multinational corporation even after hours.

And there at the entrance of Havana, was his towering frame. He had kept the jacket and shirt he wore earlier sans the tie and changed into a pair of Levi jeans. It didn't look like he put a lot of thought into this look, but the results were caramel Idris Elba on a fashion shoot. Right on cue, he turned around just as the cab was pulling off and threw a half wave.

He was with two other men, who were introduced as Nathi and Thabang. Thabang had a striking resemblance to Ben, but looked a bit younger than the two men, and he seemed to be the one very familiar with the place. Lungi saw prey and was nudging Maserati for proper introductions.

'Hey,' Ben leaned over to Maserati and gave her a hug. Oh, that was unexpected. This was the first time they had touched each other. He smelled divine. The hug lingered a second longer.

'Hey.'

'These are my colleagues Lungi and Pearl.' Thabang and Nathi were very eager for the introductions.

'This way, we booked a table.' Thabang led the way into the club; clearly he had been there many times.

I wonder if Ben has been here and with whom. Maserati was silently curious.

They got to their table, one of those VIP types where you have to buy thousands rands worth of alcohol to get it booked. Maserati did not peg Ben to be the type that did that, but the uncomfortable look on his face showed that Thabang ran the show.

They settled into the seats, and within ten minutes four more people had joined the corner table. Drinks were already flowing. Ben ordered a bottle of sparkling water which he drank while the rest of the group were already downing shots. The place was buzzing. The DJ was playing Afro-beats from across the diaspora. Lungi was already on the dance floor. Maserati was still seated, but the rhythm of the music was way too powerful.

Maserati loved dancing and was pretty good at it. On the occasion that she went out dancing with her friends, and there was a good dancer in their midst, she couldn't help but watch them. She was always drawn by their rhythm, as if she was right there in spirit with them, in their zone. As the Afrobeat jammed, she saw a girl behind Lungi dancing by herself, clearly having a great time, unperturbed by her lone dancing status. Her movements were deliberate, measured, elegant, hands periodically touching her chest, eyes often closed as if transported to some haven, just the right amount of motion, nothing exaggerated.

And then, there was Lungi! Lungi was the kind who knew all the latest dance moves and had them down to a tee. But she needed to go to etiquette school. Everything with her was so exaggerated; her movements were big, creating enough wind to stir windmills. Her movements were so wild, dancing near her was dangerous. But you could not fault her for having a great time.

Ben was watching her, silently fascinated by her obvious longing to be on the dance floor. He could tell rhythm was in her blood, as one dancer to another. Yes, as stoic as Ben was, he could throw a smooth get down if the mood called for it.

Maserati could no longer hold back. She joined the lone dancer behind Lungi who welcomed her and they grooved away. Maserati knew she was sexy when she was dancing. People often stopped and stared. She wondered if Ben was staring. With a quick smooth turnaround, she met his eyes. Yes, he was staring, and so were half the men in the club. But she only cared if he found her sexy. She held his gaze as if there was no one else in the club but the two of them and she was dancing for him.

Another popular song came on and the entire table was now on the dance floor. Except for Ben who continued sitting, sipping on his sparkling water. He only had eyes for Maserati, who was now shimmying down close to Thabang. She turned around and motioned to Ben to come and join her. When he didn't budge, she went over and pulled him from his seat. Thabang was laughing because Ben on a dance floor at a club was a rare sighting. When she paid no attention to his objections, he eventually got up, and danced face to face with Maserati. He followed her lead, her rhythm. She was quite surprised to see how good and smooth he was.

Clearly this guy can dance, so why did he insist on sitting? she wondered.

'You are such a good dancer, Dr Bušang Nkosi,' she said in a way that confirmed her shock. Plus, you know what they say about good dancers!

He smiled. 'Not as good as you are.'

'Ben. Himself. On the dancefloor! Miracles do not cease,' Nathi and Thabang teased him. Thabang even looked proud. When the DJ switched to another song, Maserati took pity on Ben and motioned for them to take a break. It was just the two of them by the table.

'Whoo, that was fun. The music is amazing.'

'It is. And deafening too.' As much fun as this was, it would be more fun for Ben to get Maserati in a quieter place so they could have a civil conversation, rather than this screaming match they were having. There was no competing with a rowdy crowd and an even rowdier DJ. Maserati read his mind.

'Do you want to get out of here, take a walk?'

Chapter Twenty

The breeze outside was a welcome refresher compared to the hot, stale air in Havana.

It was close to midnight, but you couldn't tell from the number of people still arriving at the club.

'Oh, the breeze feels so refreshing.' Maserati twirled around and raised her arms as if to draw more of the breeze from the heavens. Ben was following right behind, amused by this free spirit in front of him. He had enjoyed dancing with her just a few minutes ago. He even surprised himself that she had somehow managed to get him to loosen up in a way he hadn't done in... ever.

She was laughing and smiling. Her eyes had a spark that the night could not hide.

They walked in the direction of the Waterfront, enjoying the breeze and the sound of the waves from the nearby Sea Point promenade. He wondered how she was going to walk in those shoes but was smart enough to know you don't ask a lady such nonsense.

'You're such a good dancer.' Her voice sounded like music. 'Not only are you a world-renowned healthcare key opinion leader, but a good dancer to boot. Well, well… What else are you good at Dr Nkosi?' she teased.

Ben blushed and was glad to be under the protection of darkness.

'Thanks. You were not bad yourself.'

'I love dancing. I think I would have pursued dance as a career, but there were future bills to be paid, so I opted for medicine.' She laughed. She felt so light.

Maserati called herself a high-heel Technical College graduate, but her pinkie toe was screaming bloody murder. Thankfully, there was a bench along the sidewalk, and she motioned for them to sit down. He had been wondering about those shoes.

'My feet are killing me.' She took off the Louboutins, massaged her feet and reached into her tiny purse for some foldable flip-flops that she put on.

'Every girl carries these in their purse for a night on the town.' That laugh again. The girl was having fun tonight. 'It's such a beautiful night. I forgot how Cape Town nights can be so magical.'

'Do you come up here often?' he asked.

'I spent six years of my life here. UCT, medical school.' It seemed like a lifetime ago when Maserati was a broke, focused student, dreaming about a future with endless possibilities. 'Your hundred-page biography indicated you also studied at UCT?'

'Hundred pages, huh? I need to have a word with Grace and Nathi.' Noticing her questioning eyes, he continued, 'Grace is my PA. She loves to embellish. It's unnecessary. And you met Nathi. He's my business partner, and he insists that people want to hear that stuff. I disagree.'

Ben had always found these accolades unnecessary if they didn't do anything to help people. A list of titles was not something that impressed him.

'Yeah, I studied medicine here. I had planned on being an oncologist, but the world of public health called.' He shifted uncomfortably on the bench, like he had overshared. 'And I'm glad I followed that path. I'm passionate about making health for all a reality.' Ben was hoping this would not turn into more business talks. He was interested in the laughing, dancing Maserati.

'I'm inspired by your passion for people,' said Maserati. 'There was no mistaking it during your speech. You must be proud of the work that you do.'

It did not need a rocket scientist to tell that Ben wasn't just about talk, but that he really believed in making changes.

'Thank you,' he replied. Maserati could not have known how much this compliment meant to him. 'And you, how did you get to cross over to the dark side?' he teased, as he had earlier in the day.

'After serving my time in the public health sector, I just got so disillusioned by the poor management, the constant under-resourcing, being overworked and underpaid. Nothing broke my heart more than knowing a solution to patient's healthcare problem and not being able to provide that solution because of resource mismanagement. An acquaintance passed my name onto someone, and I found myself at Tobbas. It's been wonderful doing what I do, contributing to helping solve some of the world's most unmet health needs. Hearing from health care providers and patients alike about the impact we make is priceless. I also have an opportunity to travel to some of the most amazing places across the world.'

'So, you love to travel?'

'Sir, what kind of question is that? Who doesn't love travelling?' Maserati answered.

'Indeed. And I wish more of our people had an opportunity to travel. It's through travelling that my perspective on things and the world changes. Travelling and reading.'

Maserati was enjoying the fact that they shared these two important things in common.

'They do say that the nearest way to oneself is around the world.'

They both smiled in agreement.

He looked down to check on his vibrating phone. He'd been ignoring it for a while now. But knew it would not stop vibrating. She was curious to know who that was. He read her mind.

'Oh, that was just my brother, Thabang. He was just wondering what happened to us.'

'Thabang is your brother? The resemblance now makes sense. Does he make a habit of attending these conferences with you?' Maserati did not recall if Thabang's professional background was discussed when they met earlier in the night.

He laughed as hard as if he'd just been told a joke by Dave Chappelle. *This guy laughs at anything*, Maserati noted.

'Thabang has some work in the healthcare space, albeit in a more fundraising role.'

'Ah, I see.' She didn't quite see.

Ben's charisma, passion, and expertise alone should have many people ready to empty their pockets to donate to his cause. That speech he gave earlier today would have been reason enough to ransack her savings account.

'So, is it just the two of you?'

That uncomfortable shift again.

She got it. Family dynamics are some of the most controversial topics to talk about with strangers, or people you just barely met. Hell, with anyone, frankly.

'We have a sister. Thabang's twin. She lives in Senegal and comes home once or twice a month.'

For a moment, he had a distant look, like a memory he wished to avoid. Maserati interrupted the awkward silence, just he started to speak again. They both laughed.

'Ladies first,' he said. Maserati wished she had not hurried to close the silence. He clearly had more to say about his siblings.

'So, I imagine the two of them gang up against you?' she responded. 'I hear twins are mischievous that way.'

There he was laughing again. How does anyone have a ready laugh like this? He kept churning them out like freebies. Maserati had a sense of humour, but she was no queen of comedy. But it was so refreshing to see him laugh like that. This guy whose stature reminded her of a baobab tree; strong, statuesque, sheltering, and steady.

'They certainly did. It didn't help that they were the apples of my parents' eyes. They got away with anything, those two. They still do. But they're good kids.' There was something paternal about his tone. Thabang was hardly a kid. But you could tell Ben had a parental fondness towards them. It made sense as a first-born child. Maserati could relate to that. She was the older daughter, with a ten-year age gap between her and her sister.

'I know that feeling as an older sibling. My younger sister, Malebo, calls me deputy parent. She says not even our mother gives her as much grief as I give her. But that's because like your twin siblings, they let her get away with literally everything. I got spanked for half the things they let slide with her.'

'That's why us older siblings need to start a deputy parent support group.' This time he was the comedian. She laughed so hard she made a snorting piglet sound.

He wanted to get together with her for many other reasons too.

It was getting late. Neither wanted to leave this moment but they had responsibilities in the morning.

'It's getting late,' she said regretfully. 'And I have an early breakfast meeting with my international colleagues.'

'Where are you staying? I can call for a car.'

Within ten minutes, an S-class black Mercedes had pulled up. The driver got out and greeted Ben with familiarity.

'Good evening Mr Nkosi.' He opened the back door, and Ben ushered her in. Ben directed the driver to the Southern Sun hotel where she was staying. They drove in silence. She had questions about the car and driver but chose to stay quiet. He considered explaining the car and driver but also chose silence. They sat close together and although their shoulders barely touched they could feel each other's warmth. He did not want this night to end. He found her hand and ran his fingers softly over it. She felt the undeniable electricity and responded to his touch by opening her hand to his and they locked fingers. It was a short ten-minute ride to the hotel, but that handholding moment was an eternity.

They sat outside the hotel reluctant to let go. The driver read the room, got out of the car, and gave them space as he stood attentively outside.

'I leave for Joburg first thing in the morning. I would love to see you again when you get back, take you out for dinner.'

She turned to look at him, their hands still locked together,

'I would love that.'

He lifted their hands and kissed hers softly. He tapped the door, and the driver, on cue, opened it wide. Ben walked her to the hotel lobby and gave her a hug. She took a deep breath and breathed in his calming essence. They said goodnight aware that neither wanted the night to end. At least they had the promise of the dinner to look forward to.

Maserati went to sleep that night with her heart singing.

Chapter Twenty-One

W hat a beautiful day to meet for lunch with her friends.
Maserati could not wait to tell them about Ben.

They chose Level Four, a chic restaurant at a boutique hotel in
Sandton. She had known Mantwa, and Tebo since high school.
Khutso came into their lives incidentally, at a house party during
a varsity break, and they had hit it off. And here they were today,
pursuing happy lives and success in completely different career
paths.

The ever-ferocious Mantwa Mahlo chose to study law and
was recently named Director at the prestigious law firm, Sizwe
Incorporated, whose client list included some of the richest busi-
nesspeople and the biggest names in politics. And one of these
rich clients was the flamboyant billionaire, Sam Khanyile, affec-
tionately known amongst his friends and the entire country as
Bra-Sam. Bra-Sam was a self-made man, but his wealth grew
exponentially thanks to Black Economic Empowerment policies.
His wealth would quadruple due to his connections to the country's governing party. He had his paws in every industry, but it
was mining that catapulted him to billionaire status.

Mantwa hated to admit it, but Sam Khanyile made her world
twirl. Mantwa held the belief that men were hunters and

providers. And Sam Khanyile had hunted her down and when he got her, had provided her with the moon, the stars, and the world beyond. And the fact that he was already married with three children was a footnote where Mantwa was concerned. As much as she was a strong independent woman, Mantwa held some traditional beliefs about the roles of men and women. For her, all men cheated. The difference between good and bad men had nothing to do with their cheating ways, but rather how efficient they were at keeping one life hidden from another. Any man who flaunted his philandering ways to his wife was trash. And Sam Khanyile was no trash.

He kept his wife in the dark about his extra-marital activities. He provided a lovely home and grand lifestyle for his wife and teenage kids. They had all the help needed from housekeepers to drivers and everything in between. Bra-Sam was a good father. Although his wife, the former beauty queen, Portia Khanyile, was left to the primary role of rearing the children, he tried to be aware of everything going on in his kids' lives and made it a point to go to most of their extra-curricular activities, even if that meant hopping on a helicopter from his office in Sandton to avoid the deathly Joburg traffic, to attend a sport game and not miss a board meeting.

Mantwa met Bra-Sam at an industry function. Her law firm had represented a medium-sized company in a mergers and acquisition transaction, which saw Khanyile Conglomerate acquire a major stake in an oil deal that would make Sam one of the richest men on the continent. He first noticed her during the negotiations but had kept a respectful distance until the M&A was concluded. At the announcement party, he was ready to make his intentions known. A man of his stature was not used to being turned down, but he knew someone like Mantwa would require more than his usual moves. He had pursued her with a skill that had impressed her all the way to his penthouse suite. Sam even cut down his philandering ways.

And they all lived a polygamous happily ever after.

Khutso Malema had been married to her husband Lesetja Malema for ten years. They married young, she was twenty-one and he was twenty-five. They did not waste time building a family. Three years into their marriage they welcomed a daughter, and their son was born two years later. Khutso had just completed her diploma in Public Relations when she got married and was planning to start looking for employment shortly after. Lesetja had other plans for his wife and family and preferred that she stayed home. Certainly when the kids came along, a career in the big corporate world was out of the question.

Truthfully, Khutso did not mind this plan at all. She found homemaking to be a noble service to her family. She leveraged her PR education and was active in her community, church and on the PTO at the kids' school. Lesetja's career as a banker was blossoming. He was a wholesome family man and lived to provide for his family. Now, at thirty-five years old, he could be considered a little bit too traditional and too settled compared to his peers, who were still out chasing skirts, chasing dreams and the illusion of Black Diamond status and all its trappings. Many of his peers mocked his lifestyle.

Maserati and Tebogo Maponya had both studied medicine at UCT. Tebogo loved the public sector and stayed on when Maserati branched out to the private sector. Not only that, but she decided to pursue a fulfilling career without making the move to Johannesburg like all upwardly mobile professionals tend to do. She became one of the youngest hospital CEOs at twenty-eight years old, at one of the district hospitals in the beautiful province of Mpumalanga. In her two years at the helm, she introduced many progressive changes and made her hospital a Batho-Pele award-winning hospital. The Provincial Health Department had been noticing her efforts. It would not be surprising if her career led to the government provincial offices, although she loathed the bureaucracy and political manoeuvrings of governmental departments.

Even though Tebo was born and raised in Polokwane, she

loved the serenity and simplicity of the Lowveld. She and her husband, Lefa Rametsi, had carved out a comfortable life with their three-year-old son, in the posh neighbourhood of Steiltes in Nelspruit. Lefa, a doctor himself in private practice, was part of a consortium of Black doctors who were in talks to build the first Black-owned private hospital in the city.

As settled as Tebo seemed, she was also a lot of fun. And as much as she loved the Lowveld, she made it a point to visit Joburg at least once a month, to re-energise and to connect with her gals. Every time she came to Joburg, she would organise a night on the town, often insisting that they visit some unusual party spots. If it were up to Mantwa alone, fun times would involve some five-star place with no rowdy crowd. But Tebo was always down for whatever, as long as there was some fun and a little flirting with strange men, before going back to her 'normal' life back in Nelspruit. She and Lefa had gone through some marital problems recently, but they seemed to be holding their marriage together.

And then there was her, a failed five-year relationship and ready to mingle.

They all arrived at the restaurant to find her seated at a corner table. She had already ordered a bottle of crisp Chenin Blanc. But then again Mantwa was forever in the mood to celebrate something or the other and they would in all likelihood switch to champagne as the afternoon went by.

'Oh my gosh. You won't believe this stupid driver that was in front of me.' Mantwa had the patience of an overeager child at a candy store.

'This driver, you could tell, was driving in their fresh-from-the-floor German machine and had some of the worst drama queen moves I have seen in a while.'

The girls were already laughing because they knew the story was about to get even juicier. Mantwa had a way of telling a story.

'All these moves were to avoid a pothole. Now calling that

defect in the road a pothole is a little bit of exaggeration if you ask me. You haven't seen a pothole until you have driven on the stretch of road between Limpopo and Mpumalanga provinces, although there are probably worse roads elsewhere in the country. So, this little one was more like a pan hole – you know, very shallow. Anyone could easily drive over at normal speed especially in a machine like that with generous inches on the wheels.'

'Maybe he didn't want to damage his car especially since you say it looked new,' Khutso reasoned. But Mantwa was clearly not buying that.

'This drama queen was doing all kinds of manoeuvring, all kinds of twirling around the pan hole. The amount of twirling this guy made put Cinderella's twirling in her fairy princess dress at that ball to shame! It was like watching that male ballet dancer, Mikhail Baryshnikov executing a perfect triple pirouette. Did I mention that this drama queen was a male driver? And they have the nerve to call us bad drivers!'

'And what did you do when all of this was happening?' Maserati was out of breath from laughing so hard. It was never a dull moment with Mantwa around.

'I swiftly overtook on the left as I left him there auditioning for a role in Swan Lake!'

All four screamed at the top of their lungs. The other patrons looked around curiously to see what was making the ladies cackle so loudly.

Their waiter who had eavesdropped on this conversation had the widest grin when he came over to get their food order. They all settled for some light lunch, knowing these dates easily turned into dinner dates too.

'So, tell us about this cosy walk with Dr Ben in Cape Town,' said Mantwa, wanting them to get right on to the real reason why they were meeting today. Forget that this was their usual bi-weekly luncheon.

Maserati felt her face flush as she described every detail of her evening with Ben. It was clear she was besotted.

'Wow, that mesmerising, huh?' Tebo was now also curious because they had not seen their friend like this in a while.

Her friends were very happy that Maserati was finally moving on from that debacle with Tshepo. They had watched her emotional turmoil over the last year, but it was good to finally see her heal and move forward.

And this Ben sounded like what the doctor ordered.

Chapter Twenty-Two

I t had been two weeks since that beautiful night with Ben in Cape Town.

Maserati was unusually nervous as she pulled up to the parking area. She took one last look in the rear-view mirror, happy that she had chosen minimalist make-up to avoid looking like she was trying too hard. She stepped out of the car, walking the short distance towards Sage, the swanky restaurant in the heart of the suburb of Rosebank.

She had decided to drive herself rather than have him pick her up from her house. This was always her modus operandi in case a date tanked and then she could feign some excuse. That emergency excuse always worked like a charm.

She went against the typical first-date little black dress, and went for slimming black cigar pants, a cream bodysuit with thin spaghetti straps, and a matching black blazer, finishing the look with her black Tom Ford pumps, embellished with a padlock anklet. She was a vision of understated class.

As she entered the ground floor entrance, her phone beeped. A text from Ben.

'Come up to the restaurant level, I'll wait for you by the entrance.'

He keeps time. Maserati made a mental note, as she thought about her own tardiness.

She found the elevator and made her way to the first floor. As she exited and made her way to the entrance, she caught sight of his silhouette and at that same moment, he turned around to meet her gaze.

Ben hoped that his face did not betray him, but wow, she looked beautiful and so confident. It was sexy as sin.

'Hey, you made it,' he reached out to give her a peck on the left cheek and a hug.

'Of course I made it!'

The hostess ushered them to their table. Ben had specifically requested a table right smack in the middle section of the restaurant. He reckoned first dates were not for clichéd cosy corner tables. Besides, he wanted to admire her properly under the brightness of the well-lit section.

'You look amazing,' he complimented her, his hand on her back guiding her towards their table.

'Thank you. And you aren't bad yourself.' He was slightly formal in a navy suit, with a well-fitting white tee underneath. He completed the look unexpectedly with brown leather boots, a look that screamed rebel with a cause.

Causing me to fall in love, Maserati chuckled to herself.

The hostess left them and their waiter came for their drink orders and the menu of the evening's specials. Ben ordered a bottle of their finest red wine.

'I am glad you came tonight.'

'Me too. My friends and I have tried many times to get into this restaurant and, for whatever reason, we just never got lucky with reservations. Sage is always booked out for months.'

Maserati wondered how Ben managed to pull it off. They were even thinking of resorting to asking Bra-Sam Khanyile to leverage the power of his billions to score them a reservation.

'Thabang. Somehow, he knows everyone there is to know in

Joburg. Not even the best concierge services in the world can beat him at this.'

He seemed amused at his brother's talent.

Maserati could tell when she first met Thabang that he had a much more outgoing personality than his older brother. Thabang seemed much freer, unburdened and a 'dive in first and think later' kind of guy.

'Well, tell him that my friends and I will be calling upon his services soon.'

Ben loved the twinkle in Maserati's eyes every time she laughed. A twinkle that had been missing a couple of months ago.

'Tell me about your friends,' he said.

She lit up when it came to talking about her friends. They say good friends are a family you have a choice in. And the universe was very kind when it blessed her with Mantwa, Tebo, and Khutso. Though very different, theirs was a complimentary friendship that permitted each of them to show up fully as they are. She could never relate to common sayings like 'when days are dark, friends are few.'

Her friends had been her pillars through the good and the bad. They bickered occasionally like in every relationship; however, it was the growth that came from such crucial conversations that she appreciated.

'They sound like amazing people and friends.'

'They are. You'll love them when you meet them.'

That was not meant to have come out of her mouth. And the 'when' should have been an 'if.' Ben was not about to pass up on that opportunity. They say half the battle of winning over the girl is winning over her friends.

'I'd love to!'

Just then, she realised the idea of her friends meeting this guy soon was not a bad one. She really liked him. And the signs from him suggested that the feeling was mutual.

The waiter came with their food. Maserati had ordered the

braised short rib with a medley of assorted vegetables. He had chosen Sage's award-winning ribeye steak. When their meals were placed before them, she was surprised at how miniscule the portions were. Fine dining establishments were known for being conservative with their portions, but Sage was taking it to a whole new level. She was hungry and hadn't been able to eat the whole day thinking about this date. And the girl loved her food. And so, first-date etiquette was thrown out of the window as she ordered a second meal of seared salmon and mashed potatoes. Better that than a growling tummy for the rest of the evening.

'So, not only does she love shoes, but she also loves food,' Ben commented. He enjoyed a woman unashamed of her appetite. But they were few and far between; Maserati was like a unicorn. He was finding out even more things he liked about her.

'And she loves books too,' Maserati added. She could never pretend to be a dainty eater. It was futile; a good plate of food would always betray her.

'Tell me about your name, Maserati. I don't think I've met or heard of a Maserati before. Was Mercedes and Bentley taken?'

Maserati nearly choked on her wine with laughter. The other patrons glanced around, searching for the hyena howling in such a classy establishment. Ben joined in. Only he was laughing at her laughing.

'Oh, wow, Dr Nkosi! No… My mother abbreviated the Sepedi idiom 'Mmapelo o ja serati' to come up with my name, Maserati. She wanted me to be someone who chooses what they love, regardless of the consequences.'

'It's a beautiful name,' he complimented her.

By now, she was completely relaxed and comfortable in his presence. She didn't know if it was the wine or the food that did the trick, but she felt she could be completely free with him. The space between them was full of permission for her to be herself. Their conversation was flowing, unforced and easy.

Maserati often went philosophical in conversations. In the

past, this had made her feel uneasy and measured in conversations with new people. However, with Ben she felt safe being authentically herself even at the risk of being misunderstood. She settled back in her chair, feeling at peace that he didn't seem to find her monologues dreary.

A few months after her debacle with Tshepo, she had dipped her feet into the dating pool. That experience was a cesspool of conversations about Slay Queens, butts, *big* butts in particular, bank balances, and the cars parked in people's garages. It was all so shallow. One date had told her to loosen up and be like all 'these other fun bitches out for a good time.' That date had ended abruptly!

They had finished their mains and the waiter cleared the table, leaving a menu for dessert. She didn't like this. Dessert was a sign of a date nearing an end.

'I am not big on dessert.' She perused the menu for something suitable to prolong the night.

'Don't let my kids hear you say that.' He dropped that bomb on her waiting for the detonation.

Did he just say kids!? Maserati thought, as she looked intensely at the menu, avoiding eye contact as she processed this new information.

Kids usually came from wives. Was she being courted for a side-chick role? She did not see this coming. Ben didn't seem the type. But then again Tshepo had not seemed like the type that would dip his third leg in every hole this side of the equator.

Ben had been waiting for an opportune time to bring this up. He liked her so much that he needed to know if this was a deal-breaker for her. He had been dreading this. Women had tried to make him choose in the past. The energy at the table was shifting and he needed to preserve the magic they'd had throughout the date until now.

'My ten-year-old twins, my boy, Leano and girl, Masa, swear ice-cream is an entire meal.' He tried to lighten the mood. By this time, Maserati had regained some composure, and she might as well ask the necessary questions.

'You have twins? So, twins run in the family then?'

'They do. And so now I have much empathy for my parents.' He tried a light laugh. She got the reference and smiled.

The big elephant in the room loomed large.

'Much to their mother's, my *ex-wife*, disdain.' The emphasis on ex-wife was unmissable.

'You were married?' Baby-mama drama was the kind Maserati had always tried to steer clear from. But then again, at her age – not that thirty was old – there was a high probability of meeting men with baggage.

Are we calling kids baggage now, Maserati? She thought. Unbecoming of a lady, really.

'Yes. We were married for five years and have been divorced for five. I guess five is the magic number.' Bad joke. Nervous bad joke. He was trying to lighten the mood, but the truth could not be dressed up.

'We remain close and have been blessed to be able to co-parent well.'

How close do they remain? Maserati was thinking about how her friend Mantwa would handle this situation. She'd always been one to say, 'Follow your heart.' But surely there were circumstances where the heart's GPS should be disabled. But he sounded genuine and appeared vulnerable. She knew too that such circumstances are deal-breakers for some. Certainly, they were for her in a past life. But life had taught her that things aren't always what they seem, and that perfection comes in many imperfect forms.

'That's great that you've both found a way to co-parent amicably. It sadly isn't always the case, much to the kids' detriment.'

Ben let out a deep sigh of relief. Maybe she understood after all. It was his hope.

'Tell me about them.' Maserati took it upon herself to restore the mood from earlier in the evening. She didn't want her experience with Tshepo to breed irrational mistrust about everything.

His kids were one of his favourite topics. And Maserati could tell from the way he responded with laughter.

He laughs so easily, she thought.

'They're real rebels. We call them Thing 1 and Thing 2…'

'Oh, from The Cat in the Hat? I love that movie. It's hilarious. And the Things, my God, I could tell as soon as they got out of that fun box that they would be so mischievous,' she responded.

Ben had not expected the reference to land with Maserati. It was a common joke amongst parents.

'My friend Khutso has two kids, eight and six years old,' she said. 'And every time we visit her house, that movie is playing somewhere in the background.'

'So, you know what I mean when I say they are Thing 1 and 2?'

'So where do they get it from?' she mocked him.

'It beats me. And for Aquarians to be this mischievous?!' Ben wasn't going to take the blame for his kids' rebellious nature.

'Ah fellow Aquarians. We do have a fun, naughty side.'

'Oh, so now it's called fun and naughty? When is your birthday?'

'The 9th of February.'

There was that shift again. What had she said that made him shift so uncomfortably? But there seemed to be a mixture of sadness and pleasant surprise in his eyes.

When had Maserati become so attuned to people's subtleties?

'The twins were born on the 19th of February. But you share a birthday with my brother.'

'Oh, interesting. Thabang as well? He has such Sagittarius energy though.' This was why Maserati had never really been into horoscopes.

He shifted again.

'No. My brother… ahem. My late brother, Rori… Rorišang.'

Maserati instinctively reached out to touch his hand, which

lay on the tabletop. She squeezed it sympathetically. She hadn't known him that long, but in those few words, she could tell how much his late brother had meant to him.

'He passed away a long time ago, almost thirty years ago. We were kids. He was only ten years old. A fatal brain cancer. Everyone loved him.' He spoke of his brother with such deep fondness.

Maserati did not let go of his hand. She cupped it now with her other hand, and was unaware that she had started caressing it softly as a form of comfort. She really empathised. She first became aware of death when she lost her beloved maternal grandfather when she was ten. Her maternal grandmother died suddenly at age seventy-two, a year before she graduated from medical school. That was a devastating blow that took time to get over. She was particularly close to her grandparents because of the role they had played in her formative years by raising Maserati before her parents took on full parenting responsibilities when they started stable careers as public servants.

'Bušang, I am really sorry for your loss. The good ones seem to go early. And when you look, they seem to have lived such larger-than-life lives in their short time on earth. From how you describe your brother, he was one of the good ones. They are God's messengers.'

Her words came from a place she didn't know she possessed. For a moment she thought she saw him tear up. It was such a vulnerable moment that they shared. He moved his free hand to cup her hands.

'Thank you.'

The waiter had been hovering in the wings, careful not to interrupt this beautiful moment. He had witnessed many moments before, but none this genuine.

At the right time he stepped up to their table. 'Are you ready to get dessert now?'

'You know what, on behalf of all Aquarians everywhere, I will have a triple scoop of ice-cream.' Maserati brought some lightness to the moment. She smiled that big smile and his brown eyes danced with delight at her kind humour.

'Make that two.'

By all standards, the date was a success. A beautiful night of great food, wine, and conversation. It was refreshing to meet a man so candid and unafraid of depth and vulnerability.

'I really had a good time tonight,' Ben said as he walked Maserati to her car.

'Same here.' The closer they got to her car, the quicker her heart raced. *You would swear, I had never been on dates*, Maserati thought.

She opened her car, dumped her bag on the passenger side and turned to face him as she leaned against the body of her BMW.

'All good things come to an end.'

'I hope they needn't come to an end. I would love to do this, see you again. Soon.' Ben offered.

'Let me know when and where and I will be there.' Maserati hoped this did not make her seem too eager, but she did want to see him again. Or at least talk to him again. And again and again after.

'I will do just that.'

'Well, Miss, I mean Dr Mojapelo, let me not keep you here in these unsafe streets longer than necessary. Drive safely and let me know when you are home safe.'

With that he moved forward to lean in for a kiss. Maserati met his lips which felt warm and soft. Just as her eyes were closing, she felt him stop. She slowly opened her eyes to meet his which seemed to be searching hers for permission to continue. Her eyes consented. He moved even closer as he pressed his lips against hers, kissing her so softly and yet with an unmistakeable passion. She let out a soft sigh.

After what seemed like minutes of tongue wars, he slowed down to a halt, continuing to hold her in an embrace. He kissed her forehead and the tip of her nose.

'Goodnight Mmapelo.'

Only her late grandmother and mother called her that. Her heart melted into mush.

'Goodnight Bušang.'

Just then, it started raining softly.

She got in her car and drove off with speed, heading down Jellicoe Avenue onto Jan Smuts Avenue. There was no telling what staying a minute longer in that strong embrace would have led her to. But she knew without a shadow of doubt that she wanted to feel that again.

Soon…

Chapter Twenty-Three

I t had been a month since that beautiful first date.

She had not stopped thinking about that kiss in the parking lot. They'd had four other dates since, three lunches and breakfast, and lots of phone calls and lots more texts. There had been other memorable kisses from those dates, but nothing like that first kiss. They say you don't forget the first kiss. Beyond the electricity, there was something very thoughtful about it. Her consent was important to him.

Maserati was giddy. It was almost two months before the year ended, so work was slowing down a bit. Which was just as well because she would not have been able to concentrate on anything else other than Ben. She sometimes caught herself in the mirror, smiling for no reason. Well, technically there was a reason. She had not expected to find herself in this space again. She remembered her friends assuring her that she would eventually find happiness again.

Mantwa and Tebo had encouraged her to play the field a bit, and not settle just yet.

'Dear, free your cookie. And sample as many specimens as possible.'

But Khutso was adamant that she should focus on finding her happily-ever-after very soon.

It was too early for happily-ever-after thoughts, but Ben felt like a strong contender. Just that thought alone made her spin. She had some fears though but for now she wanted to enjoy this moment for as long as it could be enjoyed.

During their last date, they shared some of their best travel memories. And somehow, he had ended up suggesting that they should do a road trip together the following weekend. Road trips can bring out the best and worst qualities in a couple. It's often a window to how people handle the unexpected. And really, what's a road trip without the unexpected happening?

A few years ago, she, Mantwa and Tebo had decided to take an impromptu long weekend trip to Maputo for Mantwa's birthday. They drove in Maserati's new BMW 1 series. A less-than-ideal make of car to take on the notoriously potholed roads of Maputo. They had not even booked their hotel, that's how impromptu the trip was. One of the hotels they were hoping to stay at was fully booked when they arrived after 9 pm that Friday. Instead of panicking, they found a dinner spot near the ocean and had a time of their life until it was time for bed. Then they settled on some dodgy mosquito-filled 2-star lodge nearby. To this day, they recounted this as one of their best trips ever. Now, depending who had been on the trip, things could have been stressful.

How would Ben react in a scenario like that?

Ben suggested the picturesque town of Dullstroom, in Mpumalanga, and offered to take care of all arrangements. This was great. Maserati had welcomed the road trip idea with excitement. A four-hour trip from Joburg was just enough time to get to know each other even better.

It was a dreary Monday midmorning and the time seemed to tick by with the speed of a snail. Friday morning seemed in the faraway distance. She was at the office trying to do some work, but the external expert engagement insights report she needed to submit to her manager in Chicago lacked some of her usual depth; it had no chance competing with infatuation.

'Mmapelo.'

She melted as a text from Ben flashed on her phone screen. Ben had started calling her that at their first date. He said it so organically with so much affection. No other person besides her mother and late grandmother had called her that. It was their special name for her.

'Bušang.' Calling him Ben wasn't always appealing to her. Bušang was regal. He who ruled. And this man was becoming seriously successful at ruling her heart. She suspected he loved it when she called him that.

'I am looking forward to the weekend.' At least she wasn't the only one getting impatient about the time to the weekend.

'Me too.'

'I miss you.'

At that point Maserati was ready to pack up her office and go. Her mind was conjuring images of them together under the misty clouds of Mpumalanga.

'I miss you too,' she texted, with a blush emoji.

Speaking of images of the weekend... Exactly what were the arrangements for the weekend? Would they be sharing a room, a bed? She hadn't asked for specifics and would go with the flow. But nonetheless she needed to be prepared for whatever.

Was she ready for whatever though?

In the month they had been dating, it was clear they had an electrifying chemistry, the magnitude of which could power up the entire electricity grid of a small town in the Northern Cape.

But not once had Ben tried to take it further than a kiss. She had told herself she would wait at least three months before she became physically intimate in her next relationship. But who was she kidding? Every time Ben had kissed her, or she had kissed him, she would have gone all the way had he pursued it. But there had been nothing further than second base.

She had shared this titbit with her friends.

'Whoa. Could he be on the downlow?' Mantwa asked.

'You mean gay? Taking time to know someone before getting into their pants does not mean being gay, Mantwa!' Khutso was often exasperated by Mantwa's antics.

'It's actually refreshing for a guy to take things this slow,' said Tebo with her usual wisdom.

Maybe he followed the ninety-day rule. We will see this weekend. It had dawned on Maserati that in this day and age, women had just as much freedom to initiate sex. And it was just as much about what she wanted and not only what he wanted. The real question here was, was she ready to take it to the next base?

She took Friday off as they wanted to leave just after noon to avoid the peak Friday afternoon traffic on the N4 highway. She hardly slept from excitement and her bags were all packed and ready to go. That part of Mpumalanga's climate was known to be unpredictable; the days were often warm, and the evening could get quite chilly. So, she packed for all four seasons of the year.

Mantwa called her in the morning.

'Dear, did you buy new underwear like I told you?' Mantwa was a standing member of the La Senza club. Bra-Sam stood no chance. 'Are you neat down there?'

'Jesus. Yes, I have new underwear and sexy lingerie ready for any occasion. And yes, downstairs is neat and tidy. I even packed condoms. Just in case.'

'That's my girl. You must have fun, dear. And remember, go with the flow. Don't over-analyse anything, because, wow, we know how you get with that brain of yours.'

Maserati loved Mantwa's frankness. Not many people can survive such frankness, but that's what made their friendship special. There was no sugar-coating things.

It was almost noon, and he would soon be there. Maserati looked around the house one last time, making sure she had closed all the windows and locked all doors. It was a warm day, and she had chosen a pair of denim shorts, paired with an off-the-shoulder top, leaving her neck bare of accessories. Her collar bones were enough accessories for this look. Nothing elevated a look more than large hoop earrings. She left her face bare of make-up except for a smudge of eyeliner, and a popping red lipstick. She adorned her feet with gladiator sandals.

Road trip perfection.

The doorbell rang. He was here.

She opened the door to be greeted by his back. In that split second, she soaked in his silhouette. He turned around and swallowed hard. She could tell from the way his Adam's apple moved up and down, that he was trying to swallow his delight at the creature before him.

He was a tall glass of caramel Idris Elba, in a white Polo T-shirt, showing off the most perfect strong arms, a pair of faded jeans with white Converse sneakers.

Those arms could soon be carrying me effortlessly in the throes of passionate lovemaking, Maserati thought. *Calm yourself, girl!*

He had on aviator sunglasses that just made him look even more handsome. Irrespective of what he wore, sex appeal just oozed from his pores with no effort on his part whatsoever.

'Hey…'

He took off his sunglasses and leaned in for peck on the cheek and a hug. He wrapped one arm around her back and took in her scent. She had her arms loosely around his neck, on her tippy toes. Her head rested on his chest, and she took in his scent, a mixture of freshness and Yves Saint Laurent. And being there in his arms felt just right. They held each other a little longer than it was perhaps necessary.

'You look amazing.'

'Thank you.'

'Are you all ready?'

'Yeah. Let me just grab my bags and we are all set.'

He moved in to help her with her luggage. Maserati was

terrible at packing light. She was the girl that brought a suitcase to an overnight stay. She always packed a stash of just-in-case, extra clothes for any weather or circumstance. However, this time, she was proud to have fitted everything in one bag, even though the bag would exceed the requirements for carry-on luggage of any airline.

'Are you sure we are coming back on Sunday?' he teased her.

He had one light Mont Blanc duffel bag. But men were known to be extremely light packers.

'I need to stop by the petrol station,' he said, as he opened the passenger door of the black Range Rover. For someone who had kids, the car was spotless and smelt so masculine. She wasn't really surprised. Ben was so together.

They stopped at the petrol station just before the N1 highway.

'I'm going to get a few things from the store. Do you need anything?' he asked. Maserati had not slept much due to the excitement of this road trip, and she was known to be a terrible passenger. As soon as the car got on the road, she would usually be knocked out by sleep. She wanted to stay awake the entire trip and absorb as much of this man as possible. So, she suggested some energy drinks.

'I have water and some drinks in the cooler box,' said Ben.

Maserati checked and there were no energy drinks. Nope, this wouldn't do.

'I'll be back,' she said, crossing the garage forecourt, oblivious to the fact that she was almost causing the few cars that were pulling in to fill up for their respective trips to come to a standstill.

She doesn't realise the effect she has on people…. on men, thought Ben, as he watched all this with glee, spotting a man follow Maserati into the store. *Predictable!*

There weren't any other shoppers in the store, so naturally as the only shoppers, they acknowledged each other's presence. But then he started gazing and adjusting his belt. The sunshine hit the metal; the reflection was almost blinding. Hermes.

He had a look of satisfaction. He knew Maserati recognised the big 'H' on his waist.

Maserati proceeded to the till to pay, and there was the gazer, forging right in front of her to place a black credit card on the counter for the cashier.

'What's this for?' the cashier asked confused as he had no goods to pay for.

'Paying for the petrol, station 6, where *MY* blue Mercedes is.' He looked at her again. Maserati gave him a blank look, finding the whole spectacle amusing. *So, all of this, so he could have the pleasure of showing off his car?*

'These wanna-be new money types are exhausting.'

She returned to Ben laughing.

'What's funny?' Ben asked. He had a suspicion it had to do with Mr Blue Mercedes.

Maserati narrated the whole story to him.

'I guess Mr Black over there feels validated now that we all know what he's driving.'

'Did you just call him Mr Black?' Ben laughed so hard, she shushed him. 'You are the funniest person I know.'

Ben's easy laughter always seemed to cover space with its purity and sincerity.

Maserati had been called many things, but funny was never really one of them. They do say humour is one of the top ways to a person's heart. He probably just found her funny because he was infatuated with her.

It had been thirty minutes since they hit the highway, and Maserati was itching to check out the playlist. You can tell a lot about someone by listening to their road trip playlist.

Reading her mind he asked, 'Do you want to change the music?'

'No. I am just curious about the type of music you listen to.'

'I have an eclectic taste, I think. It just depends on the occasion. But my go-to are the oldies, jazz, soul, and now and then I throw in some hip-hop.'

'Hip-hop, hey? Now this we have to see.'

'You sound surprised.'

'No. People are dynamic, so I am not saying I am surprised. Just curious. Let's play a game called testing your hip-hop grade.'

'So, you Dr Mojapelo are a hip-hop head? Let's play then.' Ben never shied away from a challenge.

'Tupac or Biggie?'

'Oh, right off the bat, huh? I see you are playing hardball. Biggie.'

'What?!'

'Jay or Nas?'

'Oh, now you are not playing fair. Jay.'

'Last one. Wu-Tang Clan or A Tribe Called Quest?'

'How is that even a comparison? Hands down Tribe Called Quest. So, what do my answers say about me?'

'That you are indeed eclectic Dr Nkosi. But I don't know how to feel about you choosing Biggie over Pac. If Tupac was alive, he would be my baby-daddy.'

There was that laughter again.

Have I ever made anyone laugh like this? Maserati wondered. It was as if she was also discovering this side of herself as well.

They do say the best love connections tend to activate the dormant sides of us.

'My older cousin used to listen to these guys all the time. I prefer that era of music rather than the things they play on radio now. Rubbish.'

She didn't need that energy drink after all. She settled in by lowering the backrest slightly and took off her sandals and propped one leg on the seat. Ben tried his best not to peek at her beautifully sculpted bare legs, but it was impossible. Thanks to the sunglasses he could hide his stare.

It was a beautiful afternoon and a beautiful drive. The

greenery along the way made her feel at peace. But it was his hand reaching out to lock with hers over the armrest that made her give a peaceful and anticipatory sigh.

Hmmmm…

It was going to be a beautiful weekend.

Chapter Twenty-Four

Dullstroom is a peaceful, rustic town.

They say God took his time when he created the beautiful province of Mpumalanga and even left His window in this province, through which humankind could watch his creations in awe. They drove a short distance out of the busy town centre into a long winding driveway to an amazing piece of real estate.

'We're here,' Ben announced their arrival, parking by the front entrance. He had chosen self-catering accommodation, a perfect way to spend time alone with someone you are trying to get to know better. He opened the front door to an amazing hallway, from which you could see all the way to the back of the house and into the backyard.

The front was indeed deceiving, as the backyard was even more exquisite, with a deck that had perfect views of the open space and made an ideal spot for watching the sun set. The backyard was an expanse of greenery and a big elm tree created a divide between the deck and a stream, whose flow created a soft background sound for this haven. A narrow, cobbled pathway led from the house to the stream, at the end of which lay two lounge chairs, as if viewing the sunset from the deck was not satisfactory enough.

'This place is amazing. You should give me the booking agent's details; I'd love to come back here with my gals.' Maserati was so full of awe that she hadn't noticed the lack of response. But she had noticed that Ben seemed quite familiar with the house. It was also surprising that the kitchen was fully stocked with groceries. She'd assumed they'd buy food when they arrived.

She followed Ben as he went upstairs with their luggage. There were four bedrooms upstairs, each leading to an outdoor balcony with incredible views of the river. Two more bedrooms completed the downstairs area. It was a big house though for a two-people weekend away. Ben left his duffel bag in one of the bedrooms and led Maserati to the main bedroom, which had an outdoor shower overlooking the same stunning view. Maserati knew she would make good use of it before the weekend was over.

However, the business at hand was this separation of luggage. They hadn't discussed sleeping arrangements, so Ben did not want to make assumptions. Maserati could not help feeling a twinge of disappointment. She would have loved to spend the night with him and it needn't lead to anything beyond just being in his arms as they slept the night away.

It was almost 5 pm. Just in time to experience the beautiful sunset.

Ben made himself comfortable in the kitchen as he laid out the groceries ready to prepare a meal. Maserati did not feel like slaving away in the kitchen on vacation. But he seemed to have everything under control and insisted on cooking. This would be the first time they had a home-cooked meal together. He looked like he knew what he was doing.

How lucky was she? God seemed to be throwing cooks her way. Tshepo had been an equally enthusiastic cook. This was the first time since she had met Ben that she had made any comparison between them. She quickly pushed that thought aside. But she felt blessed. Lightning never strikes twice yet here she was with an eager man in the kitchen waiting to show off his culinary skills.

This house was tastefully decorated with high-end furniture and unusual art. Interesting that someone would spend so much on a holiday home they rented out to strangers. Ben seemed quite comfortable with where everything was located.

Was this where he brought girls? The thought crossed her mind, but she wasn't going to spoil her weekend with ridiculous thoughts. Mantwa had reminded her of her tendency to over-analyse and that she should go with the flow.

Go with the flow, Rati. Go with the flow.

Ben poured her a glass of chardonnay as the food simmered and beckoned her to the deck to view the sunset.

'Thank you for being here.'

'I wouldn't be anywhere else.' And she meant it.

What an amazing sunset. God is such a show-off. And this was just the beginning of the weekend.

Dinner would be ready in about forty-five minutes, just enough time for her to take a shower in that glorious outdoor shower under the stars. Ben stayed in the kitchen putting the final touches to whatever dish he was making.

The shower was amazing. The stars and all their galaxy cousins seemed to have come out tonight. She put on matching black lacy underwear and covered it all with a long flowing spaghetti-strapped white maxi dress and flip-flops. It was a comfortable but subtly sexy look for dinner for two.

As she walked downstairs, the mood had changed. The table was set with candles, the kitchen was spotless, and the fireplace was cracking with a wood fire. The acoustics of Maxwell played in the background. As she was admiring the set-up, he came down the stairs, refreshed in loose beige linen pants and a white tee, barefoot.

For split second, she thought she saw some extreme swinging.

Was he wearing underwear? Get your mind out of the gutter, Rati.

She had also noticed he had been barefoot since they'd arrived. Some people connected to the ground that way. Maybe he was one of those.

Could the man get even sexier?

'Your seat awaits m'lady.' Ben pulled the chair out for her to sit. On the table was a spread that would make top Michelin-rated chefs green with envy. Roast leg of lamb with rosemary sprigs in a red wine reduction, on a bed of spring vegetables. Because by this time he had learned that Maserati without starch was an unhappy girl, there was a side dish of the creamiest mashed potatoes. The food was so good, she could cry.

Dear God, thank you, she prayed silently.

'Bušang. This is amazing. I didn't know you could cook like this.'

'I aim to please,' he smiled. 'My mom cooked for us all the time when we were young. Being in the kitchen was therapy for her. And I loved spending time with her, watching her. I found creating meals to nourish people such a gift. My kids would rather I bought McDonalds, though.'

Kids.

'My mom loved baking,' she responded. 'Cooking was secondary but she would create such hearty comforting dishes. But I didn't really learn. In fact, I rebelled against cooking because she insisted that I needed to learn to cook 'for my future husband.' So, I made it a point to never learn. It's only recently as an adult that I find that I actually don't mind cooking at all. What I know for sure is I love eating.'

'As long as you eat, then I am happy to cook for you. Anytime, anywhere, anything you want.'

Did he say anytime, and anywhere?

'The way you speak about your mom, she seems amazing. Can your siblings cook like you?'

'They are useless,' he laughed. 'Mom tried to domesticate my sister Lethabo, but she shouldn't have bothered. I would pay a million dollars to anyone that could ever achieve such a feat.'

He spoke so fondly of his mom and siblings. She hadn't heard him speak a lot about his dad. She hoped he'd had a different experience than the pervasive experience so many Black kids of their generation had with their often-absent fathers.

He seemed a bit uncomfortable when she raised the topic, but there was respect and fondness there.

'Dad is my hero.' He didn't elaborate further, but she saw how earnest he was in that statement. She could sense some complexity but also a deep love for his father.

Maserati imagined his dad must feel the same about his son, who Maserati thought was the most amazing human being she'd met in a while. For a moment there, she had lost all hope in men. But Ben felt different.

'And you, what about your parents?' he asked. I've heard you talk about your mom. What about your dad?' Ben was hesitant in the question but knew this was something to know if he was ever to fully understand Maserati. We are all made up of our past and present.

'Hmmm…'

'You don't have to talk about it, if it's difficult.' He noticed the change in her mood.

'No. It's okay. I don't mind sharing especially with you.' She felt safe with him.

He reached out for her hand and kissed it.

'My parents have had a difficult marriage. My father cheated with a neighbour when my mom was on maternity leave with my younger sister. I wanted her to leave him. She stayed. I love my mother. My father on the other hand… I love him, but we have a complicated relationship. He could have done better as a father and shielded my sister and me from some of his behaviour. I often wondered why my mother never had the courage to leave for good. But people choose who they choose.'

'I'm sorry you had to go through all of that. I do wish therapy was a readily accepted option for our parents' generation. They carried traumas, causing generational havoc in the process. I bet your father loves you but lacks the wherewithal to express it in a way that's healthy for you.' His empathy was kind.

'I credit my maternal grandparents for who I am today. They raised me until the age of ten, and they were the first mentors I had in my life.' She hadn't meant to get emotional about that but thinking of her late grandparents was a sore point. They had meant the world to her. They were the blueprint of what selfless kindness was.

'Lucky you,' he said. 'By the time I was born, there were no grandparents on either side. So, all I had was my mom and dad. I envy my children and the relationship they have with my parents. I have never seen two people so spellbound by kids before. Those twins have my parents wrapped around their little mischievous fingers.'

That's grandparents.

'My grandmother was so generous, and such an optimist...' she trailed off. It had been over five years since her grandmother passed on, but her memories lived with her.

'She must have been a Leo,' he lightened the mood.

'Yes, yes. She was. Wait, are you a Leo?' Maserati didn't really believe in zodiac signs but now and then she found some truth in them.

'I am. The 11th of August.'

'Shut up! My grandmother's birthday is the same day!'

He almost choked on the wine when she revealed the coincidence. First she and his late brother shared a birthday and now his birthday was on the same day as her grandmother's.

Those who knew Ben, knew he did not believe in coincidences. Every sign was the universe communicating and affirming. Could this revelation be a confirmation of some predestined future between him and Maserati?

'You and Rori, and me and your grandmother? What do you think the universe is telling us, Mmapelo?'

Suddenly she was overcome with the fear of 'could it be' and 'what if'. Maserati had taken many of those personality tests at work and they had all confirmed that she was an analytical person, who relied on empiric data for her decisions. Any sign not backed by data was not to be trusted. She had missed many red flags with Tshepo. She wasn't going to be blinded by a few coincidences to create some illusionary conclusion about their destiny, no matter how much she liked Ben. And she liked him a lot!

But she couldn't lie to herself. There was something to these coincidences.

Go with the flow, Rati. Nothing like silent pep talk to encourage oneself.

'Maybe we should listen to the universe,' he said. Flirting 101.

They locked eyes. He seemed to be deep in thought, like this was not something to take lightly.

She changed topics.

'My grandmother passed on a year before I graduated from medical school. I was devastated that she would not witness and experience the fruits of her labour. I had so many plans on how to repay her for all those years she poured into me.'

'So, what made you choose Medicine?'

'Ah, you know how it was back then. You show a little bit of intelligence and an affinition for the sciences, the next thing, your teachers are encouraging you to consider medicine or engineering. I chose medicine because my mom is a nurse. When I was six, I visited her in the hospital. I was fascinated by these men in the white coats and thought it would be grand to be like them. And I love helping people. I got lucky and got a scholarship from the RAIN Foundation, which paid for my full tuition to study at UCT.'

While Maserati was blabbering about her aspirations in medicine, she hadn't noticed Ben shift that uncomfortable shift again, and go quiet.

That was another coincidence Ben was not going to confirm nor discuss.

Chapter Twenty-Five

D inner was done and dishes were cleared.
Darkness had now enveloped the day and the night
was cool. From the backyard came a symphony of chirping crick-
ets, rustling leaves, and the flowing stream. Maserati took her
wine glass and headed to the deck to stare at the stars. They
were the brightest bright. The crackles from the indoor fire
added to the ambience.

One could only describe the night as magical.

Ben watched her as she gazed up at the stars, their sparkle
reflecting gloriously against her skin. She was beautiful. Topping
up his wine, he joined her.

Silence.

She felt his towering presence behind her. His breath seemed
synchronised to the sounds of the night, like he was one with all
this nature. Though they both kept silent, the energy between
them was loud. Words were redundant. His proximity caused
her skin to tingle, he placed his free hand in his pocket to stop
himself from touching her.

As she took a sip from her glass the right strap of her dress
slipped off her shoulder. He instinctively caught it and slowly
slid it back up to her shoulder. The power of that touch sent a

million electrical shocks all over her body, including the nether regions. Her knees got instantly weak. She held her breath.

Breathe.

Maserati slowly turned around and laid her head against his chest. She breathed him in and knew in that moment that she wanted to feel all of him. Ben lifted her chin, and they looked each other in the eyes as he slowly moved in for a kiss. He placed his glass on the table, doing the same with hers. His kiss started slowly and became intensely passionate. He swooped her up, leading them to the rug by the fireside. Her dress was swiftly removed as she lay on the plush rug, in her sexy black underwear. Soon enough he had removed the bra and tossed it. Each moan was a sign that she liked everything that was about to happen. His tongue's GPS was leading him to the holy grail. He airily kissed her belly button and lifted one leg after another as she removed the last piece of cloth separating him and the pleasure haven.

And he went to work.

'Aaahhh. Hmmm…' Her hands were on the head buried between her thighs.

Now tongue and finger were on a mission to give her ultimate pleasure. She felt her legs tremble.

'Aaahhhhhhhhh… Bušang. I want all of you.' She reached out to pull him to her. The linen pants had come off and indeed no underwear was in sight. He knelt before her as he slid the condom on.

God was generous, thought Maserati, delighted by what was in front of her. He held his member, directing it to her pleasure cave.

'Hmmmm...' he moaned.

She began panting, feeling like her head was going to explode.

He steadied her. 'Breathe, baby, breathe.' He looked at her, encouraging her to take a breath.

With each deep breath she took, her sensation heightened.

She breathed, he pumped. She breathed, he pumped.

Deep breaths and deep strokes were the doorway to heaven.

'Oh god, oh god, oh goooooood.'

And they fell asleep to the sound of rain against the windowpanes.

———

She woke the next morning with a wide smile as she recalled the night before.

How did I get here? She looked around, realising she was in the main bedroom upstairs. She didn't recall coming up here after…

That wide smile again, as she caressed her belly.

I think I love him. She laughed at herself, clearly still impressed by his stroke game.

The smell of bacon and coffee got her out of bed. She found Ben preparing breakfast in the kitchen. As she passed the scene of the crime from last night, she could not help but smile again.

And there he was in barefooted glory, making her breakfast.

'Good morning.' She gave him a light kiss and hugged him.

'Good morning, Mmapelo. Did you sleep well?'

What kind of question was that? Of course she had slept great.

'I slept, ahem, wonderfully.' Smile and deep blush. 'You should have woken me up, I would have helped with breakfast.'

'You looked so peaceful. I didn't want to disrupt your sleep. Besides, I wanted to make you breakfast.'

He was right. Sleep was one fourth of her quartet of pleasures: shoes, food, books, and sleep, in changing order. But this quartet may soon become a quintet, with Ben.

He had set up for them to eat out on the deck and watch birds flying over the stream. It was a warm beautiful day.

After the scrumptious breakfast, they took a drive to the town centre for a bit of sightseeing and shopping. The downtown area had some amazing shops and art galleries, with unique offerings you would find nowhere else. She picked a few silk scarfs from a boutique, and a couple of art pieces for her home office and bedroom, which Ben insisted on paying for. Maserati had always been independent and had strived to pay her way whether single or coupled. After all, she was a well-paid professional who could afford her lifestyle. She didn't always know how to receive such gestures from the men she had dated. Mantwa had encouraged her to let men provide for her if they wanted to.

'Dear, men are providers. Sometimes this is how they show they care. Don't emasculate them. Let them provide.' Even Khutso agreed with her on this one, even though they hardly ever agreed on anything. She did let Ben pay, despite feeling some discomfort. It was work in progress for Maserati.

They passed a small shop selling items made from gemstones – everything from small pieces of jewellery to ornaments. She liked a couple of pieces, but she wasn't their target audience at those ridiculous prices.

'Do you like anything?' Ben enquired.

'Uhm. They are all beautiful, but maybe not my style,' she lied. She was not about to let her new lover part with thousands of rands on a gift for her.

After all the shopping they headed back to the villa. He seemed quiet. And nervous.

'Thank you for a wonderful time today,' she said.

He kissed her hand. He had a habit of holding her hand, as if he needed reassurance. She wasn't big on being touchy-touchy, nor public displays of affection. And this had been criticised in past relationships.

When they got to the house he directed her upstairs, as if he didn't want her seeing what was downstairs.

'Do you want to freshen up before dinner?' he asked.

'I can cook tonight. You don't have to slave away in the kitchen the entire weekend.' Maserati offered.

'Thank you. Not necessary tonight. I thought we should both rest tonight. We have a long drive tomorrow. We could order in?'

'Do they even do door deliveries in this part of the country?'

She really did not mind but he seemed to have decided for them. He sensed she was a bit disappointed.

'I would love to have some of your food, very soon,' He reassured her.

'Yeah. I would love to cook for you.' She seldom offered to cook for anyone.

Even after sharing bodily fluids last night, it was weird that he chose to freshen up in the adjacent room. Maserati chose a short simple strapless loose-fitting dress, and Tory Burch flat pumps. Whatever the food order was, she wanted them to eat on the deck, to spend one last time soaking up the stars. He was already downstairs when she made her way there. She hesitated midway down the stairs. There he was, waiting at the bottom, looking like he came straight from a James Bond film, wearing black formal pants, a white shirt, buttoned just up to the collar, and a black jacket to finish off the look. His feet were in Salvatore Ferragamo.

What was the occasion? She suddenly felt way underdressed.

'Oh, I didn't know we were dressing up.' She felt self-conscious with her casual look.

'You look amazing,' he reassured her.

Thank God, she had spiced up her look with a deep red lipstick. Otherwise, her face was completely bare of make-up.

'What is the sound?' She could swear she heard music coming from the backyard. Live music.

'Come.' He reached out to her, walking hand in hand towards the backyard.

Maserati froze.

The cobbled pathway was lit on both sides with fire torches. Underneath the leafy elm tree was a gazebo adorned with plants and flowers, and a candle-lit table for two. A violinist serenaded them as Ben led her down the pathway to the table. A waiter was holding a bouquet of a dozen roses which he handed over to Ben, who gifted them to Maserati.

When did he set this all up?

Her face was still stunned as they sat down. This was by far the most romantic thing she had ever experienced in her life. She was speechless.

And the tears came down without warning. She hoped she wouldn't break out in an ugly cry, with snorting and all. He let her go through the motions, while holding her hand.

She got up to give him a hug. They stood in a warm embrace as he showered her with kisses on the top of her head, and forehead.

The waiter opened a bottle of Dom Pérignon and brought their starters. He then disappeared somewhere in the house, while the violinist continued playing in the background albeit a couple of feet away from the table to give the couple some privacy.

'Cheers,' they toasted.

He had the nervous look of those people in romantic films, about to propose.

Lord, help me. I hope he's not about to do that, she thought. She liked him a lot. But it was too early for nuptials.

'Mmapelo…'

Her legs turned to jelly.

'It is not often that one meets someone by chance and gets the opportunity to meet them again. And discover that they are not only incredibly beautiful, and sexy, but they are intelligent, kind, smart and extremely funny too.' He smiled. She still didn't get why he found her so funny.

'But I am lucky. From that first time I saw you at the shoe store, I prayed that our paths would cross again. And what a pleasant surprise when we met at the conference. I wasn't going to let the chance go to waste. The last few weeks have been incredible, getting to know and spend time with you. And I want to continue getting to know you, exploring life adventures with you. You bring me so much joy. You make me laugh all the time.'

Then he cleared his throat, which he tended to do when he was nervous.

'I love you.'

He was looking directly into her eyes. And his brown eyes were not deceptive. Through them, she could see he was genuine.

'I know it's early…'

'I love you too.' A loud pin drop!

Maserati could not have stopped those words even if she had tried. Her true feelings for Ben had been niggling at her in these weeks they had spent together. With him, she felt free. It was in the way that he laughed at her 'jokes' that gave her permission to be herself completely. It is such a heavy burden to be anything other than yourself, to walk on eggshells trying to conform to an idea of who you should be in a relationship.

A month may be short, but her intuition didn't care so much for arbitrary timelines.

He leaned across the table to give her a kiss.

'This is for you.' He pulled a small box from the inner pocket of his jacket.

Lord, please don't let it be a ring. She loved him, but a ring? Too soon.

It was a dainty platinum necklace, with an amethyst pendant. He had seen her admire it earlier during their shopping excursion and had sneaked back into the shop to get it while she was at an art gallery. As if this night could get any better.

'An amethyst for my Aquarian.' He helped her put it on. Good thing she had decided on this strapless dress. Now the stone was the centrepiece of her chest.

'This is beautiful, Bušang. Thank you.' She held it to admire again. And swallowed hard as she remembered the price tag. Let's just say it was the equivalent of six months' school fees at a top-tier Joburg private school.

His business must be doing well.

The four-course meal was a hit. As the night was drawing to

an end, Ben asked her for a dance. He gestured to the violinist who serenaded them as they slow-danced.

And the heavens opened.

Maserati was about to run back to take cover in the house, but Ben held her and continued to dance with her, while being showered with rain underneath the Mpumalanga stars.

If last night's lovemaking was about discovering him, tonight would be about giving herself to him.

Chapter Twenty-Six

Maserati was not big on New Year's Resolutions.
But she was looking forward to the coming year and what lay ahead. The previous year had ended on a high, and this one held the promise of even better things to come.

She decided to drive back a day after the new year celebrations to avoid the traffic jam as everyone trekked back to Johannesburg from their homes in Limpopo. She had spent a surprisingly drama-free Christmas holiday with her family. Even she and her dad had not gotten into one of their famous blowouts. Much to her mother's delight.

Mrs Mojapelo had noticed her daughter's glow and concluded it must be due to a new boyfriend. Maserati was not big on sharing and had kept the source of her new-found happiness under wraps except for the midnight gossip with her sister Malebo, who also was home for the holidays. Ben and his entire family had made prior arrangements before their relationship took off, to visit Ben's sister in Dakar, and from there the family would spend the rest of the holidays in France. Ben had extended an invitation to Maserati who gracefully declined. She felt it too early to meet Ben's parents and let alone his kids. And she wasn't ready to meet his ex-wife, Moyahabo, who was also going on this trip with family.

How is she even still a part of the family trips? What's this dynamic all about?

Besides, Maserati needed to be home this Christmas, as the year before she had all but abandoned everyone for the holidays. She had stayed in Johannesburg alone. It had only been about three months since her break-up with Tshepo and she was in no mood for her mother's optimism. And she certainly didn't want to face her father with his 'I told you so' face. Her pride would not let her see her father win over this. During a past argument, she had let her father know what she thought of him and how he had treated their mother in the past.

'One day I am going to have a man who will be nothing like you.'

'Good luck with that Rati. Remember, no person is perfect,' her father had retorted.

No, she wasn't going home to give her father the satisfaction of hearing that she had a failed relationship. That her man, who she loved, who she thought was a perfect angel sent from the heavens, was in fact a philandering bastard. She had stayed in Joburg, which was great because Joburg was deserted that time of the year, as everyone trekked back to their childhood homes for the holidays. She even spent New Year's Eve alone with a bottle of champagne, in front of the TV watching CNN and Mariah Carey usher in the new year.

The drive back to Joburg was easy. She passed by Woolies to stock up on groceries. Ben and his family were only returning on the fifth of January, so she had three days to kill. The days dragged on like months. She missed him so much. Never in her life could she have anticipated to fall so deeply and so hard for someone she had only known for five months.

She had always been cynical of Khutso's rants on true love.

'When you find the one, time does not matter.'

It usually felt like people were justifying lust. But here she was, very sure that what she felt for Ben was more than lust. Cupid had aimed the arrow perfectly into her heart.

She shared with him without filter. This was very important to her. At this stage of her life, all she wanted was an authentic relationship. There were still some things they didn't know about each other due to the short time, but she had no doubt that everything that needed to be in the open, was in the open.

She was curious about Moyahabo though. It wasn't 'jealous girlfriend' energy. But it would be a lie to deny that she had some niggling concerns and she wanted to bring up the subject at the appropriate time. Perhaps after the twin's birthday lunch to which Ben had invited her via a text from somewhere in Monaco. The kids had had a big blow out for their tenth birthday party the year before and so this year only a small lunch with just family was the plan.

The lunch would be at Moyahabo's place.

She arrived home and plonked herself on the couch and opened a bottle of wine. She checked on Mantwa who had jetted off to Cape Town for the new year celebrations with Bra-Sam.

'Hello, dear. Happy new year. How's Cape Town?'

'Happy new year, dear. Perfect here. When is Mr Nkosi coming back?'

'Three more days. I miss him.'

'You mean you miss Little Ben.' Mantwa and her shenanigans.

'I'll have you know, there's nothing little about Little Ben,' Rati replied. She did miss Little Ben, though. 'How's Mr Money-bags?'

'In a meeting with some Russians here on vacation, discussing business prospects in Russia.'

'Russians?' For Bra-Sam, every day was a business opportunity waiting for execution. The man did not rest. Yes, his strategic connections may have opened several lucrative doors, but the man was a work beast.

And just like that, three days had gone by. Her man would be landing that morning. But would only come over to her place later that day after dropping off the kids at home. She was restless.

She had spent the whole day cooking – oxtail and creamed mealie rice, with the table set for dinner for two. She added a romantic touch to her house with flower petals from the doorway leading to the stairs, a sign of things to come that evening. She showered and wore nothing else underneath the little LBD – the easier and quicker the access, the better for everyone involved.

She spritzed her body with Baccarat Rouge 540, a scent that always drove him crazy. Her man deserved the pleasure that was coming his way tonight.

When the doorbell rang exactly at 6 pm, it was like music to her ears. And there he was. All 1,9 metres of him. That caramel had tanned slightly from the December Dakar sun, and he smelled like Dior.

'Hey.'

'Hey. I missed you. So much.'

That lasted a second before they lunged at each other like crazed animals, kissing and hugging. He scooped her up and followed the flower petals trail leading upstairs. He sprawled her over the spacious bed, his hands under the LBD. He welcomed the lack of barriers to the goods he cravingfor. He explored with his finger. The anticipation of tonight had gotten her moist already. That drove him even more crazy. His pants were off quicker than the speed of light. The LBD stayed but was pushed up enough to gain the necessary access.

'Aaahhhh…'

'Baby. I missed you.'

'You feel so good.'

'Yeah?'

'That feels, hmmmm. Good.'

'Just like that.'

'I love you.'

137

'I love you.'

Dinner was a 9 pm affair after another sensual session, this time in the kitchen. Ben found the sight of Maserati in his over-sized shirt distractingly sexy. She had been warming the food so they could finally have dinner. As she stretched up on tiptoes to get the plates from the cupboard, the shirt rode up her thighs. She still wasn't wearing any underwear. You can't blame the man for being tempted. He kissed the back of her neck as he bent her over the counter ever so slightly, lifting one of her legs onto the granite top. It was an earth-shattering quickie.

'You need to stop so we can have this food,' she murmured. He had missed her. Three weeks without her was no joke.

After all the energy they had expended, they needed some nourishment and the meal tasted even more scrumptious.

'So how was Paris?'

'It felt like it lacked something special,' he answered. 'I kept thinking I needed to bring you back with me next time, just the two of us to fully experience the magic that is Paris. It is, after all, the city of love.' Ben didn't usually do clichés, but Paris was a cliché she would be happy to experience with him.

'Frankly if I never go to any Disney World Park ever again, that would be too soon. Moya says I should give it two more years and they will be over it.' In his wishful thinking, he'd brought up Moya's name, a name Maserati wished she didn't have to hear during their intimate time. But Ben was Leano and Masa's father. There was no separating him from that. And therefore, there wasn't always much separation from Moyahabo.

'You and Moyahabo. What happened exactly, why did you break up?' There was no better time than now to get into it. When he'd mentioned the break-up with Moyahabo in the past, he had not gone into many details. The atmosphere tonight was laid back enough to have the crucial conversation without feeling like an interrogation.

'We just grew apart.'

'How do you mean? Because from where I sit, you two are close.' Generic answers were not going to do tonight.

He did that shift he always did when he got uncomfortable. But today she was ready to ask the bold questions.

'Did you cheat?'

'Huh?' Ben was taken aback, as if he'd just been accused of being a world terrorist.

'What? They say the three things that break up a relationship are infidelity, finances, and poor communication. I made a pick.'

Finances didn't seem to be a problem for either Ben or Moyahabo. They were great parent partners, so communication was not likely to be an issue. So that left infidelity. And 'things didn't work out' seemed an insufficient reason for people as close as the two of them.

'No. I did not cheat.'

'Did she?' asked Rati. Ben shifted again. He seemed to be in deep thought about how to respond to the question. Moyahabo was the mother of his children and honouring her with respect was important to him.

'I knew Moya from childhood. Then her family moved, and we lost touch. We reconnected again by chance at university, and it wasn't difficult to quickly re-establish our friendship which slowly turned into a romantic relationship. We thought we wanted more from the relationship, so we decided to get married. The twins were born shortly afterwards, but two years in, we realised we had mistaken our friendship for more than what it was. So, we decided we were better suited as friends and co-parent partners than husband and wife. It took another three years before the whole thing was formalised.'

He hadn't answered her question. But as if he knew it was still on her mind he continued.

'In those three years we were both free to do as we pleased, including meeting other people.'

'Did you both meet other people?'

'She did. Ahem, things didn't work out.' He sounded like he was being careful not to spill Moyahabo's business.

'And you?'

'Twenty-one questions, tonight, hey?' Ben teased.

Maserati was glad the mood was light, and she could finally get better answers to this Ben and Moya mystery.

'I did,' he admitted. 'It was nothing to write home about.'

There had been some women, mostly introduced to him by Thabang and Nathi, his friend and business partner. Their choice of potential dates was always problematic, it wasn't too long before the true motives of the women eager to date him would become clear. They saw dollar signs in Ben. The Nkosi name had become a burden around his neck. So, he decided to lie low for a while. Until that fortuitous day he met one stunning shoe-lover browsing at a Sandton shoe store. And he knew his life would never be the same again.

'And then I met you at the conference,' he said happily. He was happy. Truly and utterly happy with Maserati.

'Met me and never looked back, baby.' She leaned over and gave him a kiss, careful not start the kinky stuff they had gotten up to a few hours ago.

'Maserati, I love Moya, and she loves me too, and that will always be, because we are family. But that is where it ends. Mmapelo, I want to promise you one thing. I know you got your heart broken in your last relationship. I understand when your ex cheated, it caused trust issues. I will never leave you wondering where you stand with me. You've asked me where I stand on monogamy. I am true to you and what we want this relationship to be. I have no interest in being with anyone else. I want us to build a relationship that we both want, that makes sense only to us, that gives us immense joy. I want to create for you and with you, a space in which we can both grow, be safe, vulnerable, be everything and anything. That I promise you.'

Ben's eyes and tone were serious. Those eyes, that always

managed to communicate so much of his heart, those eyes that always made her feel safe.

She walked over to his side, as he stood to welcome her embrace. They stood in the dining room, in each other's arms, a place that felt like a haven.

Home.

Later they went to bed, secure in their love for each other.

Chapter Twenty-Seven

'I want to introduce you to my family. The kids and Moyahabo.'

Ben had asked her while they were lying in bed a few weeks ago. This was one of the few times Maserati had seen him unsure. It was as if he doubted that she would agree to meet with his family so soon. He'd been talking about his children quite freely and she knew that this day would come. Their relationship had been growing solidly over the last few months.

'Oh, you want me to meet the kids?' Maserati intentionally omitted to acknowledge the ex-wife.

'Yeah, and Moyahabo.' *There we go with the ex.*

'Moyahabo is hosting the kids' birthday lunch. I want my family to meet the lady that has been the source of my smiles lately. And I think the kids will love you,' he said, uncharacteristically shy.

The source of his happiness. Maserati loved the sound of that, momentarily forgetting her earlier concerns with the ex-wife.

'I love making you smile, baby. And I would be honoured to meet with your family.'

Now, what does one wear to a lunch date with your man and his previous woman, the mother of his children? The anxiety started setting in as Maserati already started pondering the lunch.

Meeting the family is one of the most significant milestones of a relationship.

It's when your partner lets you know that they see potential for the relationship. But then again, meeting a family is no guarantee that a relationship will have longevity. She had met Tshepo's family. His brothers, sister, and his mom. She had hit it off with his mother. When their relationship soured, his mother had tried to reason with Maserati to stay.

'Men cheat, my dear. You need to be strong. No woman should make you leave your home.'

Well, it wasn't the woman that had driven her out of their home. It was Tshepo and his own doings.

Meeting Ben's family included meeting his children and ex-wife. That was completely new to her. She had met cousins, siblings, and best friends in previous relationships. But never kids and an ex-wife.

Ben had texted her the address to the Waterfall Equestrian Estate. She didn't need to be a rocket scientist to understand the level of wealth that lived in that estate. Their divorce settlement must have been a sweet deal for Moyahabo as this home belonged to her.

Her Uber was right on time. She carefully balanced the gifts she bought for the kids and Moya as she got into the back of the car. She didn't know what eleven-year-olds liked, but Ben said she would not go wrong with video games. So, she got them two games each. She brought a bottle of Meerlust Rubicon and a bouquet of flowers for Moyahabo. Mantwa had thought she was trying too hard to impress Moyahabo, but doesn't one bring such gifts to someone's lunch?

The Uber made its way to Waterfall. After clearing the security checks at the estate entrance, Justice, the driver, drove slowly towards her fate. He was visibly impressed by the massive homes.

The house sat on just over a hectare on a corner stand. As they approached, a Rolls Royce was going the opposite direction. She was able to get a glimpse of the occupants. An elderly couple, she guessed they were Ben's parents. They must have come early to celebrate with their grandkids. Thank God they were leaving. She could only handle one stress at a time. Maybe meeting his parents was the ultimate step in the relationship.

The grounds surrounding the house were amazing. Over to the east was a man-made stream dividing the huge garden. Was that a chicken coop? A mini park with biking trails and a large playground with all amenities to make this any child's dream playground, completed the east side. Why would the kids ever leave their home to play elsewhere?

Towards the south of the house was an infinity pool, and a patio decked out fully for entertaining, with views of the stream and garden. The sunsets here must be amazing.

The driveway zig-zagged around a large water fountain, which created glimpses of rainbow when the sun hit it at the right angle. The driveway was adorned with cars befitting an exotic car dealership. The sight was so contrary to Ben's humility.

And amongst those shiny wheels, a white Maserati Ghibli.

Huh!

Justice found an empty spot in the driveway, his 15-year-old Toyota looking decidedly out of place alongside the grand cars. Ben was waiting at the entryway. He looked happy and anxious at the same time. He gave her a big squeezy hug and a kiss – no tongues today. He helped Maserati out of the car, and thanked Justice with a generous tip.

'You made it.' He helped her carry the packages. 'I'm so happy you're here. Everyone is going to love you. Like I do.' The excitement was obvious.

She had lathered on layers of deodorant because the last thing she needed was her nerves to be betrayed by a copious flow of perspiration running down her sides.

And then the twins came from nowhere. They were miniature versions of their father. Leano was going to tower over his friends when the growth spurt hit. Masa was more effervescent, something she must get from her mother because Ben was toned down.

'Kids, meet Dr Maserati Mojapelo.'

'You're named after Papa's car?' asked Masa.

'Yes, she is,' Ben teased.

'No. The car is Italian, and I am Pedi,' Rati answered, with a smile.

'Dr Mojapelo, do you have your stethoscope in your bag?' said Leano.

'Uhm, no. Uhm, please call me… Mase..' Maserati was stumped. What should the kids call her without resorting to her professional names?

Should they call me Auntie? What is the appropriate protocol here? She had forgotten to consult her friends.

And while she was still trying to decide, there *she* was.

The woman's energy was unmissable. She had both grace and that effervescence she had noted in Masa, only extra. She was wearing a flowing skirt to her ankles, in the style of Stoned Cherrie. Hoop earrings framed her almond-shaped face. Her hair in faux locks was gathered in a bun at the top of her head. And she was barefoot.

So, she shares the barefoot look with Ben? What else do they continue to share besides, well, everything?

The woman was not an Instagram beauty. Hers was the kind that truly exuded from within. Maybe it was the effervescence, or maybe her overflowing confidence, or her friendliness? Whatever it was, she understood why Ben hadn't completely let go of his bond with Moyahabo.

And before Maserati knew what was happening, Moyahabo came in for a hug, the kind where you feel someone's entire soul. Maserati froze for a second.

'Hello, my darling, welcome. Welcome. Did you find this

place alright? Oh, my word I love your dress. Oh, you got me flowers. Carnations are my favourite. How did you know? You are so kind. Meerlust? Oh, I love your taste. Please come in. Come in.'

What just happened? What is happening? It was a whirlwind. Ben was watching with bated breath, hoping that all his favourite people would take a liking to one another.

The house was massive. And quite open. The entryway was grand, leading to an even grander gourmet kitchen. Moya led them through another exit leading back to the patio where Ben's siblings were lounging, already with drinks in hands.

'You remember Thabang? And this is Lethabo and her partner, Amadou.'

'Hello.' She had planned to either just wave or shake hands, but the family was full of huggers. The Senegalese added kisses on both her cheeks.

'Have a seat.' Moyahabo directed her to a chair next to Lethabo.

Ben came to join her, sitting on the armrest of the seat. He rested his hand on her shoulder giving it a reassuring squeeze. She looked up at him and smiled still not settled.

'Are you okay?' he mimed to her.

She nodded.

'What can I get you to drink?' asked Thabang. Party animal, concierge extraordinaire, and host, he knew how to keep guests happy.

'Some water please.' Maserati wanted to ease into this visit.

'Water?!' Lethabo sounded like drinking water was a cardinal sin.

'Come on now. This is a no-judgement zone,' urged Lethabo.

'Water and a glass of that chardonnay, please.' Maserati relented to the light peer pressure. It had been explained to her that Lethabo was the rebel of the family. The one that pushed boundaries and can be up to no good.

'Leave my baby alone.' Ben gave her another squeeze on her shoulder. She was surprised by his casualness around his family.

'So, Thabang tells me you convinced Mr Stiff here to dance that time in Cape Town. I want your secret, girl. Because anyone who can convince this one to get on a dance floor has superpowers I need to mine.' Lethabo was an instigator.

Maserati began to relax.

Moyahabo had disappeared somewhere in the kitchen. The twins were frolicking around the large grounds. Thandiswa Mazwai's soulful music filled the background.

'And you should have seen him, Thabo. Like the man was doing young get-downs. I thought I was imagining things.' Thabang had clearly told this story too many times to too many people.

Ben was grinning sheepishly as he got roasted by his siblings.

'You guys are talking about the dancing?' Moyahabo was back.

'Thabs, did you get this on camera? That's some good blackmail tape right there.'

'Stop teasing him. He is such a good dancer.' Maserati was getting in on the light-hearted rant.

'If you say so, because no one we know has seen the dancing with their naked eye.'

Laughter.

Maybe it was the laughter or maybe the wine, but she was beginning to relax. They were all so welcoming. She was curious though how Moyahabo remained so closely integrated with the family.

Moyahabo was back in the kitchen putting the final touches to the lunch. Ben went over to help.

Ben and Moyahabo were the quintessential real-life example of a healthy post-divorce existence. The world-famous actor Will Smith, his equally famous wife, Jada, and ex-wife Sheree, had shown the world that a mature relationship can be forged between current and past spouses, in the interest of happy, healthy, and well-adjusted children. Even they would have been jealous of Ben and Moyahabo's harmonious post-divorce life.

Sadly, it appears to be the norm that when couples go through divorce, the post-divorce relationship is almost non-existent and where it exists, it's such a classic toxic mess that there might as well be no relationship at all. Children who get stuck in the middle of this toxicity bear the brunt of such adult pettiness. Couples who choose maturity and healing are few and far in between, but when they choose that path, it can be a beautiful thing to watch and certainly the best outcome for the children involved.

Ben and Moyahabo appeared to be the PhD version of that rare breed!

'I have never seen my brother this happy. You make him happy. And that makes you alright with me.' Lethabo brought her back to her senses. She must have noticed Rati's discomfort while watching her man with his ex. She didn't know how to respond, but her blush was enough for now.

'Yeah. The man is smitten. And he deserves to be this love-struck puppy.' Thabang added his two cents.

They seemed genuinely happy for their brother. But beyond that, they seemed grateful to her for being the reason for his joy. This allayed her discomfort about Ben and Moyahabo. Maybe she was over-imagining things.

'Besides, *Moya* is not the one to worry about.' Lethabo's emphasis was unsettlingly cryptic. But before Rati could question her, Moya swept into the room.

'Lunch is served,' Moyahabo announced, as she ushered everyone to the beautifully laid dining table. It was a table full of good nourishing food, laughter, and love. Maserati watched it all as an outsider, even though Ben's reassuring love and presence was close by.

Watching the blissful interaction of the barefooted Ben and his ex-wife of five years, was disconcerting. Five years post-divorce, and here they were lovingly exchanging laughs, ideas, and peacefully rearing their twins. Watching them was like watching two ethereal beings, they seemed to function in sync and at such an elevated spiritual frequency. To be in their midst was to be exposed as a mere mortal. Even though Maserati considered herself a student of life and truth seeker, in their presence, she felt very deficient.

There was no mistaking the awkward silence as they drove quietly down William Nicol.

It was just after 8 pm when they left Moyahabo's house. Maserati had so many questions. Should she be worried at how close Ben was to his ex-wife? Was that level of closeness even normal?

I bet even psychologists would agree, Maserati thought, as she made a mental note to schedule a session with Dr Mosibudi.

But why do these two remain oblivious to the abnormality of their closeness?

Ben could sense the tension but knew it was better to wait the moment out. Maserati needed to process the afternoon they just had. She would raise the questions he knew she had when she was ready. He let the silence exist without interruption.

He'd been down this road before. With Palesa.

A year after the divorce Ben had started dating again. He met Palesa, a successful HR executive at a top petroleum company in the country. A mutual friend had introduced them at a party. Palesa was fun, had a loud presence and commanded attention. She made it a point at every gathering to remind people of her accolades. Palesa was a beautiful woman, her face exquisitely symmetrical and always contoured to perfection. Her body was a silhouette synonymous with Instagram models, an unnaturally perfect hourglass. Palesa was the opposite of every quality Ben had looked for in women. Although that could have been a turn off, there was something extremely alluring about her. You don't get to be a top executive in a leading company without some grey matter between your ears. So, Ben had thought perhaps he needed to look outside his normal purview and bring some unexpected excitement to his life.

Well, maybe Palesa was more excitement than he could handle. Because under that beautiful facade lay a woman with extreme insecurities. And this was revealed when Palesa realised the relationship between Ben and Moyahabo was not just as co-parents, but they were truly friends and a family in every sense. Instead of discussing her concerns with him, she went full crazy girlfriend, found Moyahabo's mobile number and started sending her texts to stay away from her man.

The one particular event that broke the camel's back, was when Palesa stalked Ben on his weekly Sunday brunch with Moyahabo and the kids. She showed up unannounced at the restaurant, pulled a chair from the next table and sat next to Ben. She started hugging and kissing him, while glaring jealously at Moyahabo. The kids were nearly seven years old at the time and while too young to understand, there was no missing crazy when crazy was right in front you, slurping up your daddy's face.

With empathy, Moyahabo tried to appease her.

'Oh, Palesa, nice to finally meet you. Ben talks about you all the time.'

But Palesa was too far gone. The commotion was now becoming a scene and the restaurant's patrons were staring.

'Bitch, this is my man!' hissed Palesa. 'You think just because you popped out some kids for him, that gives you the right to infringe on my space. He is MY man now; do you hear me?!'

Ben caught her by the arm and led her to a secluded area of the restaurant to try and reason with her. But he knew just then that Palesa, despite her beauty, was not for him.

He drove her home. He explained yet again how much Moyahabo and the kids meant to him. And he did not blame Palesa for not being able to accept that arrangement, but because of that, it was best for everyone to part ways. She was still livid, screaming non-stop. He hated that it had to end in such a manner, on a driveway, but there was no reasoning with Palesa. He drove off and blocked her number immediately. On the Monday she called him on his other phone asking him to choose between her and his family. There was no contest for Ben, although she asserts to this day that it was she who dumped him.

So, driving Maserati home in this silence, he knew the mental conversation that was going on in her head. But he knew that even with those swirling questions, Maserati would act nothing like Palesa.

He waited with a bated breath for when she would eventually ask the questions.

'Well, thank you for dropping me off. I had a good time today and will call you tomorrow.' Maserati leaned in to give him a hug, and she might as well have given him a handshake because that was the most rigid hug she had given him to date. And her body language was clear.

'Likewise. Good night, Mmapelo.'

He had begun calling Maserati Mmapelo Ya ka, 'one who owned his heart.' But tonight, he wasn't sure if she received his heart still.

He watched Maserati step into her house before he drove off. And although it was 27 degrees Celsius outside, he instinctively turned the car heater on, as it felt like the interior's mood had dropped to below zero degrees.

I don't want to lose her, he thought as he made his way home.

Chapter Twenty-Eight

When Maserati told her friends about the relationship between Ben and Moyo, she was trying to assess whether her discomfort was unwarranted.

She didn't know anyone in her circle who was in a similar situation. Her discomfort was caused by her mistrust of people, of men, due to her experience with Tshepo. There probably would have been a time when this would not have bothered her so much. But she had trusted Tshepo with everything in her. And look where that had led to. So, she reckoned she was within every right to question what seemed questionable.

'I find it very refreshing,' said Tebogo. 'We have seen this with famous people like Will Smith. My brother's best friend is married to two women who have forged a great friendship for the sake of the family unit.'

'Over my dead body!' Mantwa did not mince her words. 'They are divorced for a reason. I find it disrespectful to you, dear, as the girlfriend. And it's up to Ben to set the tone. He must be a man and take charge of this situation and put you first.'

'Do you feel he is not putting you first?' Khutso chipped in, ever so diplomatic and peaceful, truly living up to her name Peace.

'*I* would feel disrespected,' said Mantwa. She did not even understand why this was a topic of debate. It was as clear as day to her. 'Mrs Nkosi is an ex for a reason, people. Ben must let her stay in the rear-view.'

Maserati kept quiet but was soaking in every perspective that her friends threw out. This was the reason she loved her friends – they were always on hand with diverse opinions. And the best of all, they never tried to force an opinion on one another. There was mutual respect that as adults, each could make the right choices for their lives. Of course, this knowledge never stopped them from churning out their viewpoints.

Tebogo turned the conversation back to Maserati. 'Dear, what do you think is the real reason they broke up? You clearly don't completely buy what Ben said.'

'My concern is not really the reason behind the break-up. I guess I am concerned about them deciding to get back together. Based on what I have seen from their interactions, it could easily happen and where would I be left?'

'In the cold!' said Mantwa, disregarding the fact that Maserati had asked a rhetorical question.

'I don't want to invest in a relationship that may not lead anywhere. And I don't want to be a third wheel in their perfect family. I mean I'm the stranger in this whole equation.'

And there it was. Maserati felt like she was coming into this perfect set-up as an imposter, who was likely there as a transient distraction for Ben to find his way back to the true love of his life, Moyahabo. That Ben and Moyahabo had been divorced for five years did not seem to matter for Maserati. It was just a matter of time. A love like that doesn't die. At least that's what the romance novels said. That kind of love always finds its way back home. And she didn't think she was home.

'From what you said about Ben, I doubt that he would lead you on or lie to you,' said Khutso. 'And he wouldn't have invited you over to meet his kids, forget the ex. But his kids? That's a big deal, dear.' Khutso felt a guy would only introduce a woman to his kids if he believed the relationship to be of some importance.

'And that's the mind-fuck,' said Maserati. 'Plus, I do believe deep down he is a good guy. I just can't shake my questions, though. Anyways, enough about me,' she said, as she turned to Mantwa.

'And then you? How's Mr Money-bags?' The girls roared with laughter. Mantwa hated that nickname for her billionaire boyfriend, Bra-Sam.

Maserati had come to appreciate her sessions with Dr Mosibudi. She wasn't going as frequently as she had when she was working through the failure of her relationship with Tshepo, but she had kept steady bi-monthly visits to her for perspective and sanity checks. When she brought up her concerns about Ben and Moya's relationship, she had probed her to look deep within herself to make sure there weren't any other reasons for her concerns.

Could she finally have found something lasting in Ben, that she was looking for reasons to sabotage it? Were her concerns about Moya and Ben's relationship the real concern, after all Ben had been upfront about it and had reassured her of his love. Nothing to date had happened that had been contrary to that assertion.

'Are you concerned that your relationship with Ben is too good to be true?' asked the psychologist. 'Or is your concern that Ben's familial relationship with his ex-wife seems too true to be good? Your concern about their relationship is valid. Talk to Ben. Be clear about your true concerns and not those that you project. Don't conflate things with stories.

'Ask for what you need from him. You may feel tempted to run because this is a new experience for you. But lean forward. Trust that goodness and truth can share equal estate in your life, Maserati.'

———

A Sunday afternoon drive to Hartbeespoort, followed by lunch at one of the many charming restaurants in the town was always a beautiful way for them to connect and talk. She needed for them to talk about the lunch at Moyahabo's house and her feelings that night as he drove her home.

Her friends were right, she was overreacting. Dr Mosibudi was right, she needed to lean forward and trust in the goodness of her relationship with Ben. He had made a promise to her that he loved her and only her, and wanted their relationship to work. He had been honest and upfront about Moyahabo and her role in his life. He had assured her that it was nothing more than a friendship and co-parenting relationship.

She would need to work on her insecurities.

She trusted Ben. She trusted their love.

It was just after 12 noon when he showed up in his Maserati GranTurismo convertible. The man had told her when they met that Maserati was his favourite car.

I guess he was not lying.

Maserati had sent him a text late that night after he dropped her off.

'Bušang. I am not mad. I am processing. I love you and I know you love me.'

Ben had gone to bed somewhat relieved but knowing that this was a hurdle they would need to handle. A large part of the responsibility of handling this would fall onto his shoulders. How could he change his relationship with Moyahabo to accommodate the needs of his new love?

They'd had a busy work week and were unable to see each other, except for a quick lunch on Thursday. However, this Sunday drive would give them a chance to connect and talk about the day at Moya's house. He needed to reassure her of his love.

Maserati opened the door to let him in as she put the last touches to her make-up.

'These are for you.'

Two dozen red roses are better than one. He always made it a point to bring her fresh flowers. He was thoughtful in the selection and meaning for each of the bouquets he brought her.

'Thank you, babe. I'm almost done, and we can get going soon.' Maserati looked sexy in a short pale-yellow dress that made her look younger than she was. Ben could not help but get really hot and heavy very quickly. The sight of his sexy girlfriend was enough to make him think of activities other than a drive to Harties. He pulled her close to him and they locked lips for ages. It was a passionate kiss that communicated all the things they had been feeling since the lunch: security where insecurity existed, assurance where there was mistrust; love where had been doubt.

They had missed each other.

His hands were under the pale-yellow fabric, pulling down the white flimsy panties that covered the place he wanted. The bedroom upstairs was too far for what needed to happen urgently. She pulled him towards the long couch in her living room and unbuckled his belt. His hand found its way between her thighs. He circled her throbbing bean with his fingers, she responded with warm moisture. She found his hard member and caressed it between her hands before guiding him into her warm mouth as she circled her tongue on the tip of his nether head. She gently sucked and kissed. When he was on the verge of eruption, she let him go and lay back. He parted her legs and entered her with slow precision.

'Mmapelo…'

'Bušang…'

They had missed each other.

There was nothing like sweet love on a hot Sunday afternoon. And there was nothing like a beautiful drive along the winding road of Harties after sweet lovemaking. Maserati was now in a tangerine short dress, as the yellow one lay somewhere under her sofa.

They had a beautiful lunch at a lodge restaurant overlooking the dam and then strolled in the gardens. Just as she was readying herself to have that talk, they were interrupted by a phone call.

It was Moya.

Ben hesitated before answering, knowing what conversation they were about to have. But the parenting protocol was that a phone call from either of them was warranted in an emergency. Any non-urgent issue could be communicated via text. Plus, Moya knew he was here with Maserati and would not have called if it wasn't urgent.

'Moya?' He answered casually, glancing at Maserati apologetically.

The greeting on the other end was not casual at all.

'Ben! Ben! Where are you? Are you nearby?' Moyahabo sounded unlike her usual jolly self. Maserati was within earshot and could not miss the fear and panic in Moyahabo's voice.

'Moya, what's wrong?' He didn't want to sound panicked, but she could tell he was.

'It's Leano.'

'What about him?'

'He hit his head against something while they were playing outside and a few minutes later he just collapsed. We are at the Waterfall Hospital. Can you get here, quick? Now?' It was a half-question and half-instruction.

'I'm on my way. Is he okay? Moya, is our son okay?' He was afraid. Maserati didn't know just how bad his fear was.

She didn't need to be asked, she had started packing up their things as they both ran to the car.

He put his foot down on the pedal. Maserati read the speedometer, 120km/hr in a 60km/hr lane. He drove like a crazed maniac down the winding road. She held on to the side for dear life, as the seat belt barely kept her steady in her seat. Her fitness watch beeped as her heart rate soared.

He's going to kill us both, was her fearful thought. But the panic

157

on his face made her much more fearful than the thought of a car accident.

It took them less than thirty minutes to get to the hospital. There was no time to find a parking spot, he stopped right in front of the emergency room like an ambulance. The car had hardly come to a halt when he was out and running in a flash towards the emergency room. Maserati was unsure what to do in the car alone, clearly illegally parked, but he had left the car key in the car, so she drove towards the designated parking for hospital visitors. She quickly made her way to the emergency room, unsure what her role was going to be when she got there.

They stood at the end of the hallway. Ben was already reunited with Moya, Leano nowhere in sight. They were in full embrace. The fear in his eyes transitioned to anger at his perceived slowness of the medical team to stabilise his son, then anger turned into an overwhelming flow of tears. He kept going back to Moya for an embrace, staying locked together until his need to pace the corridors overwhelmed him.

Maserati planted herself against the wall watching them like an intruding stranger. When he seemed somewhat calmer and less pacy, she went over to see if he needed anything. His response was dismissive, and he seemed irritable at her unhelpful presence. She did feel helpless. Her man was fearing for his son's life and all she could do was be a spectator and watch him repeatedly seek comfort in Moyahabo's open arms.

Moya seemed to have her fear under control and tried to reassure Ben to calm him down and remind him that things were being handled. She repeated that their son was a trooper and would be fine. Maserati could tell Moya had probably been the stronger one in the matters of their kids' well-being. She probably suppressed her fears for Ben's sake.

'Moya, I'm scared.' Maserati overheard Ben's vulnerability to Moya.

Why is he not allowing me to comfort him? Why is he not coming to me with his fears? Maserati could not help it. Her fears about

Ben and Moya resurfaced with a vengeance. Her suspicions about them were right. These two have unfinished business and will always come first to one another. Standing there watching Ben ignore her was all the evidence she needed to confirm whatever doubt she still held about them, and to remove whatever hope she held for her and Ben's future.

She was going to be a third wheel in a relationship that would be everlastingly cemented by their two children, who will always bring them together in moments like these. And she would always be the bystander trying to forge her way in. Her heart sank to the pit of her stomach. She tried not to be selfish at that moment. A child's life was at stake.

Thabang arrived and immediately embraced his brother and looked to Moya to give an update.

He had zoomed past her; she might as well have been the paint on the wall.

But as soon as he noticed her, he came over and embraced her so tightly she wished it was Ben giving her the hug instead.

'Hey Maserati. I didn't see you there for a minute.'

'It's okay. I understand. Leano is a priority'

'Let me see what my brother and Moya need. I'll catch you later?' There was empathy in his voice. He could tell she'd been placed on the outside.

A few minutes later, Leano was wheeled back into a cubicle. A doctor came out to announce that Leano was fine, stable, and responsive. And that the brain scan was clear, and he suspected Leano only suffered a minor concussion. He should be well in a few days with enough rest and a break from any sports activities. Certainly, a break from climbing the tree he had fallen from. Moyahabo was sure that tree was not going to survive a week in the backyard. Ben would likely have it uprooted.

Just then a drowsy Leano called for his parents who both leaped to be at his bedside. Mom and Dad were kissing and embracing their son. Ben was trying hard to hide his tears. Tears of relief. But the fear hadn't completely subsided.

Maserati attempted to be useful and picked up Moya's belongings which were lying on the chairs outside the cubicle. She stepped quietly into the cubicle without interrupting them and placed them on the chair for safety. Just as she was about to sneak out, Leano caught a glimpse of her.

'Auntie Maserati, hello. You also came to see me?' Leano spoke slowly, but also relishing all the attention he was getting from everyone.

'Of course I came. I am glad you are okay, Yano.' She had become really close to Leano, more so than Masa, and the gradual affection turned into the endearment name.

Leano tried to say something, but everyone urged him to rest, which he did by immediately falling asleep. The doctor wanted to keep him overnight for further observations, so he was wheeled to a private room in the children's ward. Ben who was still completely oblivious to Maserati's presence, was at his son's side when they wheeled him to the ward, Thabang by their side. It was finally Moya who acknowledged her.

'Thank you for being here. And sorry for the panic and frenzy. Let me call you tomorrow when Leano is out of hospital.' Moya felt some guilt at how Ben had completely ignored Maserati. But she knew the dark fearful place Ben's mind had gone to, imagining the worst for his son. She suspected Maserati did not have all the background.

'It's okay Moya. I completely understand. And I am so sorry that this happened to Leano. Let me know if there's anything I can do to help.'

'Thanks, Maserati. I will call you tomorrow.' With that, Moya turned into the direction of the children's ward to join her ex-husband and their child.

Alone in the corridor, Maserati felt the sting in her eyes. The tears flowed down her face without shame. She felt completely ignored, useless and betrayed by Ben. And she cried even more at the guilt of feeling this way when the man's child was in a critical condition and he was more focused on him than her, as he should. But there was something else, his fear seemed irrational and the need for comfort in Moya's arms was excessive. Why would he have not come to her?

Maserati made her way out the emergency room, into Ben's car and drove home, straight into her bed.

Everything hurt. Thinking hurt.

Chapter Twenty-Nine

Maserati got out of the shower the next morning, still feeling sluggish.

The shower had not re-energised her like it normally did, and it certainly had done nothing to wash away the pain from yesterday's events. Thank God, her work had flexible working schedules. She would have struggled to make an 8 am appearance at the office. It was just after 8:30 am, and the earliest she would get to the office would be 10 am. The first of her five meetings thankfully would start at 11am.

She blasted music in her car to stop herself from thinking about Ben and how he had treated her at the hospital. She didn't think she was going to be able to get through her day, but thanks to the meetings, she breezed through Monday without stopping once to feel sorry for herself. It was the end of the day, and Moyahabo's call had still not come. She probably had said it as courtesy rather than a promise. She remembered that she'd never exchanged contact details with her. Maybe that was the reason she hadn't called.

It was just after 7 pm when she decided to call it a day and head home when the text came through.

'Sorry I didn't call. Leano had to stay an extra day in hospital. Nothing major, he's fine. Will call later in the week. Love, Moya.'

Maserati felt shitty. Here she was worrying about her feelings getting hurt and Leano had to be in hospital one more day. Moya and Ben must be in a state.

'Sorry to hear that, Moya. Please send my well-wishes and big hugs to Leano. Focus on him, don't worry about the call. We will catch up when you are settled.'

She wondered if Ben was okay and sent him a text.

'Hey, my love. Moya tells me Leano had to stay an extra day in hospital. I am sorry that he's going through this. I wish him a speedy recovery. How are you? I am sending you my love. I am here for you if you need to talk, and if you need a shoulder to lean on. Whatever you need, always. Love, Maserati.'

She hadn't expected him to respond right away but receiving a 'Thanks' four days later from him was like adding salt to a very raw, very painful, wound. Why was he so completely withdrawn?

Her work week had been hectic and a welcome distraction. She was in no mood for weekend things and planned to call it an early Friday night much to her friends' disappointment as they were itching to go out for drinks at the Sky Bar in Sandton.

She ignored the phone until it rang again incessantly. She didn't recognise the number and it was too late to be receiving call centre or spam calls. She didn't make a habit of answering her personal phone when she didn't recognise the number, but eventually her curiosity won and she picked up the phone.

'Hello?'

'Oh, hello darling, did I get you at a bad time? It's Moya.' There was no mistaking that effervescence. Leano must be back to normal.

'Oh, hello Moyahabo. Nice to hear from you. How are you? Is Leano okay?'

'Everything is fine, darling. Leano is a trooper. It was just a minor concussion and no permanent damage. At least he will learn not to go up that tree again.' Her laughter was enough confirmation of Leano's well-being.

'I wanted to invite you for lunch, tomorrow, just the two of us.'

Maserati had plans. Albeit solo plans, but nonetheless important, as this was part of her monthly self-care routine of a solo escapade to art galleries in Rosebank, followed by a late lunch in Parkhurst and then home. Nothing and no one came between her and her me-time.

But this was an unexpected invitation. And she was curious.

'Oh, sure. Tomorrow is perfectly fine.'

'Great. How about 12 noon? Should we do Peas in a Pod? It's a beautiful new restaurant that a friend just opened off Monaghan Farm in Lanseria. It's part of this new Green Spaces Project. It's heaven, everything is organic, and I absolutely die for their ravioli and homemade pesto cream sauce. You'll love it. I'll text you the details. Okay, darling. Have a good night. See you tomorrow.'

She was a bundle of energy. It was clear to see why Ben had fallen for her and why he insisted on keeping her in his life.

The group WhatsApp chat was busy that morning. Her friends were anticipating this lunch just as eagerly as she was, well probably a little more eager than her. They were just as intrigued about the close relationship that Ben had with his ex and wanted the details.

'How do you feel about the lunch date with Mrs Nkosi today?'

'Let's create a code word to come rescue you if things go pear-shaped.'

'Please share the deets afterwards.'

'Dear, don't let her disrespect you in any way. This first-wife club doesn't know how to let go and think they have perpetual ownership of the man.'

Maserati had never allowed anyone to disrespect her, and ex-Mrs Nkosi was not about to beat that score. Besides, Moyahabo was not the type; the woman was self-assured and confident, but most importantly, she was kind. She certainly was raising kind kids.

But her curiosity about this lunch was almost too much to bear.

Maserati wore a white short A-line linen dress with the hem ending just above the knees. She adorned her feet with tan wedges that showed off her perfect calves, thanks to being a running-track star in high school. She completed the look with big wooden earrings in the shape of the continent of Africa.

I am also in touch with Mother Africa, Maserati thought, not about to be outdone by the Afrocentric look that seemed to be a preferred style for Moya.

Peas in a Pod was as divine as Moya had described it. How come she and her friends hadn't heard about this place before? It smelled like earth; with the kind of comfort she would get out of her grandmother's kitchen. She settled into her chair, forgetting the anxiety that had been promising to suffocate her just minutes earlier. Moya had said just the two of them, but somehow, she imagined both her and Ben walking in to break the news to her that they were back together.

Imagination is a powerful tool for the foolish.

Where was she anyway? Maserati did not have to wonder too long.

Moya arrived fifteen minutes late, looking simple and yet spectacular in blue skinny jeans, slightly torn at the knees, a cream dashiki shirt with ornate orange embroidery around the V-shaped collar, and equally orange tassel earrings reaching down to her clavicles. Her face was flawlessly radiant. Her presence filled up the room. Watching her walk across the room, the woman was a vision. And she wasn't even trying.

She is gorgeous, Maserati thought. Moyahabo caught sight of her, waved, and shot her that glorious smile.

There's no way to hate someone with a smile like that.

'Oh hello, darling!' Moya extended her arms before she even

got to their table. Maserati stood up to meet the embrace. She smelled like cocoa butter. 'You look amazing. I love those earrings.' Moya pulled a chair and settled across from Maserati.

Maserati felt a strange sense of delight that Moyahabo approved of her look. It dawned on her that she was feeling a little insecure around her. Watching her with Ben, she had wondered if she measured up to this woman who held a special place in his life.

'What do you think? Isn't this place divine? My friend owns this place. And I loved it so much I decided to come on board as a silent partner. So, my choice was completely biased. But the owner, he is a fine specimen of a man. Italian.'

Did Moya just wink at her when she said Italian? She didn't need further explanation around the myths of origins of men and their special giftings.

As if he had overheard them talk about him, the said fine man came over to their table and exchanged pleasantries with Moya. His name was Marco. Maserati's experienced eye could tell there was some extra familiarity between them. Drinks and starters were ordered.

Moya shifted in her chair and Maserati sensed a tinge of nervousness.

'You're probably wondering why I invited you here, just the two of us. Well, I needed to share a bit of my history with Ben. I know it's something you may have questions about. Many people do.' Moya took a sip of her iced lemon tea.

Many people… or many women? Maserati concluded silently that it must be other women who had been in his life.

'He and I are family. And we will be family forever.' This could have been said as a threat, but Maserati realised that Moya mentioned this as a matter of fact, with no hint of threat. She also sensed an apologetic tone from Moya, as if she knew that this fact was a source of many contentions and a huge barrier for Ben's love interests. Ben had pretty much said the same thing to her, so Moya's confession came as no surprise.

'But Ben and I are not and could never be together again. Our life as husband and wife ran its course and fulfilled its purpose. And that is just our truth.' Moya raised her eyes towards Maserati because she wanted this truth to land. It was important that Maserati believed this because she knew how much she meant to Ben.

For things to make sense to Maserati, Moyahabo needed to start at the beginning.

Chapter Thirty

'**B**en's older brother, Rorišang, died at the age of ten. It was an aggressive fatal form of brain tumour, glioblastoma. Ben was seven at the time. His brother's nickname was Rain – Rorišang Aaron Israel Nkosi. They were Rain and Ben.

'Despite their three-year age gap, they were like a finger and nail, close and always together. Ben admired his brother. He loved that Rain let him hang out and play with his friends. Ben never made many friends with boys his age or in his class. He was part of Rain's clique. I was also part of that clique. I was this awkward twelve-year-old girl, and couldn't make friends with any of the pretty girls on our street. Somehow, Rain found me and befriended me.

'I had the biggest crush on this boy with an old soul. Before long, he and I were inseparable. I don't know if kids are meant to experience soulmates at that age, but I honestly think Rain came into my life for a purpose. We were always together: Rain, Ben and me.

'Rain's illness was quite short-lived. As quickly as he was diagnosed, he was gone. Ben was too young to process or under-stand. All he knew was that one day Rain woke up feeling sick, complaining of a really bad headache. Ben ran to his parents' bedroom to call them. By this time, Rain was crying and clutching at his temples. As his mother rushed to his bedroom, she was met with projectile vomiting coming at her like water from a firehose. She got to him just in time to catch him as he fell towards the ground jerking violently in a fit. Mrs Nkosi screamed for her husband to call the ambulance.'

Moya's face appeared calm, but the serviette she was shredding betrayed her emotions.

'Ben stood by the door witnessing his brother, the hero of his life, shaking like a leaf in the wind in their mother's arms. He was terrified. He had never seen his parents so frightened. Rain's eyes were closed and he was moaning from the pain in his head as they tried to calm him.

'The housekeeper ran upstairs to let them know the ambulance was outside. His mother went in the ambulance with Rain, while his father followed behind them with a change of clothes as they still had their pyjamas on. The housekeeper got Ben ready for school, which was useless, because only an hour into class, the school called home for someone to fetch him as he could not stop crying. The driver picked him up.

'When Rain got to the hospital, a whole host of tests and scans were done. Mr Nkosi was expecting nothing less than the best medical care for his son. His parents were still trying to process the diagnosis and had assembled a team of the best oncologists and neurosurgeons, but exactly six weeks after he was diagnosed, Rain succumbed to the disease. Apparently no one had ever seen Mr Nkosi cry before until Rain took his unexpected last breath in the hospital ward. The man's wail reverberated throughout the hospital corridors. It was the most gut-wrenching display of grief the hospital staff had ever seen. His mother was broken.'

Maserati felt the tears pricking her eyes and swallowed hard.

'Ben was too young to fathom death or understand that he would never see his brother again. Every day since Rain had been admitted to hospital, he had asked his parents when his brother would be coming home. His mother is religious and tried as best as she could to explain that his brother had gone to heaven and would never come home.

'I, on the other hand, had experienced a death in my extended family when I was ten. I understood as much as any twelve-year-old could. When Rain died, it was the saddest day of my life.

'The day of the funeral was overcast. As we were about to leave for the church, the rain began to fall. Ben stood transfixed, staring upwards, getting soaked. He called out 'bye Rori' and waved as he was ushered into the car.

'Mrs Nkosi had wanted a small intimate funeral, with just family, close friends, and Rain's school mates, at the school's request. But for a man of Mr Nkosi's calibre and network, a small funeral was a 500-people strong crowd of community members and business associates. It was a beautiful send-off for a beautiful boy. Speaker after speaker, old and young, spoke of how Rain touched their lives. Even at his young age, he had made an impact.

'It was an impact that Ben tried to emulate as he grew older – often to his disadvantage. He lived in his brother's shadow for so long. His parents were devastated and grieved for many years. So, he always wanted to please them, to compensate for the loss of their older child.

'By all accounts Rain was a brilliant boy. Ben, at the time, was an average child, who looked up to his brother and always did what he did. But as the years went by, he worked himself to the bone to be a close replica of his dead brother. It pleased his parents to see glimpses of Rain in him, but he could never fill Rain's shoes. No one can live up to a ghost.'

Maserati felt her heart constrict, imagining the little boy's pain.

'Shortly after the funeral, my family moved to Pretoria and I lost touch with Ben. Until we met again at medical school, over ten years later.

'Ben is a good person through and through. And a good son. I think that's why he became a doctor. He has a passion for people, even though I don't think his passion is necessarily limited to medicine. He could have been anything, really, if it meant helping people, and creating solutions that have positive societal impact.

'Ben and I reconnected at university when he started first year medical school at UCT. I was in the fifth year, fantasising about life as a qualified doctor. I volunteered as a mentor for the junior students, and he fortuitously got assigned as my mentee. It was such an emotional reconnection because for the longest time we had gone through individual grief for Rain and we could finally share our grief with someone who could understand. We became very close, very fast.

'It was during that time working together, and my experience seeing many Black students excluded from graduating due to lack of funds, that we came up with the idea of honouring Rain in the form of a foundation that would not only fund childhood cancer research but would also provide scholarships to talented Black and underserved kids to study medicine.

'Ben took the idea to his parents and they established the RAIN Foundation: The Nkosi Family Foundation for the Advancement of Science and Medicine in Africa.'

Maserati could not believe her ears. How had she not connected the dots before? She had studied medicine because of the RAIN Foundation scholarship. What a coincidence! Ben hadn't said anything when she spoke about it in Dullstroom. But she remembered his discomfort when she had mentioned it.

As a star student in high school, Maserati's grades and leadership qualities had won her the all-inclusive scholarship. She and her mom had driven from Limpopo to Johannesburg to attend the gala dinner that the Foundation hosted for all recipients of the scholarships before they jetted off to university. They were the first cohort of recipients since its inception. She remembered her excitement and gratitude for the beginning of her new life at medical school. She recalled that the chairwoman of the Foundation had welcomed and encouraged the future doctors and scientists. The 17-year-old Maserati was too absorbed in her teenage life and the excitement of going off to Cape Town in a couple of months and had not ever bothered to research the origins of her scholarship donor.

What a small world! It is amazing how the universe works. What were the chances that Maserati and Ben would have the RAIN Foundation as another coincidental connection? If that wasn't destiny, then nothing else was.

'But why on earth hasn't Ben told me?' asked Maserati.

Moyo shrugged. 'Ben has an uncomfortable relationship with his family's wealth and their good deeds. It's something he doesn't talk about to anyone.'

Maserati could not help feeling a sting in her heart at the thought of being considered as 'just anyone'.

Moyo sensed the unintentional hurt. 'He doesn't talk about it even to the ones closest to him. It's something he's working through in therapy. It's probably a trust thing. People from wealthy families don't always trust people's motives. And he believes his family's good deeds should speak for themselves. Even though he sees the good in everyone, he prefers people to get to know him without that connection.'

From what she already knew of Ben, Maserati could see why he would hesitate to share details of his family's accomplishments. She remembered the medical conference in Cape Town: he'd been uncomfortable with the accolades showered on him.

Maserati was curious about his twin siblings and asked where they fitted into this whole story.

Moyo smiled. 'The Terrible Two? Everyone loves them. They were born exactly a year after Rain died. They were the first twins of the family – maternal or paternal sides – so everyone believed this to be a gift from the gods for taking the beloved Rori away. Lethabo and Thabang were the joy everyone needed after a year of grief.

'Their parents were devoted to them, and not surprisingly, they were very overprotective and vigilant with the twins. They didn't miss a single clinic visit and insisted on all sorts of tests to make sure the twins remained healthy.

'Ben adored the babies. He couldn't believe he'd got two at once. He helped to change and feed them, and was equally protective of them. And just as anxious that they may become sick like Rain. But over time it was clear that the twins were as strong as oxen and full of life.'

Maserati remembered Ben always speaking fondly about his siblings. And she'd seen their lively and confident personalities first-hand at Moya's house.

'How do they feel about the family wealth and the foundation?' she asked.

Moya considered her question for a moment. 'Lethabo has always had a rebellious streak, probably as a way of trying to separate herself from her older brothers. She didn't want the pressure that comes with being an Nkosi kid,' she answered. 'She got her Masters in Contemporary Art in London, but she fell in love with Senegal – and those tall, dark French men – and now she works as an Art Curator in Dakar. She's a very talented artist.'

'Yes, Ben has some of her art in his home. It's stunning,' Maserati answered. 'And I can understand that she loves Dakar, it's such a vibrant, lively city. If I were to live in another African city other than Johannesburg, it would have to be Dakar or Kampala in Uganda.'

'Fortunately, she comes home regularly,' said Moya. 'It's always a whole family get-together.'

'What about Thabang?' asked Maserati. 'How does he feel about the public spotlight?'

'Thabang embraces it!' said Moya. 'He's living his best life as a flamboyant Joburg heartthrob, totally unashamed of his Nkosi legacy. He's still lives at home as the prince supreme much to his parents' delight, working for the family business as the Chief

Executive at the RAIN Foundation. He has a degree in Marketing and he's a real technology wizard, so he's responsible for keeping the Nkosi's business ahead of global technology advancements and staying on trend and responsive to consumers' ever-evolving needs.

'Thabang loves the limelight, and the limelight loves him. His dad would never admit it, but Thabang is easily the apple of his eye. For Lethabo, this worked exactly in her favour as it's allowed her the freedom to follow her own dreams while her parents were both preoccupied with their sons' accomplishments.

'However, don't get it wrong. Although they have quite different personalities, these three would kill for one another. Cross one of them and you have crossed all of them. And Lethabo and Thabang both love the Things. Ben often comments that if something were to happen to him, his kids would have another father and mother in his siblings. It is so beautiful to see.'

Maserati could still not quite figure out why Ben and Moya weren't together.

She asked Moya, 'With so much shared history between you and Ben, I still don't understand why you got divorced?'

Moya sighed. 'Ben and I got close again at university because of our childhood friendship and our common ground. However, chemistry between us never exploded. I loved him and he loved me, but there was something missing. I sensed it. It was a relief that we didn't need to explain how much Rain had meant to us. After I graduated, I stayed and worked in Cape Town as Ben was still in medical school. We got married a couple of months after he graduated. We had Leano and Masa and they were the family's joy. We were happy, but something had always been missing for me.

'I finally figured what was missing, the holy trinity: Body, Mind and Spirit. Ben and I got the latter two right. We felt like home to each other. We were meant to procreate and birth our two beautiful children. We connected in mind and spirit, but I wanted the entire tripod. A tripod with only two legs falls eventually.

'I was restless. I got into philanthropy work particularly around children's literacy. I started doing this work around southern Africa, it grew to east Africa and west Africa. Then I started travelling to Uganda… well, let's just say my world collided with a tripod on two muscular legs.'

Moya laughed at her own comment which came out sounding like a love-struck teenager.

'I finally met my soulmate in Psalm Kambugu,' Moya said, smiling. 'No need to guess what his mother's favourite Bible book was, right? I didn't mean to fall in love, but I knew the second that Psalm and I held a conversation that I had met my person. I came home and broke the news to Ben that I found my spirit mate, and did not want to betray him by conducting an affair.'

Maserati was surprised at the ease of it all. 'Can you meet a soulmate and break up a seemingly perfect marriage just like that?' she asked.

'Yes, you can,' replied Moya. 'Ben and I were very good at being honest with one another. Good or bad, the truth always prevailed. It is such a rare thing to find an authentic partner. And I think that's why the end of our relationship was so confusing to many, not just you. Some of our friends still don't get it, even his parents who didn't like me at first, were devasted when we ended our relationship.

'We didn't get divorced right away, but I couldn't deny my feelings for Psalm any longer. To cut a long story short, Psalm and I started a very hot, and very healing relationship. I finally let go of the ghost of Rain and I wished Ben could do the same. Psalm and I had a blissful two years of soul-filling connection and romance. Whoo, bless the Lord. That man was my spirit!'

And then Maserati saw it. She saw an indescribable love in Moya's face when she spoke of Psalm, one she had not seen when she spoke of Ben. And in that moment, she knew her insecurities had been baseless.

'But why are you referring to Psalm in the past?' she asked gently, hoping she wasn't prying into a sensitive zone.

'Psalm died in a freak car accident almost two years ago. He was on his way to Entebbe to board a plane bound for Joburg to visit me. I was devastated and useless for a long time. Ben moved back in with me and the kids, to take care of me. We have been through things, Ben, and me.

'Don't mistake Ben's kindness to me as romantic love. We love each other, we are honest to ourselves, our kids, and the people in our lives about that. We are a family and that will remain forever even when the Things are grown. But nothing more than that.

'Ben doesn't know this, but Lethabo hooked me up on a date recently with one of her artist colleagues, a very sexy man from Dakar, who moved here recently. Between him and Marco, my hands are full!

'But enough about me and the others, I know you want to talk about Ben. When Leano had his concussion, it sent Ben to a very dark place, one he thought he had overcome. It was as if he was reliving Rori's seizure and he feared for the worst. He insisted on Leano staying an extra day in hospital for observation and another brain scan. He's been working from home watching Leano like a hawk. These are things he needs to work through in therapy, and I am glad he's started going again. His reaction at you at the hospital wasn't a true reflection of his feelings for you. That was just a trauma reaction. Ben cares deeply for you. Heck, I think you are The One, but that's not my place to say.

'You know it rained when he first met you. I believe you were getting shoes at some shoe shop in Sandton. Then it drizzled when you met again in Cape Town, again on your first date, and in Dullstroom.'

Maserati did not recall it raining on those occasions, except for Dullstroom when he insisted they danced in the rain. 'How do *you* know it was raining, though?' she asked.

Moya smiled. 'Ben called me every time, excited that he may have found 'The One'. Ben believes Rori communicates with him, and blesses him, through rain. There's been rain during almost all the significant moments of Ben's life. When the twins were born, when he registered Digital Health, on the steps of the courthouse when we got divorced, and those occasions with you.

'Through rain, Rorišang has always been with Bušang. Like I said, finger and nail through eternity. But it has been raining less and less with you in his life. I believe Rain's job of supporting Ben is done. Ben has you now.'

It was late afternoon when they ended their lunch.

Maserati drove away with a lot on her mind.

Chapter Thirty-One

Maserati hadn't slept well last night.

She had rerun the information overload from her lunch with Moyahabo, over and over throughout the night. It was like waking up with whiplash: her head was still spinning. She tried to still her mind, so she could think and get clarity on what to do next. Ben had still not been in touch beyond one-word answers to her texts. But her mind was in overdrive. She needed a distraction.

What better place than Sylvie's, one of her favourite restaurants at Cedar Square. It was usually crowded with the after-church crowd still in their fine designer wear, ready to show off before going home. And the entrepreneur types, that liked to advertise that they did not subscribe to the 9-5 schedule like the working slaves. Sunday could very well be a Tuesday for that crowd.

That's where she would go.

It would be good distraction to watch people and wonder what crazy life problems they were solving in that moment. Hers were certainly getting complicated.

She found a perfect table on the outside patio with great views of the comings and goings. She ordered a glass of merlot, hiding her people-watching behind wide dark sunglasses. But she could not run away from the matter at hand. There was a lot that needed processing.

Hard as she tried to believe in Ben's love, his reassurance, and those non-lying eyes, she could not ignore her doubts. Was she being unreasonable?

Ben had shared much of what Moyahabo had told her about his family, but not in such depth.

Why had he not opened his soul like that with her? Granted, they had only been together for just over six months, but for her it had felt like a lifetime.

She loved Ben – in a way that she had never felt before. Her mind drifted to one of their first dates and how quickly they had deeply connected and shared such philosophical points of views on life. She thought back to their conversation...

'What makes you tick?' Ben asked, as he sipped his wine.

'Hmmm, let me see... Except for my love of shoes, you mean?'

He nearly spat out his wine. 'Of course, except for your love of shoes.' Ben laughed. 'I do remember when I first saw you at the Sandton shoe store, you were completely in heaven, gathering from the glow you exuded with every pair you tried on.'

'Life. Life makes me tick.' She paused and assessed his face for the 'oh here we go again with those wanna-be gurus of life' bored expression.

Nothing. He seemed to be readying to hear more.

'How so?' He *did* want to hear more.

'Life is such a mystery,' she said. 'There was a time in my life that I wanted to understand it all. You see, I'm a bit of a control freak. I don't always do well with uncertainty. And life in general is such a mystery. I think we need to accept, even when we don't always understand, that we are all here for a given purpose. And when we live out that purpose, we elevate God.'

She took a sip of her wine. He took a sip of his wine.

'Hmm... I think this is going to be a beautiful night.' He

smiled, seemingly intrigued even further with this woman in front of him.

'Should we place our orders and continue with this thought-provoking conversation?' He signalled to the waiter, who took their orders and disappeared.

'You know the saying 'I dance to the beat of my own drum', right?'

'Yes. Why?' Ben was curious where this was leading to.

'Well, I think if we all lived in isolation, alone on some island, this would be completely true. However, we live amongst people who beat their own drums producing their own rhythms and melodies. But sometimes, we find ourselves adjusting our beats trying to blend in with all these other beats. And then the beat of our drums gets drowned in all the other sounds. Our sound gets lost.

'You are still with me, right? I haven't lost you?' she teased him. The wine may have been lubricating her sense of humour a bit.

'I am still with you. I'm intrigued that we are so deep and haven't even gotten to dessert yet. Anyway, go on Oprah Winfrey.' He reciprocated the humour.

She surprised even herself with such a hearty laugh.

'Haha, you're funny.'

'Anyway, I used to think I danced to my own drum, but I was dancing to the meshed beats of all the drums surrounding me, never just my own drum. So, now I am learning to synchronise my beat, finding my own rhythm within and without all these other sounds. I am at my best when my reason for being makes sense in the grand scheme of life.'

'Wow. Uhm… Okay. In English please.' They both cracked up laughing.

'Are you always this deep on first dates?' Ben chuckled.

'Uhm, technically this is not a first date.'

'Technicalities aside, I completely get what you are saying.'

Maserati threw her head backwards, rolling her eyes, 'Yeah, yeah.'

'No, seriously. I do completely get what you mean. I agree that when one is perfectly synchronised in an orchestra for example, the audience should be able to make out your beat, as uniquely yours. We all add to the music of life, to the beats of other drums, but we should also be able to produce a mean solo performance and dance to the beat of our own distinct drums.' Ben appropriated Maserati's analogy to drive the point that he truly understood and shared in her point of view of life.

'Absolutely!' was all Maserati could say, delighted at the fact that Ben understood.

He absolutely gets me, she thought, feeling strongly attracted to him at that moment, with a slight flutter in her heart. And a tingling warmth between her legs.

'That's exactly it. It's a balance between the alone time necessary to replenish our spirits and the need to interact with others in order to grow spiritually.'

'But as people, we generally suck at being alone,' said Ben 'We have a need for attachment. Don't you think?'

'I agree. I think it stems from fear," replied Maserati. 'As people we are generally much more motivated by fear than love. There's power in being alone with oneself. I wonder though, if maybe subconsciously we are afraid of our own power?'

'Of course we fear our own power,' replied Ben. 'And perhaps that is why as people we get stuck in the same failure patterns. We allow those failures into our lives because success is too scary.'

Maserati considered his comment. 'I admire people who are willing to try over and over again at this life game, people who understand that life's destination lies in the trying.'

'Well, while you admire these trying people, I am going to be admiring this dessert menu.' Ben diverted the conversation back to the meal that seemed to be secondary to the date at this point.

'Oh my gosh, that's so cheesy.' Maserati laughed at his attempt at a joke.

'Cheesecake it is then.' They both laughed out loud, oblivious to the judgemental eyes of their fellow patrons.

Sitting alone now, remembering that date, she missed him and those conversations so much. Now all she was getting was silence, and one-word answers. In their love, she had found plenty of room for the freedom to just be. She had trusted that he loved her too. There was no perfection required. And as a recovering perfectionist, she had enjoyed the freedom from the shackles of the perfect images she had conjured up during her time with Tshepo.

But she could not help but feel like an outsider in this life story he had had with Moyahabo. As reassuring as Moya had seemed, she felt really jealous.

There it was!

She was jealous of Moyahabo, jealous of the life they had lived together. It made hers and Ben's love story pale in comparison. How could she compete with a woman who not only shared Ben's childhood but his adulthood too? Where would she fit in?

She would be the square peg in their perfect round hole family.

'Hello stranger.'

The waft of Tom Ford was clouding her already foggy mind. And he needed to reinvent a new and better greeting.

'Tshepo.'

She called his name with such bold diction, daring him to approach her with caution. Feeling courageous behind the safety of dark Dior sunglasses, plus the added benefit of liquid courage did not hurt.

He always just seems to appear from somewhere. And why here, and why now?

'I never got that call from you.'

'I never said I was going to call.'

The words were not spoken, but they both knew the eyes had implied a promised call.

'Semantics.' The well that Tshepo visited to drink up his arrogance must be plentiful.

'It's good to see you, Rati. What has it been? Six, seven months?'

'I wouldn't know.'

'I was here for a meeting when I saw you walk across. And couldn't wait to come over and say hello.' He was in a navy blazer, which meant the meeting was an important business deal. He always said blue blazers were his lucky business charms.

'Every day is a deal-making day,' Maserati recalled this to be his mantra.

'One hundred percent! You remember?' He smiled.

The conversation had been going on for close to ten minutes; if she was going to dismiss him, she would have done so by now. But she still hadn't extended an invitation for him to sit, so he remained standing in front of her.

'Please. Sit.' This *was* the distraction she needed. It was also the merlot making this decision on her behalf.

It was two in the afternoon, and she was hungry. Sylvie's had the meanest oxtail in town. She ordered a refill, but a full bottle this time. The waiter brought a second glass for Tshepo.

As Tshepo settled across her, still hiding behind the sunglasses, she watched him closely, noticing differences in mannerisms between him and Ben.

Tshepo had an eager confidence. Ben's confidence was still.

Tshepo's expressions were explicit. Ben's expressions were subtle.

Tshepo name dropped. Ben was THE name.

Two plates of delicious-smelling food were placed in front of them.

'No oxtail can ever beat yours, Rati.' Tshepo laid on the charm in between bites. But it was true.

Ben had the same reaction to her oxtail. It was appalling that

her oxtail had not garnered many marriage proposals. Well, technically one proposal, which had ended in the dumps, thanks to
the philanderer in front of her.

'Really?' A little flirting was just part of the distraction,
Maserati convinced herself.

'Absolutely! What do you put in that meal, love potion?' His
jokes were still textbook cheesy.

She laughed, her elementary school acting lessons coming in
handy.

'So, was your meeting successful, did you secure the deal?'
Maserati needed him to talk more so she could talk less, lest she
started talking about Ben. And what better way to rev him up
than talk deals?

'Yes. As part of the Premier's manifesto promises, Economic
Development is looking at various infrastructure expansion
projects including township malls, road revamps, et cetera.
Private and public partnerships are essential for such projects, so
we have been in talks with Sexwale, Motsepe and others, on
strategic partnerships. The MEC and Premier are meeting with
the President soon to brief him before the next lekgotla.'

Name drop 101. He was going to be a great politician one
day. Soon.

She had never really paid attention to this. But if truth were
to be told, she had found this name dropping quite impressive,
at some stage in their relationship. She had assumed that having
political and business bigwigs at the tip of your tongue to be a
necessary networking ingredient, for someone with Tshepo's
political and business career ambitions. This kind of talk had
certainly impressed her parents. She was convinced her mother
bragged a little about her future son-in-law.

Maserati wondered what she told the church ladies now.

Ben was completely the opposite. She'd had to find out just
how wealthy his family was at lunch with Moyahabo. She
remembered how uncomfortable he had been at that conference

in Cape Town during the standing ovation. Tshepo would have soaked it all up.

The waiter cleared the table. She was onto her third glass of wine, a bit much for a Sunday afternoon. She considered sending a 'not coming to work' email to her manager for Monday.

'Rati, I know the last time we saw each other, I sprung that apology on you abruptly.' Tshepo redirected the conversation. He didn't think he'd made a mistake when he thought there could be a second or third chance in this case, after their last encounter in Parkhurst.

'I meant every word of it. For what it is worth, I wanted to reiterate what I said. I'm truly sorry for how I fucked things up. You deserved none of the things I did. I would like to remain, you know, friends.' Shot fired.

She removed the sunglasses. Tshepo noted the tinge of red and swelling around her eyes. She must have been crying. Tshepo shined his armour, getting ready to be the knight to the rescue from whatever had caused the sadness.

'I did appreciate your apology. But sometimes words aren't enough.' Her mind drifted to that night when she almost called him.
What would have happened if I'd called him?

'I understand. I just want to be friends. You are someone I cherished… still cherish, and I would like to believe we were friends once. And could be friends again.'

What do people really mean when they say, 'let's be friends' after a nasty break-up?

'Hmmm…' Maserati took the last sip from her glass. The bottle was empty. She had drunk three quarters of it. He was never much of a drinker. It was probably best not to get another bottle, otherwise she would need to crawl home.

'Do you want another glass?'

'No. I think I should call it and head on home.' She tried to stand up and stumbled a little.

He caught her arm. 'Are you going to be okay driving home?'

He knew she wasn't. She must have started drinking on an empty stomach. She always got over the edge if she drank without first eating. Plus, those eyes meant she had been crying. There was some opportunity here for him to save the day. To redeem himself.

'Rati, I can drive you home. I'll leave my car here and take a cab back. Is that okay?'

She suddenly felt sorry for herself for getting this sloshed in front of him. But she also remembered why she came here in the first place.

Ben and Moyahabo's dream love.

She wanted cry. And sleep. But she was not shedding a single tear in front of Tshepo. However, she needed a ride home. That much was clear.

She handed her car keys to him. He strategically held her hand as they walked slowly to her car. He was careful to steady her, so she didn't stumble. He knew how embarrassed she was going to feel the following day. This was already embarrassing enough.

The drive to her house was a short ten minutes.

Tshepo had not lost his way around her house. Maserati had fallen asleep in the car, and he had to carry her upstairs to her bedroom. He carefully undressed her for comfort and got her under the covers.

She opened her eyes just as he was about to go and pulled him by his collar and kissed him, first like an exploration and then more passionately. He responded without hesitation as he'd been waiting for this chance to feel her lips again.

'Ben, I missed you.' She moaned in between kisses. Tshepo stopped, taken aback.

Who the hell was Ben?

Just then he realised that Maserati was not only drunk, but was yearning for someone else. He had known that she must have already moved on but hearing her calling that name with so much passion was like being karate-kicked in his balls, such was the fragility of his ego.

'I miss you and love you so much, baby,' mumbled Maserati, before she turned and fell right back to sleep.

Tshepo walked downstairs, a thousand thoughts going through his head, wondering if the house had any telltale signs of this Ben. The house had a different energy. Another man's energy. Whoever this Ben was, he had a huge impact on her. This wasn't the outcome he had hoped for when he saw her walk into the restaurant four hours earlier. He could have left at that moment but decided to wait until she had sobered up. It didn't feel safe to leave her in that state.

He eventually found the telltale he'd been looking for, a framed picture of Maserati and a tall guy, taken from what looked like a vacation. Tshepo recognised that face. Every businessman worth his salt made it their business to know this man, or his family. How did Maserati find herself in that circle? It was a coveted circle he had not been able to crack.

Then he was drawn to something in Maserati's eyes. In the picture she looked really happy, her eyes sparkled ever so brightly, and her smile was radiant. Not only did she look happy, but it was the way she was looking at him. She looked at this Ben like he was her world! He'd never seen that look from her before.

This lit up a young rage in Tshepo.

He'd worked hard to be in the calibre of men like Ben, and this picture had just set him back many years. After all this time, Tshepo still hadn't realised that it wasn't 'what' men like Ben were, but 'who' they were that made all the difference. He was still chasing the elusive high of external accomplishments.

———

It was close to 11 pm when she woke up. Her bladder needed emptying and her body, hydration. She was confused for a minute before she remembered her afternoon with Tshepo and her alcohol-gulping ways, and how she got home. She was in her underwear and realised he had taken her clothes off. And she vaguely remembered a kiss.

Fuck.

She had kissed him.

I hope that fool doesn't think it means anything.

Assuming he'd caught an Uber back to the restaurant as he'd said, she walked downstairs in her underwear to get water. When she got to the bottom of the staircase, she glanced into the lounge area and let out a scream when she saw the man lying on her couch. She was about to reach for the panic button, when Tshepo called out her name.

'Rati, it's me.'

'Fuck, you gave me a fright. I thought you left.' She suddenly felt naked. She grabbed the throw blanket from one of the couches and covered herself.

'What are you still doing here?'

'I couldn't leave you in, uhm, you know, in that state.' He knew better not to emphasise her drunkenness.

In her defence, it had been the alcohol plus the lack of sleep the night before that had pushed her over the limit.

'Thanks. That was kind of you.' She was sober now. 'I'm fine now; I don't want to take up any more of your time. I really appreciate you helping me this afternoon.'

Tshepo wasn't ready to leave yet. Mostly because of his curiosity over that picture.

'You are welcome, Rati. And this is no bother at all.' Tshepo was all in on the chivalry.

The displacement of her picture with Ben caught her eye, and she knew that Tshepo had seen it. As a man who made it his business to know the influential people in Johannesburg, she was pretty sure he knew who Ben was or knew of his family. And she knew he probably had questions, to which she would offer no answers. He may have helped her in her time of distress, but she did not owe him access to information about her private life and certainly not Ben's.

Tshepo wanted to play his cards right.

'Are you sure you're okay, Rati. I couldn't help but notice at the restaurant that you had been crying.' If this Ben was the reason for her being upset, he wanted to remind her of that fact. May the shadow of doubt be upon her.

'I am okay.' Keep it short and sweet.

'Yeah? Because it was so unlike you to, you know, exceed the limit like that. Especially in public.' He was relentless.

'One has to live on the edge now and then, don't you think?' Two could play this game.

'I was just concerned.' He needed to shift gears. 'Hey, this picture, I thought I recognised this guy. That is Ben Nkosi, right? How do you two know each other?' No one could ever accuse Tshepo of not being brazen.

'How do you think we know each other?'

Tshepo chuckled nervously.

'I mean from this picture I would say you two are an item?'

'And how do *you* know Ben?' Maserati was not offering a single confirmation.

'You know the business circle can be small.' If Tshepo knew Ben, there would be no modesty in sharing how and where they met and the accomplishments they had together. He didn't know him. He had no business deals with him or his family. And that was eating at his ego.

'True. The business circle can be small. Tshepo, once again, thanks for tonight. I didn't mean to put you out of the way. But let me also not keep you here longer.'

It was time to nip this interrogation in the bud.

Tshepo knew he had been kindly asked to leave. Maserati had indeed moved on. There could never be another chance of rekindling things here. But his materialistic opinions assumed it was due to Maserati capturing a wealthy boyfriend rather than his own doings.

'I am glad you're feeling better. And I meant what I said earlier. I hope we can be friends. I'll call an Uber.'

'Goodbye, Tshepo.'

This chapter was fully closed!

She picked up the picture and the love between her and Ben was apparent. She had been worried about Moya and Ben's love story when she should have been fighting to continue to tell the Maserati and Ben's love story.

She messaged him.

'Bušang, this silence and wall between us is killing me. I may not fully understand what you are going through, but I want you to know that I am here for you. Let me be there for you. Can you come over in the morning for breakfast, to talk? I love you.'

The response was immediate and brief.

'Yes. I'll come over. Love, B.'

It wasn't perfect, but it wasn't silence either.

Chapter Thirty-Two

Surprisingly, she slept like a baby. Maybe it was the thought of finally seeing him or finally getting answers.

Maserati woke up refreshed. She made all the things he loved for breakfast; freshly baked English scones with jam and cream, poached eggs, avocado and smoked salmon, and toasted bagels. It was 10 am when the doorbell finally rang. She took a deep breath and opened the door, unsure how they would greet each other after not really speaking for over a week.

And there he was, a little rugged but as handsome as ever. He looked tired, and slightly defeated, like he had been battling a demon and lost dismally. She instinctively reacted by reaching over to him with a hug. He seemed surprised and frozen, clearly he hadn't anticipated that she would be welcoming him with warm hugs after everything. The awkwardness could not be missed.

'Hey.' Maserati tried hard to mask it all with some enthusiasm.

'Hey.' His voice sounded rough. What had happened in this last week that had turned that confident, assured, charming, laughing-at-all-her-jokes man into this defeated creature?

'Come in. I hope you're hungry. I made some of your

191

favourites.' She thought she saw a tinge of a smile in his eyes, but at this point she could just be imagining things.

They settled at the dining table with the breakfast spread. She made a plate for him and got the brewing coffee from the kitchen. He took his coffee, with two sugars and a dash of cream. She got a cup too and settled across him because the only way to have this conversation was facing each other. He may lie with his words, but his eyes could never be deceptive.

The light in his eyes was still there even though the sparkle was missing. The light was clouded by guilt, doubt, hurt and hesitation. The shade of earth brown that exuded life and breathed essence into hers, had gotten darker. She almost reached out across the table to touch his hands in reassurance of her love. But he had to want it. This man that had been so open, months ago had become shut down.

He had to open up.

There they were, like strangers, trying to find the perfect words to bridge the thick silence between them.

'How's Leano?' She might as well start the conversation.

'He is fine. Thankfully,' he said, the gratitude for his son's well-being very clear.

'He is such a trooper. I am glad that it was nothing too serious.' She wanted to be careful not to minimise what had been a scary situation.

'Yeah. It could have been worse.'

And therein lay the foundation for all this tension. His fear for his son had been very evident that afternoon at the hospital.

'I met with Moya, and she told me Leano was out and about like nothing had happened. Boys!' She knew that he probably knew that she and Moya had met and what they had talked about. She wanted to see if he would talk about that.

'Both of them, Leano and Masa. They are going to age me prematurely.' He shook his head and flashed a faint smile.

There he was. Her Ben. Not completely, but her Ben, nonetheless!

'Did he scare you?' This conversation needed to be had.

A cloud suddenly hung over the room.

Ben took a deep breath and cleared his throat.

'Yeah. Yeah, he scared the living daylights out of me.' And suddenly he was fragile and scared.

Ben had thought he had worked through the grief of losing his brother Rain. But when the twins were born, it resurrected an anxiety he had long buried. Every parent worries for their children, wanting to prevent any harm from happening to them. Ben's fear for his twins was kept alive by a real lived fear. That incident with Leano scared him. Really scared him. Rain was about Leano's age when he died. In the hospital waiting for Leano's scan report, Ben relived the fear of that scared seven-year-old boy who had witnessed his brother's seizure and ultimate passing.

'I was so scared. If we had lost him, I don't know what I would have done. I don't think I can take another loss like that.' There was so much pain in his voice. If life could take someone as precious as Rain, what was stopping it from snatching his children?

'Is this because of what happened to your brother, Rain? Moya told me everything.' Maserati wanted to move closer to him, but she knew he would not welcome her embrace.

Ben wanted to open up to Maserati, but he didn't think she could understand. No one could understand this journey like Moya.

He was battling an inner conflict of keeping Rain alive and letting him go. Much of his life had been lived with the conviction that his brother was near him all the time. But to continue to keep him close was causing friction with life in the living world.

Who would he be without Rain?

How could he keep his legacy alive by letting him go?

Lethabo had told him once that she felt like she and Thabang had always competed with a ghost for his affection. It was like they did not measure up to the great Rain. There was resentment. There was envy. But how does one hate a ghost? Ben was a loving brother. But he never gave them full access to himself. There was a piece of him that would always be reserved for Rain. They never got all of him.

'I am here for you. Let me be here for you.' Maserati ignored her own pain and wanted to assure him of her support.

'I don't think you or anyone can understand that trauma. Of losing someone you love so deeply and being constantly afraid of history repeating itself through your children. No one can get it. Well, no one except for Moya.'

He pushed the dagger deep through her heart and wiggled it around to rip apart whatever was left of it. But she was not done fighting for him.

'Ben, I may not understand. But I am human. I have compassion and empathy for what you have gone through. I love you, so so much, and I want to be here for you, if you will let me. When you hurt, I hurt. Deeply. I want to make this better for you. I want your world to be better because I am in it, for you and with you.'

Maserati didn't know how else to convince him. And she truly meant every single word. She was ready and willing to move mountains for him, to bring the sunshine into his life. To be the sunshine in his life. To be a safe space from a raging world.

She knelt beside him.

'My love. I don't mean to speak out of turn, but Rain will be here, is here, for you for as long as you need. But you need to let him rest in peace, and let others be here for you just as he had been for you. Let others love you like he did. Let my love comfort you.'

He knew she was capable of being and doing all those things. But some wounds run deep. And some battles need to be fought in solitude. He had come over to have a harder conversation than she may have been expecting. It was only fair that it happened in person.

She wasn't asking him to choose but asking to be let in. It didn't feel like it though. It hurt to let Maserati go. But letting Rain go would hurt even more.

'Maserati.'

It was the way he called her name, that she knew in her bones the words he was about to utter. There kneeling by his side, the tears started running down her face. Someone had ripped out her heart and dropped it into a grinding machine.

'This past week has shown me that there are things I have not completely worked through. My grief over losing Rain lives with me in conscious and subconscious ways. It lives with me in raising my children. It is a constant presence in my life, one I cannot explain in full to anyone.

'Mmapelo, I love you, enough to know that you deserve more than I can give you right now. I need time to work through my grief, and my fears. I am not capable of loving you in depth while these things occupy my heart.' The tears welled up in his eyes, but never fell. The shame of letting her down was too much to give himself permission to cry in fullness.

Maserati's body had resigned itself on the cold tiled floor. How is it that love can be so easily taken away?

'I am so sorry, Mmapelo. I do not mean to hurt you. My love for you is real. You made me happy in ways I didn't think I was capable of being.'

She didn't want to hear that.

'How much time do you need, Ben? Should I wait for you while you work through these things you say you need to work through?' She loved him but didn't want to wait in blind foolishness for something that had no chance of ever happening.

'I don't know. And I will not ask you to wait. That would be a selfish ask.'

Like everyone else, Maserati had only gotten pieces of him. Not of all him. And those pieces were about to slip right through her hands. The fact that he could not commit a timeline and commit to making it work so they could eventually be together again, did not leave any doubt in her mind. There was nothing left to be said but their goodbyes.

Like a robot, she stood up, opened her front door, and gestured for him to leave.

'Goodbye, Bušang.'

Maserati finally understood Lethabo's statement that very first lunch at Moya's house. '*Moya* is not the one to worry about.'

She had been worried about an unresolved relationship between him and Moya, when all along it was the ghost of Rorišang Aaron Israel Nkosi that was haunting her relationship with Ben.

Chapter Thirty-Three

The universe works in mysterious and generous ways if you believe.

Two weeks after the break-up, no, after Ben broke up with her, she received an exhilarating email from her manager in the US. She wanted to know if Maserati would be open to a six-month-long assignment based in Chicago for a signature project the organisation was working on. It had been James Gaines, the VP of International Enterprises, who had proposed Maserati for the team, to bring a voice and perspective from Africa for this project which had the potential to have significant global impact and a paradigm shift in digital health care.

This was the clean break she needed, not only for her personal life, but for her career plans. This opportunity would be a big deal. She had said yes without hesitation.

A week later the legal department sent over the paperwork she would need for her US work visa application. It took her another two weeks to secure her appointment at the US embassy in Sandton. She'd previously only been at the embassy for a tourist visa. That appointment had been scary as it was her first time there. The reviews were unfavourable for first time applicants. But she worked for a well-known American corporation, so she figured the odds would be in her favour.

This time around, she wasn't too concerned. Although her appointment was at 11:30 am, she decided to forego the office and took her morning meetings from home. At 10:30 she made her way towards Sandton, giving herself ample time for incidental traffic delays. It was her lucky day. Within twenty minutes she was at the embassy.

The work visa interview was a breeze, and her visa was approved after a couple of clarifying questions. She decided to head to Sandton City for a quick celebratory lunch. Mantwa, whose offices were in Pretoria, was swamped and would not be able to trek all the way to Joburg to lunch with her friend. It was a good thing Maserati had never been afraid of lone lunches.

She craved Tasha's creamy pesto pasta. The square was buzzing for a Wednesday. Sandton, the richest square mile in Africa, hosts some of the country's top companies, so it was not surprising to see suits out for lunch. Like Tshepo always said, every day is a deal day. She chose a table facing the fountain and enjoyed the views.

While waiting for the food, she replayed the last few surreal weeks in her mind. Watching Ben walk away from her that day felt like a bad dream. Two significant break-ups in less than three years.

Was she cursed in the matters of love?

Was *she* the problem?

Was she not worth a fight and commitment?

Thank goodness for her sessions with Dr Mosibudi because she would have been a basket case.

However, her sadness had settled. She was moving towards acceptance that her promising fairytale with Ben had ended. She could not hold herself responsible for other's actions. All she could do was assess her own role in the relationships, and their eventual breakdown. And she was proud of herself for not pushing to change Ben. No one person is responsible for making another human whole.

Instead of wallowing in pain and occasional anger, Maserati was choosing to cherish the time they'd had to know one another and the love they'd shared, however brief. If anything, she had learned what genuine love felt like. Her time with Ben had taught her that one can only fail forward. That there's nothing wrong with taking a leap into love. And now, here she was ready to take on a completely new challenge, one she would have probably turned down if she was still with Ben.

The universe has good timing.

The waiter brought her food, and as he was leaving the table, a familiar silhouette made Maserati freeze for a split second. A closer look established that it wasn't who she thought it was, but Ben's younger brother. She had forgotten that Thabang was Mr Sandton. He was seated at a corner table with three other equally suited and equally dashing gentlemen. Maserati noticed that all the ladies in the restaurant had their eyes angled towards that corner table, whose net worth could mortgage a small country. Thabang mingled often with the Maponyas and Motsepes.

She hoped he would not recognise her. The less she had to talk about the other Nkosi, the better. But she had a magnetic aura. Thabang had quickly made her out in the crowd and was now making his way towards her.

'One of my favourite humans in Joburg.' He gave her such a genuine and open hug, as if to confirm that she was amongst his favourite people indeed.

'Just in Joburg? And here I was about to be flattered.'

'If you can make it in Joburg, you can make it anywhere.' His famous charm was unparalleled. And she needed the laugh.

'How are you though, Maserati, really?' With that one question, Thabang had invited the elephant in the room to sit at the table with them.

Maserati shrugged her shoulders. 'I'm fine.'

He didn't seem to believe her.

'You know he loves you?'

It was her turn to wear the sceptical look.

Everyone kept trying to convince her. She knew it too, but love alone is not enough to build a working relationship. There were many other ingredients that Ben had made clear he was not able to bring to the table, now or any time soon. A love that's surrounded by a high brick wall is inaccessible and useless. Ben had built the highest wall around himself.

'This is the first time he's been challenged to let go of the past in a real way.'

Maserati knew what Thabang meant by that, thanks to that lunch with Moya.

'When we were young, Ben was our world, he was there for Thabs and me. But something felt different once he went to UCT. He rekindled his friendship with Moya and their shared experience with Rain seemed to shut us out. Thabs and I were competing with a ghost for our brother's affections. We grew so resentful of Rain. Can you believe it, being resentful of your own brother, granted one we never knew? It was like we weren't enough for Ben. But he wasn't ill-intentioned. Over time once Moya had decided to put Rain to rest and start fully living her life, Ben slowly started to shift too.

'When the twins were born, I think it just brought up all that grief and fear for their safety.

'And then you came along in his life. It's the first time I've seen my brother so energised. That dancing in Cape Town?' Thabang smiled at the memory of that night in Green Point.

Maserati also remembered that night and chuckled at the thought of the two of them on the dance floor.

'I had never seen my brother so light, so free, so recharged. He's carried a lot on his shoulders. And being with you has allowed him to begin to let go.'

Maserati could not reconcile the confident Ben she had met at the shoe store, and watched on the podium in front of all those dignitaries, mesmerising them with his intellect, and this Ben burdened by lifelong grief.

Maybe it was true. Maybe he was different with her. Maybe being around her made him different.

Maserati had some new-found respect for Thabang. Most of what he said also explained why Lethabo didn't seem to try too hard around her older brother. She had probably got tired of competing with Rain. Maserati had also noted that Lethabo was the only one amongst the family that never really referenced Rain in her conversations at all.

Thabang pulled the chair closer and faced her. He had Ben's intensity, though his eyes were a softer shade of brown that she hadn't noticed before. It was like looking at a younger, relaxed Ben. But there was something distinctly different about them. Moya often said Thabang was the spitting image of Rain.

It was crazy how quickly she and Moya had become close. She was like a wise, fun, older sister whose take on life and love was so refreshing. She did not take herself seriously and dove headfirst into life. Life did not scare her one bit, where others crumbled at the first sign of life's valleys.

'Don't give up on him,' said Thabang. 'Allow him time to work through this grief he's been carrying his whole life. You're the best thing that's happened to him because you've opened his eyes to other gifts life has in store for him. He wants to be with you.

'Thabang, I wish I was hearing all this from him and not you or Moya.'

'I know. I know. Give him time.'

'He's not asked me for time. In fact, he's asked me not to wait. I feel for him. I can't imagine everything that he's endured. But I can't be there for him if he doesn't allow me to be there. Besides, I'm moving to Chicago next month.'

His eyes nearly popped out of his skull.

'For good?'

'For six months. I am taking an international assignment at

HQ, and that's why I am in Sandton today. My visa appointment was this morning.'

'I assume he doesn't know?' Thabang asked the question though he knew the answer.

'Your brother and I don't talk.'

'I'm sorry about that Maserati. And congratulations! Young Black South African women doing big things in the world! Man, you're awesome!' Thabang's joy for her was so apparent. The second hug signalled the pride he felt for her.

'Thanks, Thabang.'

There's such truth in the saying, don't judge a book by its cover. Thabang had been delivering surprise after surprise.

'We have to throw you a farewell party before you go.' Party animal Thabang would not miss an opportunity to party.

'Yeah?'

'Oh yeah!'

One of the gentlemen at the corner table was getting impatient.

Thabang glanced towards them. 'Does he not know we don't rush conversations with a lady? Especially one that's your favourite? Maserati, always a pleasure. Think about what I said.'

'Sure,' she said. That will shut him up.

'My brother is a fool.' He landed a soft peck on her cheek and headed back to the clearly irritated men.

Chapter Thirty-Four

M aserati was nervous. Today was a big deal.
  She presented in front of crowds quite often as part of her job. But this was different. She would be standing not only in front of a crowd, but also dignitaries, and giving a speech to honour the founding father of the foundation that had enabled her to attain her medical degree.

It was a big deal.

Her greatest nerves came from knowing Ben was going to be in the audience. She had last seen him four months ago, and didn't know how she would approach him if they encountered each other. She was hoping that the family would be too busy hosting the dignitaries and that she would be able to avoid him. Though some part of her secretly wished for a chance encounter, to see if there was still something there, to see if *he* still had something for her, because she still did. She had a great deal of empathy for his grief, and would have been there for him, had he let her in. Beyond being lovers, she had enjoyed their beautiful friendship, something she had hoped would have sustained their relationship through anything.

The event would also be recorded for the SABC Prime News

show, hosted by the MC for the night, Tom Mogale, whose show attracted millions of viewers.

Her stomach was in knots.

The invitation had landed in her personal inbox three months ago, soon after she got to Chicago.

Dear Dr Mojapelo

The RAIN Foundation:
The Nkosi Family Foundation for the Advancement of Science and Medicine in Africa.

A Journey of A 1000 Milestones
Sandton Convention Centre
Saturday, 11 August; 17h00 - 21h00
RSVP by 1 July

The RAIN Foundation is proud to announce that since inception, it has helped make the dreams of a 1000 young South Africans a reality. The RAIN Foundation alumni includes various professionals across the health sector, who serve South Africa in various capacities and settings.

We are excited to extend an invitation to the RAIN Foundation: **A Journey of A 1000 Milestones.**

In honour of the founding father, Mr Frank Kgosi Nkosi.

Regards,
Thabang Nkosi
Chief Executive: The RAIN Foundation

A week later the email was followed up by a much more personal one extending an invitation to her to be a speaker, representing the first cohort of the RAIN Foundation scholarship recipients. She wasn't sure what to make of that personal invitation; was it Ben's doing or was this just a coincidental invitation? It proved to be the latter, as the Executive Coordinator of Events at RAIN had followed up with a telephone call to discuss the agenda and expectations.

Maserati was a little hesitant to speak on behalf of a large cohort of people, most of whom she did not know. She had stayed connected to a handful of recipients from UCT, including her best friend Tebogo. However, the Executive Coordinator had reassured her that her selection was based on the essay she had submitted when she applied for the scholarship, which made her the standout candidate for the job.

She agreed to speak.

Truthfully, she had always been grateful of that scholarship. Her parents' salaries as public servants would not have stretched as far as affording six years of medical school education at one of the world's most prestigious universities. Fortunately, she had received the scholarship on academic merit. Maserati had been amongst the top matriculants in Limpopo province.

When she told her mother of the invitation, Mrs Mojapelo was over the moon. It was a full circle moment. Maserati hadn't filled her mother in on the Ben connection. It was better this way before she started conspiracy theories about how people are predestined.

The day had finally arrived. It was his birthday too. It was going to be an awkward day.

Thank goodness Tebogo was also going; they would partner up.

'Good luck dear. You will be great,' Mantwa and Khutso texted.

Getting through security was a nightmare. Thank goodness the President hadn't been invited. Amongst his top cabinet ministers on the VVIP list was the Minister of Higher Education, Minister of Basic Education, Minister of Health, and their entourages that included their deputies and Director Generals.

Several of the country's universities and medical schools' top brass were also present.

And the protocol the invitees were about to observe would drive anyone to the looney bin.

After the epic lunch with Moya, she had done a bit of googling on the family. Mr Nkosi senior was a true story of rags to riches. He started from nothing to build a property empire extending as far as Mauritius. And he did so before political connections were the ticket to riches. Besides introducing national policies for the advancement of the previously margin-alised, none of these politicians could claim to have helped him rise to his wealth. This was part of the family's allure – they had never wanted or accepted any under-the-table, brown-envelope deals.

She had witnessed Ben walk away from deals on principle – deals that could have brought him more riches. He would rather walk away than do business with someone who held none of the same passion and vision of bringing innovations and services to help people. Even Thabang, the socialite and party animal, would never cross that principled line.

After finally clearing all the security measures, Maserati and Tebogo found their seats. They had been placed at one of the front tables, the benefit of being on the programme. The place was packed with hundreds of RAIN alumni, plus many other guests. The Nkosi family's table was in the front in the middle section. The other middle section tables were for the rest of the dignitaries. The family was not yet seated.

The former Miss South Africa turned businesswoman, Mrs Peggy Kunene and the SABC Prime News anchor, the charming Tom Mogale were the MCs for the day. Two top South African musicians were billed to perform a couple of favourite hits.

A big deal.

Once the guests were seated, the family walked in a proces-sion to their table. Mr FK Nkosi was just as statuesque as Ben, with similar looks and mannerisms too, judging by their posture and way of walking. Mrs Nkosi looked regal in her classy ensemble. Age had not stolen her beauty. She was the epitome of grace, with the same caramel complexion as Ben.

Thabang and Lethabo were there too, the latter with her Senegalese beau. The younger twins, Leano and Masa, were on either side of their father. Ben looked straight ahead and held the kids' hands. He looked so handsome in his black tuxedo. Maserati was trying not stare, but Tebogo nudged her side with her sharp elbow.

'There is your man,' she whispered.

'Dear, stop!'

Moyahabo did not walk in with the family, but she was seated at same table. The Nkosi table seating arrangements were such that Ben need only look straight ahead, and he could potentially make eye contact with her. Maserati wished she had a different table. It was hard enough being here. She didn't need the extra awkwardness.

The ceremony got underway. There was a prayer opening, followed by a beautiful rendition of the national anthem, sung by a Soweto youth choir. The first dignitary to speak was the Minister of Higher Education. Followed by many others…

'If I hear one more honourable this, honourable that… And can we all agree that the first speaker has already observed protocol for all of us?' Maserati's irritation had more to do with her nerves than the speakers. She knew better than to think that any of these VVIP speakers would give a speech without the prerequisite observation of protocol.

The programme was broken into three parts with starters, main meal, and dessert; each with a musical performance. Maserati's speech was after the main meal. Moyahabo, who had seen her earlier and waved, used the break during starters to come over to her table and greet her warmly.

'Hello Maserati. It's been a long time. When did you get in? How is Chicago? Have you been well? It is so good to see you. When do you go back? We should do coffee before you return.

Are you nervous about your speech? Don't be, you will do fine.'

Maserati hardly had a chance to get a word in.

'Moya. This is my friend, Tebogo. She's also a RAIN alumnus.'

'Nice to meet you Moya.' Tebogo hadn't even finished before Moya ambushed her with a hug.

'I'm a hugger,' she said, with that effervescent laugh.

They were rescued by the resumption of the programme.

'Ladies and gentlemen, we now call onto the stage, Dr Vicky Pillay, of the University of KwaZulu-Natal.'

Maserati could hardly eat; her stomach was in complete knots.

Breathe. Breathe.

She could feel his stare from across the auditorium. She didn't look up; locking eyes with him would only throw her off. And she needed to be steady.

'Breathe. You will be fine. Just imagine everyone naked.' A text with a smile emoji on her phone screen.

From Ben.

She looked up. They locked eyes.

Those brown eyes. Those eyes that had made her feel safe and given her assurance many times. Those brown eyes that had communicated many emotions to her. Those eyes that twinkled every time he laughed at her terrible jokes.

She felt herself get calmer.

'We now welcome on stage, Dr Mojapelo. Dr Mojapelo is an Associate…' She didn't pay attention to Tom reading her short biography. She was already on her feet making her way to the stage. The instructions were to keep it to five minutes. She clutched her written speech firmly as she steadied herself at the podium.

And… action!

She was poised and measured, her voice projecting

eloquently, contrary to the nerves that had nearly swallowed her earlier…

'Ladies and gentlemen, honourable ministers, the honourable Mr and Mrs Nkosi, the Nkosi family, the RAIN Foundation, its board and staff, fellow RAIN recipients, all protocol observed.

'A young girl, six years of age, declared to her grandfather that she will one day be a doctor. This young girl made this declaration with the optimism of every child who carries a living dream within them. She didn't know of the systemic barriers that lay ahead. She worked very hard and was diligent with her academics. After all, children like her are told "With hard work, anything is possible. All of your dreams will come true". And we, the children, believe this.

'But the reality of existing in a country like ours is that systemic educational and economical inequalities slowly kill those dreams. The children realise that they were sold a lie. In the absence of opportunities, hard work doesn't get you to your dreams. Many of these children slowly let go of the dream, surrendering to a bleak future. Others continue to barely hold on to the dream in the face of great adversity. To paraphrase Ms. Oprah Winfrey, our dreams can only come true when our preparation is given an opportunity.

'The RAIN Foundation was the opportunity that the hundreds of recipients in this auditorium needed. A two-hundred-million-rand investment and commitment from a family that had a vision, and empathy for the future of this country.'

Maserati turned boldly to face the government officials' table, and her challenge was clear.

'RAIN fills the gaping hole left by our government – a hole caused by the lack of political will, inadequate commitment, and insufficient funding to address education and economic inequalities. If our government was fully concerned with the future of its children, the RAIN Foundation would not be the blueprint. To our honourable ministers of education here tonight, the future of this country relies on the self-actualisation of its children.'

Loud applause erupted from the audience.

'The RAIN Foundation requires all of us to look within ourselves and ask, "What can *I* do?" Start where you are with what you have.

'To Mr and Mrs Nkosi, on behalf of past, present, and future recipients of your generosity, we thank you for your vision and selflessness. To the RAIN Foundation, Rorišang Aaron Israel Nkosi, and the entire Nkosi family, our gratitude can never equal the gift you have given us and this country.

'May God bless you. May God bless the children of this nation. Thank you.'

Her speech was met with a standing ovation from the floor.

The table with the government officials remained seated. She sensed she had made some enemies.

Tebogo hugged her when she got to her table, and some people were high-fiving her.

She sat down and felt his stare again. She looked up. His face had that familiar look she had seen a million times on her beloved grandfather's face. That of pride. He was proud of her. He was also clenching his jaw. He did that when he was trying to suppress emotions. She wanted to go over and give him a hug. But that would be inappropriate, not only because of the official nature of the event, but because they weren't together anymore.

The main part of the event was the speech by the founding father, Mr Frank Kgosi Nkosi. Ben and his siblings called him FK.

This family and their love of acronyms and nicknames.

FK was ushered onto the stage by a standing ovation. She could tell where Ben got his tone, and assuredness.

'A journey of a thousand milestones is a journey of first steps. It is a journey birthed out of tragedy for the triumphs of many.'

Although the history of the foundation was printed at the

back of the programme, Mr Nkosi gave a brief overview of the start of the foundation and paid a proud tribute to his late son.

'My son, Rorišang Aaron Israel Nkosi, who we all fondly called Rain, was a visionary young man. And this room is filled with a thousand such visionaries and outside this auditorium, many young visionaries fill villages, townships, and suburbs alike. All of them yearning for an opportunity to change their lives and make a difference in this country with knowledge, and innovation. The young professionals being honoured tonight are making a significant contribution not only to the health of our societies, but also to the economy of our country. They work in the public, private and non-governmental sectors. They work locally, regionally, and internationally. They are putting South Africa on the world map with their talents.

The RAIN Foundation has many collaborators and donors to thank for what's been achieved here. But there are many others out there doing more. We salute you all and encourage you to remain committed to the education of the children of this country.

Eh, as the young lady so eloquently challenged you, honourable Mr Mzimba and Mrs Moloi.'

The auditorium broke into laughter again at the jab towards the governmental table.

Unlike Maserati, Mr Nkosi was a seasoned diplomat, and he knew that there was a diplomatic way to challenge the government without alienating them.

He continued once the audience had settled.

'Honourable Mzimba, Honourable Moloi. We are very grateful for the opportunity to partner with your departments and will continue to do so. We know that your departments' pockets run deep, Chiefs. We urge to you to be generous and help create a better future for the disadvantaged children of this nation.

'Finally, let me thank my family, starting with my beautiful wife of forty years and my children and grandchildren. I especially want to acknowledge one of them, my second-born son, Bušang, whom some of you know as Ben. It is his birthday today.'

The crowd clapped and cheered.

'The day chosen for this celebration was intentional because I want to honour him for bringing the idea to start this foundation to his mother and me. Not only did he want to honour his brother, but his own journey at medical school showed him there were a lot of students in need who deserved quality education. No one knew Rori better than Ben did. And he continues to carry his legacy to this day.

'Son, your brother would be very proud of the man you turned out to be. Your mother and I are extremely proud. Please, everyone, join me in wishing him a very happy birthday.'

The musician was on stage singing 'Happy Birthday.' The auditorium joined in.

Ben was clenching his jaw quite hard now. He was blinking away tears. This was a touching tribute from his father. One he had possibly been waiting to hear since he was a boy.

What a beautiful way to end the evening.

The dance floor opened and networking began. The family table was swamped by dignitaries and media trying to get pictures. Ben kept trying to spot her, but there was no getting out of this stampede. Maserati had also hoped for a chance to say hello to him. But it wasn't going to happen.

She and Tebogo decided to leave before the crowds made it out, causing a monumental traffic jam. Plus, Tebogo had promised her brother in Pretoria an overnight visit before she headed back to Mpumalanga the following day.

'Do you miss him?' Tebogo asked, as they headed towards the exit.

Maserati's downcast face beside her was all the answer she needed.

Chapter Thirty-Five

The ground floor of the convention centre was beginning to fill up, thank God they decided to leave before the crowds.

Her phone had been ringing since they left the auditorium. And now it was vibrating aggressively in her bag.

'Hello?'

'Dr Mojapelo.' An eager familiar voice was on the other end of the line.

'This is she. Who is this?'

'Dr Mojapelo, this is Primrose.' Maserati was surprised to hear from the Executive Coordinator of Events again, since the event was officially over.

'Dr Mojapelo, I just realised that there was miscommunication. All speakers have been kindly requested to come to the speaker room for a brief meet and greet with Mr and Mrs Nkosi. A token of appreciation from the family for your presence. Are you still in the building?'

She wanted to lie. But to be the only speaker not to show up would be rude. Plus, her mother would never forgive her for foregoing a chance to meet the famous Nkosis. She didn't know she had already met, very intimately, one member of the family.

'Yes, I am still in the building.'

'Great, I will be waiting for you up here.'

Shit!

Tebogo didn't need to ask as she had overheard the phone call.

'I think you should go, dear. It's not about Ben, it's about the opportunity to meet his parents and thank them in person.'

'And you can't stay, just thirty minutes?'

Tebogo shook her head regretfully. Her brother was waiting.

Maserati knew that her friend would stay if she could. She just had to don her big girl panties and do this. There was a good chance that Ben would not be there.

'But if you do bump into him, tell him how you feel.'

Oh, that ship may have long sailed. As great as their relationship had been, Ben was clear on his commitment to the memory of his brother. He had no room to love others as he had loved Rain.

'Drive safe, dear, and let me know when you get to Pretoria.' They hugged and off they went in opposite directions.

The elevators back to the top floor seemed to move at a rapid speed. She didn't even get a chance to gather some composure.

Primrose approached her with apologies.

'This way,' she said, and led Maserati into the lion's den.

The room felt more informal than the auditorium had earlier in the evening. The whole family was there, Mr and Mrs Nkosi and Thabang talking shop with the government dignitaries, the two MCs posing for pictures with some of the speakers and the RAIN Foundation staff. Lethabo and Amadou were sitting at one of the tables, engrossed in each other, unbothered as usual by all the happenings. There were a few other people she didn't recognise. She scanned the room and didn't see him. Neither were the twins and Moyahabo in the room.

The disappointment was palpable.

'Please accept this small token of thanks for agreeing to be a speaker, Dr Mojapelo,' said Primrose, handing Maserati a goodie bag filled with gifts worth thousands.

'Thank you.' Maserati felt quite awkward as she didn't know the etiquette of approaching Mr and Mrs Nkosi.

'Excuse me, Primrose. I am not sure what I am supposed to do here.'

'As soon as Mr Mzimba and Mrs Moloi finish their discussion, I'll take you over to the Nkosis.'

'You know, it's not necessary. I know they are busy people. I am grateful to have been invited.' Maserati did not want to interrupt important talk.

'Dr Mojapelo, Mr Nkosi asked for you.'

For a minute Maserati was confused as to which Mr Nkosi had asked for her. It couldn't have been the elder one. She was just Maserati, a non-dignitary. But if it was the younger Mr Nkosi, why would he have not just have called her himself? Why go through such confusing formalities?

'I can take you now.' Primrose led her to the elders, ending her confusion.

'Mr and Mrs Nkosi… Dr Mojapelo.'

Suddenly she felt really nervous. This was how it felt to meet people you admire. Nothing prepares you for such moments. She prayed that at the very minimum to not make a fool of herself.

Maserati extended her hand to each parent, and half curtsied, as one does when meeting respectable elders.

'Mr and Mrs Nkosi. Such an honour to meet both of you. Thank you so much to the Foundation for extending the invitation to be part of such a momentous occasion. I am humbled.' *Stop blabbering, Maserati.*

'Young lady.' Mr Nkosi's demeanour seemed a lot softer and friendlier than one would imagine for a magnate like him.

'What a powerful speech you gave there. Heh, I think the two ministers of education are not very happy with you.' His chuckle made him so human.

'It so good to see young women like you command change. The country needs young leaders like yourself. Your parents must be very proud.' Mrs Nkosi sounded exactly like Maserati imagined she would, very queenly-like. She was so beautiful, and her eyes were the same shade of brown as her son's.

'Thank you, Ma.' Maserati felt humbled.

'Maserati…' Thabang, who had been standing next to his parents this whole time, watching her sweat, came in for a hug.

And just then, she felt him before she heard the loud rant from Things 1 and 2.

'Auntie Maserati!' Leano rushed over to give her a hug. Maserati was touched by their enthusiasm. It had been a little while since she'd last seen them.

The elder Nkosis were perplexed by the sudden familiarity. Then it clicked for Mrs Nkosi.

Ah… *that* Maserati!

It was as if the entire group was waiting to see how either Ben or Maserati would make the next move.

'Maserati.' Ben was now standing to her right, just centimetres away. They hadn't been this close since that night he broke her heart into smithereens.

'Ben.' Her eyes slowly moved up to meet his hesitating gaze. She was hoping those eyes would not knock her off her feet, right in front of his parents.

'Powerful speech you gave. I don't think you have any friends over at Education.' He was slick, turning what could have been an emotional embarrassment of monumental proportions into a safe neutral ground.

Everyone laughed.

As reserved as he sometimes seemed, Ben was very close to his mother. She had been his biggest source of comfort after Rori's passing and made sure he didn't feel left out after Thabang and Lethabo were born.

Thabang and Lethabo had hinted to their parents that Ben was seeing someone and seemed happier than he'd been in years. And of course, Things 1 and 2 had mentioned an Auntie Maserati. It wasn't too long before his mother added things up and realised Ben was in love and that it was serious. A month after things ended with them, his mother had noticed the light had left his eyes. After some gentle probing, Ben had reluctantly shared that things were off.

'Ah, Maserati.' Mrs Nkosi smiled at Maserati with a knowing nod. Maserati realised then that she knew about their relationship. She didn't need a mirror to know what colour her cheeks had turned.

Like any good mother who wants the best for their son, Mrs Nkosi went into engineering mode.

'How is America treating you, dear? You are in Chicago, right?'

There was no mistaking that Mrs Nkosi had extensive knowledge of her son's ex. Before Maserati could answer, she quickly added, 'Maserati, dear. It's late and we don't want to keep you too long. But there's still more to discuss. We are hosting some alumni at the house for lunch tomorrow. We would love to have you there. Please come. Ben, will you make sure to share the details with Maserati?'

How does one eloquently decline an ambush like this? She hadn't seen Ben in months, their last conversation was a difficult one and here she was, being invited to lunch with his parents? He better come up with an excuse for why this was a bad idea.

Ben turned into a schoolboy who knows better than to go against their parents' instructions. It was quite endearing to see him, a grown man, who commands auditoriums full of global leaders and stakeholders, squirm like eleven-year-old Leano and Masa.

'Yes, Ma.'

The room was clearing, many people having said their goodbyes. Maserati followed suit and excused herself before things got even more embarrassing.

'Mr and Mrs Nkosi, thank you again. And have a good night.'

She did not miss the meaningful look that Ben's mother fired in his direction.

'I will walk you to your car,' Ben offered.

Or was he coerced?

Chapter Thirty-Six

B en walked her to the car.
In silence.

Never had silence been as loud in the ten minutes it took them to walk there. She stopped herself twenty times from speaking first. There was a lot she wanted, no needed, to say and ask. But he had put the impenetrable brick wall up around himself. If anyone needed to speak first, it was going to have to be him.

They exited the convention centre and crossed the road to get to the parking lot. As they stepped off the pavement, he instinctively took hold of her hand to lead her across the road, as he had done many times before, when things were good. It was his protective nature.

Her baobab. Her refuge.

The danger of being hit by a car was gone as soon as they reached the other side of the road, but he did not let go of her hand. They got to her car, and she quickly found her key. He reached out to the door but did not open it.

He finally broke the silence, but the awkwardness lingered.

'You did good this afternoon.' He was looking directly at her;

his brown eyes not giving anything away. He might as well have looked past her.

'Thank you. And thanks to your family for extending the invite. It was an honour.' She wondered if this was a window for a longer conversation.

Was he warming up?

'Well, ahem, about tomorrow…' Ben spoke or understood the eleven official languages of the country. Today, he spoke a perfect dialect of body language, and it conveyed a clear message of nervousness.

'Don't feel obligated to come.'

'Do you not want me to come?'

'No. I mean… That's not what I am saying. I know things are strained between us. I just didn't want you to feel obligated.'

'I know you probably don't want me there, but I could not turn down Mrs Nkosi's invitation.' The irritation in her voice surprised her. If Ben didn't want her there, he should have made that clear to his mother. Then it was her turn to speak a perfect dialect of silence. She pulled the car door open and got in. It was clear that this conversation had come to an end.

Ben wanted to say something but knew better.

'Have a good night and drive safely. I'll send the details for the driver tomorrow morning.' He closed her car door. As it closed, the little window of possibility in her heart closed as well.

————

Maserati hardly slept that night thinking about the lunch. What does one even wear to a lunch with your almost potential in-laws? She should have declined the invitation. Would it be disrespectful to fake some urgent illness? Before she could conspire further, her phone rang.

'Mama.'

'Rati! Rati! Did you see it?' Her mother was extra jovial. That level of optimism should be illegal on a cranky Sunday morning like this.

'Mama, see what?'

'*The Sunday Times*. You are famous, Rati. The papers are quoting your speech from last night.' Her mother's laugh had some extra oomph this morning. It is that extra laugh that proud parents have.

'You know people were even congratulating Papa and me at church. Our daughter challenged the Minister of Education. Can you believe it? The Reverend wants you to come and speak at the youth seminar next week before you go back to Chicago. Can you do it? I said you would.'

Her mother had become an instant booking agent and manager all in one morning. And her parents were basking under the spotlight. They always knew Maserati was destined for great things.

'Eh, Mahlako…' Her father only called her that in very rare, tender moments between father and daughter. And when he did, it meant he felt extremely proud, or extremely emotional.

It caught her off guard, to hear her father's trembling voice on the other end.

'Eh. The papers say you gave a great speech and have inspired the youth. They are calling you a young leader, a future leader, fearless. We, the Mojapelos are known leaders. You my child, just showed the country who we are. Eh… my child. I am so proud of you. Heh.'

She wished her phone had automatic recording for moments like these. So she could listen to them in those hard moments when she and her father didn't see eye to eye.

Maserati had stopped reading the Sunday papers two years ago. It just seemed that the news had become politicised and journalistic objectivity had become optional. After the call with her parents, she scrolled social media, and her picture was everywhere, including quotes from what they called her 'powerful awe-inspiring speech.'

'You have set Black Twitter alight.' Malebo, her sister texted her. Maserati was not on Twitter. The empath in her was averse to Twitter energy. One moment Twitter reveres you and the next minute it is skinning you alive; knocking you off the pedestal onto which it placed you.

Malebo sent her screenshots of all the tweets about her speech.

'Maserati Mojapelo for President.'

'Maserati should sponsor Maserati.'

'Is she single?'

And the tweets went on. She had no time to be mesmerised by the fleeting admiration from Twitter. She had lunch with real royalty in about four hours. A feat she would happily celebrate if she survived it.

Maserati called the only person who she reckoned knew the inner secrets of this family for tips – Moyahabo.

'Darling!' she answered enthusiastically. 'Have you seen the papers? You are famous.'

'The papers should focus on the goal of that event. I was just a small part of a big movement that should be the highlight of the news. Not me.'

'Darling, your speech was powerful. Don't underplay that. You made an incredible impression.'

'Hmmm.'

'Speaking of impressions, are you ready for this lunch?'

'You are coming right?' Maserati could not believe she was seeking allyship in Moya. Never in a million years would she have guessed she would need Moya like she did today. Moya would bring her jovial lightness to what could potentially be a tense environment.

'Oh no. I am not coming to the lunch, darling.'

'Why not?' The question was asked in shock but also a desperate plea for her to reconsider being there.

'Maserati…' Moya had never called her by name. It was

always darling. So, whatever she was about to say next must be quite serious.

'You know how I feel about you and Ben. I am rooting for both of you to work it out. You belong to one another. I don't want to be a main part in your love story. I am happy to be a small footnote at the bottom of the page or at the back of your storybook.'

Moya had always been consistent about where she stood with Ben. Maserati had come to have huge respect for her and finally understood why Ben had maintained a relationship with her. Not only was she the mother of his children, but they were true friends, and true friendships don't come often. A one-in-a-million God-ordained friendship can be intimidating in a society that would have you believe in innuendos.

'Thank you, Moya. You have always been encouraging. I appreciate your friendship. I know it's probably hard being in the middle, with Ben not talking to me.'

'Ben is working on his issues. Stay open to him.'

'So, I wanted to ask your advice on what I should wear, how to behave, you know…'

'Oh darling, you are always so well dressed. Do me one favour. Just be yourself. It's a quality I love about you and why I loved you for Ben.'

'The Nkosis may be wealthy and powerful, but I promise you, they are very down to earth. Salt of the earth kind of people. No airs. Come as you are, and they will adore you.'

After that call with Moyahabo, Maserati felt somewhat reassured, although her nerves did not go away completely. It was now two hours to go before her debut at the Nkosi's house. She had better start getting ready. One thing she had learned about Ben or the Nkosi drivers, was their punctuality. And right on cue, Ben's text with the driver's details came through. She had hoped he would have changed the plans and come himself.

She chose a mid-calf length pleated green and gold dress she had bought at a small vintage shop in Cape Town. It always went great with a pair of Giuseppe Zanotti strappy heels, but today was not the day for sexy heels. She settled for Manolo kitten heels. Trust Manolo to make you look like a perfectly groomed and demure lady. Moyahabo had said she should be herself. Well, technically while this look was on the more conservative side, the clothes were hers. So, she was being herself. Her make-up was minimal.

The driver was on time. She settled into the back seat and asked him to turn the aircon up to avoid any incidental sweating.

The Nkosis lived in a Sandhurst homestead that was previously featured in a luxury edition of the *Homeowner* magazine as one of the most expensive homes in the country. It was reported that the Nkosis bought the house from the Oppenheimers and it wasn't even on sale. So, it must have taken a pretty penny to convince the Oppenheimers to relinquish this piece of architecture. The grounds were manicured to perfection. The house itself was a grand old masterpiece of architecture, and apparently boasted ten bedrooms. Complementing the house were three guest cottages, which were used as domestic quarters for several of their staff.

The car stopped in the front driveway, adorned with an oasis of roses.

A butler was waiting attentively and led her into the house. Maserati gulped as she stepped into the entrance hall. It was as if Michelangelo himself had been commissioned to paint the ceilings and walls. There was an eclectic mix of rich fabrics, but the house mostly had an African flair without the feel of a lodge in the Kruger National Park.

Ben and Moya had mentioned that Thabang lived at home even though he could afford a place of his own. How did the most eligible and available bachelor in Gauteng manage his lifestyle at home? It would take a brave woman to be intimate with him, knowing his parents were sleeping nearby. Granted the homestead was huge. But still.

The Nkosis had taken care of several of their domestic staff's children including Nathi, Ben's business partner and Primrose, the Executive Coordinator of Events at RAIN, who were among the guests for lunch today. They had raised Nathi and Primrose like their own children and they lived at the house too. So the large house was always full. Ben and Moya's twins spent a considerable amount of time here as well. Their grandparents let them get away with absolutely everything so this was heaven for them.

What do you bring to a lunch hosted by one of the wealthiest families in the country? She made her mother's famous carrot and fruit mince squares. These were always a hit at gatherings. She packaged them beautifully in a glass container. But she was nervous. What if they didn't like them?

'Maserati. Come.' Mrs Nkosi emerged from a grand dining room, in a kaftan, with her arms outstretched. This woman was beautiful! Maserati was drawn more by the familiarity of her welcoming warm brown eyes.

Mrs Nkosi gave her a hug that only a mother can give – one that takes away all anxiety. Maserati handed her the glass container with her baked goodies. She smiled as if Maserati had just handed her a container full of rare gems.

'Thank you, my child. Did you make these yourself?'

'Yes. It's my mother's recipe, and she makes them for every family gathering.'

Mrs Nkosi did not waste time sampling one of the squares.

'Hmmm, these are delicious. Now I absolutely have to meet your mother for the recipe.' Maserati didn't think that was necessary, she could simply share the recipe.

'Come, come in. Everyone is in the other room.'

The other room was a surprisingly cosy family room, with walls adorned with pictures of their children and grandchildren at their various stages of their lives, from childhood to current.

Nathi, Primrose, Thabang, Lethabo, and her beau, Amadou, and the younger twins were there as centre of attraction. They all rushed to her with welcoming hugs. Well, for Lethabo it was more like a stroll. She had never been known to generously dish out affection except for Amadou. The girl could be aloof.

Leano and Masa were all over her, and when they saw that their grandmother had goodies in her hands, they went for them. Soon everyone was reaching out into the glass container for a piece.

'Hmm, oh my gosh, these are good.'

'Maserati made them. It's her mother's recipe.' They were about to clear the container when Mrs Nkosi put a stop to it.

'No, please. Leave some for Papa.' Mr Nkosi was apparently in the upstairs study finalising a call.

Ben was at the far end of the room, in a casual look formalised by a navy Armani blazer. He had a glass of whiskey on the rocks in his hand, watching as his siblings fought like cats and dogs over the treats. He wasn't surprised; he had tasted their goodness one Sunday morning when Maserati had made them for breakfast.

His eyes were different today. They seemed softer; a lot more welcoming than they had been the last few months. Maybe it was being in his parents' home with his childhood splashed across the walls of this room. But Maserati could have sworn she saw a slight twinkle. Her Ben emerged for a split second. And for a split second, a tinge of hope flushed her heart. Her face betrayed her as she responded with a smile. His eyes smiled back as he acknowledged her with a nod.

Just then, Mr Nkosi walked into the family room. His presence was immediate. There was a power and yet gentleness in his silhouette. The kind of power that was in stark contrast to the loud and crass shaky fame of the nouveau riche. It was silent and yet commandeering. Ben had that same powerful presence.

'Dr Mojapelo…' he said, and before Maserati could compose herself, she was enclosed in the warm embrace of Mr Nkosi. She felt awkward and humbled by the respect she was been shown.

'How are you? You made the news this morning. I just got off the phone with Mr Mzimba. The chap is still unhappy with your speech,' Mr Nkosi chuckled.

'Mr Nkosi,' was all Maserati could master as she half curtsied.

'Oh no need for that, my child. In this house, you are free to behave just like these rascals filling this room.'

Thabang's laughter broke the ice. He was indeed the apple of his father's eye, after the younger twins.

Mr Nkosi looked fondly at his wife. 'Mmago Rori tells me you came back from America a week ago for the RAIN event? Are they treating you well over there? You are in Chicago, right? We were there once for business in the middle of winter. Never again will I be caught dead in Chicago in February.'

Maserati was touched by the term of endearment he used for Ben's mother. Mrs Nkosi may have had a big hand in the Nkosi empire, but she was also Mmago Rori; mother of Rori, the first born. Mr Nkosi used the term to convey honour – a sign of his gratitude to his wife who bore him his very first child. A badge of honour rather than a reduction of her identity to her maternal role, a fairly common form of patriarchy.

Maserati found Mr Nkosi quite amusing. Moya was right, Ben's parents were so down to earth.

'So far, so good,' she answered. 'My job has been keeping me busy.'

'Ben says you are heading some technology strategies that plan to expand access to health care. You know it's amazing to see the many advances across all sectors, all thanks to technology. Amazing indeed.'

Ben cleared his throat as if to urge his father not to spill their secret discussions about Maserati.

Mrs Nkosi who had disappeared to the kitchen interrupted the moment.

'Lunch is ready.'

Everyone made their way to the sprawling dining room, with a table filled with scrumptious looking dishes. A butler and maid were waiting in the wings making sure the family had everything they needed.

While the dining room was quite formal and clearly a venue that had hosted many previous important dinners, there was an air of informality that day. They looked like any other family sitting down for a meal, albeit at a dining room table that cost nearly a year's salary for some.

Mrs Nkosi had manipulated the sitting arrangements so that Ben and Maserati were seated across from each other. She avoided eye contact with him as much as possible, but she could feel his presence. Something began to melt inside.

Gather yourself together, girl, she silently chided herself. She would be mortified if she were to embarrass herself in front of him and his parents.

Leano and Masa said a small prayer to bless the food at the urging of their grandmother. Everyone started dishing up as Nathi drew her into conversation.

'Tell us about your parents, Maserati. Your mother and father, where are their people from?'

Maserati began sharing the origins of her parents. She was surprised to see an excitement in Ben's father's eyes when she began speaking about her mother's people.

'Ah the Matjemas!' he exclaimed. 'Mmago Rori, you remember the old man Matjema? A very fine man. A man of the people. The old man built a school, and shops around his village. He was a cabinet member in Ramodike's cabinet. The man was self-taught. Growing up, it was men like that I looked up to. Your mother comes from very fine people, Maserati. Very fine people!'

Her paternal grandfather had clearly been a great influence in Mr Nkosi's life, yet another divine connection that she shared with Ben.

It pleased Maserati to hear such accolades about her grandfather. Her grandfather had been a visionary although he never achieved the level of wealth that the Nkosis managed. Her grandfather had been an innovative and hardworking man. He'd built businesses from the ground up in an arid village to which they were forcibly moved during the apartheid era, and with no formal education, built a school so that *his* children could be educated. The apartheid system had created a ceiling that hung so low that no matter how hard he worked, he could never be greater than the limits the system had set for people like him.

She was so proud that her grandpa had made such a great impact.

She was also touched by how Mr Nkosi had put an emphasis on her coming from fine people. It was as if he was endorsing her. Maybe endorsing her for his son who was sitting across from her, still slightly walled off.

Her heart was so full that she felt the overflow in her eyes. She didn't want to cry but the tears sat on the edge of her lower eyelids threatening to disrupt whatever composure she'd maintained throughout this lunch.

'Please excuse me. I must use the ladies' room.'

As she pushed her chair back, Ben half rose from his seat. Probably out of years of etiquette school rather than a true gentlemanly gesture towards her. The butler led her down the passage to a luxurious guest bathroom the size of a university student's entire flat.

The tears flooded her face in a rush. Her grandparents were the main reason she was where she was today – having many opportunities, giving compelling speeches at conferences, being here in the Nkosi family home. To hear Mr Nkosi praise them touched her in a way she didn't expect.

She called her mom.

'Mama. Just calling to say hello. I was thinking of Grandpa and Grandma today and how forward-thinking they were. Just how amazing. Mr Nkosi knew Grandpa and he's proud that I represented his legacy yesterday. I'm just so moved. I wanted to tell you.'

Her mother was softly sobbing on the other end. She had been a Daddy's Girl in her youth.

When she was done, she carefully powdered her face erasing any remnants of tears. She stepped out, poised and composed. Ben was waiting just to the left of the bathroom, with what looked like concern on his face.

'Is everything okay?' His voice had a softer tone than it had in a while.

'Hmm. Yeah. Everything is okay. What your dad said about my grandfather was unexpected and it just touched me to hear him honour him like that.'

She hadn't meant to spill her guts, but his face genuinely invited her to share.

'I was surprised to learn he knew of your grandparents too. I knew that your grandfather was a great man based on what you'd shared with me. But hearing my dad affirm your description of him... I can see how that would touch you.'

Maserati hadn't expected him to be so kind and understanding of how emotional this could make her. Perhaps Ben was finally letting his guard down and breaking that great wall of China he had fortressed around his heart.

She took a deep breath to stop herself from crying all over again. Some of it was due to seeing Ben's eyes exude that warmness she had come to know and that made her feel safe. He could tell she was holding back tears and did not want to say anything that could make her shed them. He knew how embarrassed she must already feel for being emotional in front of his family. But he wanted to hold her tight and kiss her forehead, as he'd done so many times before. All he could do was reach out and touch her shoulder in reassurance.

'You have every right to feel how you feel. And it's okay.'

'Thank you, Ben,' she said quietly, wiping a lone tear from her face before it summoned her tear glands for a flood more.

He moved forward to embrace her but stopped himself just as he was about to pull her to him. She wanted him to take another step forward. Sensing her consent, he took a step forward, gave her a hug.

Maserati could feel her legs buckle. This embrace had been home just a few months ago.

She quickly pulled herself together.

'We should get back before your mom wonders where I have disappeared to.' She hastily retreated in the direction of the family dining room, putting on a brave face and a smile as she entered the room.

But nothing goes past mothers. Ben's mom noted the hidden emotion. And encouraged her with a knowing nod. She also noted her son's composure and knew the two must have had some conversation.

'Are you alright, my dear?'

'Yes, Ma. Yes, I am fine. What Mr Nkosi said about my grand-parents was very kind and moving.'

'You are clearly their grandchild.'

'Tell us about Chicago.' Thabang was blessed with impec-cable timing to distract from heavy moods.

'Chicago is great. The summertime is beautiful, making up for the horrible long winter.'

'What exactly are you doing in Chicago?' Lethabo asked.

'I took on a short assignment at our headquarters to work on a key project to facilitate and leverage the power of digital exten-sions in bringing healthcare and medicines to those in remote areas in low- and middle-income countries.'

'Sounds fascinating. This is exactly what Ben's company does in Africa. Are there opportunities for your company to work with companies like Ben's that are already doing this in other parts of the world?'

'Absolutely! We recognise that this can only work through business-to-business and public-private partnerships. We plan through an advisory board to engage several key stakeholders, in building and rolling out this strategy.'

'Fascinating. What do you think Ben?' Mr Nkosi was orchestrating an opportunity for the two ex-lovers to engage on something other than their romantic spats.

'I was approached by Maserati's team a few weeks ago with an invitation to the advisory board. Due to the conflict of interest, I've offered an alternative referral. Dr Lamola would be a great addition to the advisory board,' Ben answered.

Maserati had also disclosed the conflict of interest to her managers, so it came as no surprise that Ben had declined the invitation.

Lunch came to a beautiful end, and Maserati needed to give the family space. Plus, she still had to make her way to Limpopo to her parents before she returned to Chicago at the end of the week.

'Mrs Nkosi, thank you so much for the invitation to your wonderful home. I had such an enjoyable time. I'll be sure to let my mother know the regard you hold for my grandparents.'

'It was wonderful to have you here, child. Thank you for honouring Rori, you have a fighting spirit and there are wonderful things we are going to see from you. It's good to know that young girls like Masa here have strong role models like you. In my time girls did not quite take up spaces that you and your generation are. Keep up the good work.'

As she hugged her, she whispered a startling remark.

'Thank you for making my son happy. Don't give up on him.'

Maserati froze for a minute. Mrs Nkosi smiled a knowing smile and winked.

Mothers!

You can't get anything past them.

The butler went to call the driver.

Leano and Masa came over to give her a warm hug.

Chapter Thirty-Seven

'I can take you home.'

Ben's offer surprised and pleased everyone, especially his parents. The statement had an instructive tone, so to the natural response was to comply.

She felt her chest instantly constrict.

Breathe Rati.

This man still had a powerful effect on her. She was a mixture of secret excitement and worry that the ride home could be a great opportunity to reconnect or further evidence of their separateness. The former would be ideal, but she would not let herself raise any false hopes.

The driver had pulled the car up front. A Mercedes S500, the grandeur of which suited Ben. As much as he loved life's luxuries, he still got uncomfortable in embracing their blessed wealth.

He shot the driver an eye that said don't you dare touch that door. He walked to the passenger side and pulled the door for her, looking her in the eye.

'Ma'am.' He flashed a smile. It wasn't really a flash but more like a slight peek of a beautiful Colgate smile.

'Thank you,' she murmured, as she slid onto the plushest

leather seats, feeling ever so first-lady-like. She admired him as he crossed in front of the car to get to the driver's seat.

They could easily fool people into believing they carried Mr and Mrs titles.

Ben masterfully guided the car down the driveway and onto the highway towards Fourways. The silence which lasted all of ten minutes was surprisingly pleasant. They were breathing in each other's air. Corinne Bailey Rae's soft sound was a perfect companion to the silence.

'Thank you for coming. Gracing my parents with your presence. You've left an impressive mark on them.' He wanted to add that 'just like you had on me.'

'Your parents are… amazing.' Was there an adequate adjective in the world to describe just how amazing, accomplished, and humble Mr and Mrs Nkosi were?

And that amid mind-blowing wealth and its trappings, they had managed to raise such grounded human beings? One of whom makes her heart swell.

'It's good to see you, Mmapelo.'

Her heart fibrillated. Her whole body warmed up. She barely stopped herself from hurling her arms around his neck and showering him with kisses. She remained composed, anchored in the custom-made leather seat by the seatbelt.

'It's good to see you, Bušang.'

The sound of his name forming around her lips sent shivers down his whole body. He could do nothing to stop the tenting in his pants. Fourways seemed like a 400km-away destination and not the mere 4km that was left.

He could not get to her house soon enough and carry her upstairs to pour his love into her.

The mood was tangible. No words were needed.

He parked the big car in her driveway, while she fiddled with her bag to find the keys. As soon as they walked through the door, he swooped her up in his arms, leading her upstairs to her large bed. Their breaths and heartbeats were synchronised in their longing for each other. He lay her on the bed and they pulled off the barriers that lay between their skins.

He found her aroused breasts and took a hard nipple into his mouth. As he circled the nipple with his tongue, she let out soft moans. She wrapped her arms around him and caressed his back, feeling the sinewy muscles that were the evidence of many hours spent at the gym. He worked his way to the other breast, while his hand found its way to her navel, and slowly across the south border to a warm flowing welcome. His finger slid in easily to which Maserati responded with an even louder moan, arching her back to allow him further access to her depth. She could not hold it any longer and found his steel rod and led it into her warmth.

'Aahh…' he moaned as he filled her with his throbbing member. She grasped his buttocks, pushing him even further, hungry for his love strokes. He obliged and pumped rhythmically, pumped some more until they both let out a yell of satisfaction.

They lay cuddled up in silence for half an hour. Ben kissed her softly on the forehead. She sensed that he needed to say something and so she relaxed her body into his, hugged him tight to let him know she was willing to hear him out.

The deep sigh preceded what he knew was a long overdue apology.

'Mmapelo… I am sorry for how things ended. For how I handled things.' He paused to see if she had any reaction.

She continued to lie limp and relaxed in his arms, which he took as a sign to continue.

'I didn't realise how much of my loss I hadn't dealt with. I held on to my brother at the expense of my siblings, my children, and you. You came into my life, and for the first time, I felt myself let go. For the first time I felt like I was giving myself permission to breathe, to let go and to look forward to a new paradigm with you. But I was afraid to let go.

'Letting go of Rori would mean betraying his memory. He

has always given me assurance that he's around, but I took those as signs to hold on to him even more. However, I now realise after many hours of therapy that not letting him go is the betrayal. I continue to use him as a crutch, an excuse to not live my life fully. I realise now that I've lived my life out of guilt. Why did God take him, and not me? Rori was a good, brilliant human being in society.

'I carried that burden on my shoulders. I wanted to be good; excellent, and perfect all the time. But no one is and no one can be. I now know that had Rori lived a long life, he would have had shortcomings, like all of us. I have missed out on many things with Thabang and Lethabo because I treated them like they could never measure up to Rori. I've caused them to build up resentment, especially Lethabo, towards someone who they never knew. Instead of meeting them as who they are, I always compared them to him.

'I got into a relationship with Moya as a way to hold on. I don't regret it as she and I created the best gifts in my whole life. But it was unfair to her. She was brave enough to realise this soon enough and was able to move on with life, and honour Rori in other ways. I lived in fear, that I kept buried deep inside, which would bubble to the surface any time my children had minor health scares. Without realising it, I started transferring this fear onto them. They are such adventurous and curious children, just like Rori, just like Thabang and Moya. But I was beginning to stifle that.

'The nail on the coffin was you showing up in my life. For the first time I allowed myself to fall completely in love, to start to fully feel parts of me I had reserved only for Rori. You continued to pour your love into me, and I soon realised that I had not created enough room in my heart for it. I didn't *want* to create the room. What I didn't realise was that the heart is expansive. Memory is expansive. Creating space for you did not mean deleting the space reserved for Rori. It's like energy, I could merely transfer the Rori energy from my heart into my memory cells. But I was a coward. Instead of that I chose to put you at arms' length. I pushed you out of my life. I let you down. I let myself down. Hell, I let Rori down as he would have wanted me to live life fully, to experience love fully and be open to life like he was.

'I am sorry. And I know I don't have the right to ask you to take a risk on me, on someone who flaked the minute he was faced with a hard choice. But if you would have me back, I will spend my days making up for breaking your heart like I did. I missed you so much. And life without you in it has been meaningless. You have impacted me in ways I didn't think possible. Your mere presence and love challenged me to step up to be the man I want to be. The man my brother would be proud of. The man you will be proud of.

'My healing journey is not done, as I continue therapy. It has been a lifesaver. I promise that I will always fail forward. I will always give it a shot and not cower. I will not let fear rule me and how I show up for you. I know right now my promises may not be worth a dime, but I can assure you, I will not cause you pain intentionally. I will be your soft landing. I will be an environment through which you realise all your dreams. I love you Mmapelo. And I am asking for a second chance to show you. I am asking for a lifetime to show you.'

She felt the warm tears against her breasts. They weren't hers.

The first tear drops that hit her bosom carried the sincerity of his apology. Each subsequent teardrop carried gallons of his sincere love for her. Her heart opened and let this flow of love reach its core. How they both thought they could escape this love that was destined, was beyond her.

She cupped her hands around his face, kissed his left eye, followed by his right eye. She kissed his forehead. And hugged him with all her might.

'I love you Bušang Emmanuel Nkosi. With all my heart. With all my being. I forgive you. And I understand. I never want to be apart from you. You and I were destined to cross paths, to heal our past and to grow into a new journey full of endless possibilities.'

In that moment, a lifetime of endless possibilities was right in front of them. With this knowing, Ben was overcome with gratitude and the deep love he had for her, he embraced her tightly as they flowed in and out of each other.

Until Ben released life into her.

They lay there intertwined in a restful sleep.

Chapter Thirty-Eight

Ben had asked her to move in with him after she returned home when her Chicago assignment had come to an end in February.

Her return to Chicago was hard, knowing she would be leaving him behind for five months. And she had not planned to return home until the end of February when her assignment would be coming to end. She wanted to focus on the digital health project and see it to conclusion for a successful launch. She knew this would be a move that would cement her career at Tobbas for a long time. James Gaines had even suggested the possibility of the team receiving one of the highest recognitions in the company: the Chairman's Award. Only a select few teams got this recognition, and the team was working hard to deliver a stellar initiative that would have lasting impact on the global health landscape.

She did not want her missing Ben to distract from her work. Ben was also not looking forward to being away from his love and made plans to visit her every six weeks even if for a week. He did not care about the distance, and it helped that he could afford first class travel comforts, so the repeated trips were not strenuous. But Ben would have endured a journey on a ship in tumultuous sea waters to get to see Maserati.

The man sure loved her.

Ben's regular visits made the months go by quickly. It was beautiful to experience Chicago through his eyes too. Every time he visited, they made it a point to visit some of Chicago's landmarks, museums, theatres, and music scene.

She lived in a high rise building and there was something special about making love to Ben with the city skyline and twinkling lights as their backdrop. It added even more sensuality to their lovemaking. And they could not stop getting it on. She opted to work mostly from home when he visited.

'Baby, you look so hot. There is something about you here in Chicago,' Ben said, every time he returned.

Autumn came with the beautiful change in colour. Trees going from green to yellow and orange hues that just calmed the soul, although the cold did not bring any calm to her bones. Chicago's wintry weather can be a bone-numbing experience. Her colleagues had warned her about the brutal winter months of January and February.

It was right after Halloween at the beginning of November, when she started feeling different. Her Starbucks coffee tasted strange. She blamed it all on the pumpkin spices that are sprinkled in everything at that time of the year. Pumpkin spice everything is synonymous with the fall season. Whoever lied to the Americans about this being a treat must have died a thousand years ago. No matter how many times she asked the barista not to add pumpkin spice, her coffee came back with a really weird taste. She decided not to order anything from Starbucks until after the fall season.

A couple of colleagues had mentioned that the cool Chicago weather agreed with her. She had assumed a dewy glow when everyone's skin seemed to be drying out. She had started using a new serum to keep her skin hydrated through the brutal wind of Chicago, and these compliments just made her happy that the hydration formula was working. Rarely does a skin range do what it claims, so it was great to see this serum work. She would likely continue using the range after the winter.

A week before Thanksgiving she had gone out for dinner with some of her colleagues to celebrate a key milestone to the digital health initiative. Everyone was overjoyed. The project was on time, within budget and they were making headway. There was a buzz already within the company. Achieving this key milestone before the Thanksgiving break was so timely. There was a sense of gratitude all round. James took the team out before everyone dispersed for the Thanksgiving break.

Dinner was at swanky steakhouse right on the riverfront. The city lights reflected by the river provided a beautiful backdrop. Everyone was feeling festive and the drinks were flowing. The recommended red wine was a total flop for her, however everyone seemed to be enjoying it. She hadn't looked at the brand, but it had a nasty metallic aftertaste.

She decided to forego alcohol and had a nice refreshing glass of strawberry lemonade instead.

'What are you using on your face? Because I need the secret recipe.' Claudia, the Marketing Director on the project was the umpteenth person to comment on her complexion. It no longer felt complimentary but an annoying inquisition. The consistency with which people gave her the compliment had also started to raise the question in her mind… What was in that hydrating serum?

'If you had your boyfriend here, I would swear you are pregnant. My sister had such a beautiful glow when she was pregnant with her youngest. I almost fell pregnant just to have her glow.' Claudia shrieked at her joke, unaware of the bombshell she had just dropped on Maserati.

Pregnant? Pregnant!

The odd flavour in her coffee. The mercury undertone in the wine. The glow.

When last was her period?

Damn.

She had not had her period since her return from South Africa. She had been so engrossed in her work, and happy to be flow-free every time Ben visited that she hadn't noticed nor questioned why Aunt Flow had decided to stay away.

Pregnant? Could she be?

Dinner could not end soon enough. On her way back to her apartment she stopped at Walgreens to get three pregnancy tests. The third would be a tiebreaker just in case.

As soon as she walked into her apartment she shot straight to the bathroom.

Pregnancy test one – positive.

Pregnancy test two – positive.

Pregnancy test three – positive.

Oh my word!!!

Joy. Tears. Dance.

She and Ben had created a life together.

She was going to be a mom.

How she wished he were there, right at that moment. Thank God they already had plans for him to visit for Thanksgiving, so he would be there in a few days. She was lucky to secure an appointment with a gynaecologist before the end of the week. And a scan confirmed the twelve weeks plum-sized life growing inside of her.

How timely. What a gift to be thankful for during this Thanksgiving.

Ben arrived a day before Thanksgiving. It had been hard not sharing the news, and she had avoided video calls with him because her face would have been a dead giveaway. She wanted to surprise him in person.

He arrived at the apartment just after 2 pm, exhausted but energised by seeing her. They went straight to her bedroom and reconnected across her king-sized bed. As they lay on the bed naked, he caressed her abdomen, and she wondered if he could feel the life inside. Looking into his eyes took on a whole new meaning. His eyes had always felt like home. And who better to create a home with than with him.

The morning of Thanksgiving, they joined the masses at the annual Macy's Thanksgiving parade on Michigan avenue. It was a beautiful day. He had sensed a joy in her he hadn't felt before but could not figure out what it was. He knew she was happy to see him but didn't realise just how much. This reinforced his commitment to her.

With restaurants either closed for the holiday or those that were open fully booked, she had planned a quiet candle-lit dinner at the apartment. Turkey was too huge for two, so she had ordered a roasted braised duck with spicy greens from her favourite Michelin star restaurant.

She waited until dessert to bring the beautifully wrapped gift.

'What's this?' Ben had not anticipated any gift exchanges and he could have sworn Thanksgiving wasn't a gift-exchanging holiday. Christmas came early.

'Open it. It's a beautiful gift, which could not have better timing than this very moment.'

Ben was curious. And intrigued.

'I didn't get you a gift for today. I didn't realise we were exchanging gifts.'

'Don't worry. Open it.' She tried to maintain her composure.

Ben nervously unwrapped the gift. The stick was the first thing that clumsily fell out. A glossy paper with grey imprint was sticking out from the paper back. He didn't know which to look at first. But when he looked at the stick again, he shot Maserati a very curious and cautious look. He picked it up instantly knowing what it was and the news it was about to deliver. He picked her up before he confirmed.

'Mmapelo… is this what I think it is? Mmapelo…?'

'Yes, yes. But take a look.'

Ben looked at the stick – positive. He pulled out the glossy paper from the gift box. There lay the most beautiful sight – a six-centimetre-long bundle of his hopes and dreams in the copy of the ultrasound scan.

Tears of joy formed and began streaming down his face. Watching him cry made her cry. He embraced her tightly, thankful for this wonderful gift of life that she was carrying – a life created with this woman that he loved like no other.

'Mmapelo... I love you so much.' He got down on his knees and kissed her belly, caressing it like it was the most precious thing in the world. To see Ben in this state fired up her love for him even more. He had grown comfortable with this vulnerability in a way that made him even more sexy.

That night he made love to her, their souls connected by a love so deep, it was inscribed in the stars.

Before he returned to South Africa, Ben had ensured delivery of her favourite things to her apartment. He returned for the Christmas holidays, this time with the biggest surprise.

He brought her parents and Malebo along. Although they had visited Mozambique, Botswana and Swaziland, these countries were unfairly considered extensions of South Africa, and therefore the trip to the USA would be considered their very first international trip.

Her father was proud and spoke of all the American history and monuments he was looking forward to visiting, especially Washington DC and the White House. This would be the biggest bragging right during his monthly gatherings with the other dads in her township. Those poor men would never hear the end of how he, Mojapelo, the son of Ngwato Mojapelo, had been to America and the White House, as if he got a personal invite from the President himself.

Her mother on the other hand, had set her sights on New York. The movies had depicted New York as the most luxurious city next to Paris. Her sister Malebo was hoping to be discovered by some big shot agent in Hollywood, so California was where she dreamed of going. Ben had made all this possible for them, in the three weeks they were there. It was such a glorious time for Maserati. To have the man she loved, carrying his child, and her parents and sister being in town, her world was complete and would be even more perfect when she returned home in just two months.

Ben had been nervous about broaching the subject of Maserati's pregnancy considering they were not married. She on the other hand was not even slightly concerned.

The trip alone was enough to have mellowed her dad. Besides, Ben had demonstrated his commitment to her and had wiped away any ill feeling they may have had for breaking her heart before. They trusted him. And that was a lot to say especially for her father – she and her dad had truly come a long way. He was making strides. And she was seeing him for the human being he was. Mostly she respected his efforts and the open affection he showed her mother. It had taken years before he would apologise outright to her, and his kids. That had meant a lot to Maserati.

In true Ben fashion, he proposed to her one night while lying in bed on the New York leg of the trip. No frills. Just a heartfelt commitment to her, their baby, and the family they were going to build.

'Mmapelo, you make me happy in ways that fail words. It is not a fleeting feeling. It is a joy that is ingrained in my being, in my bones. I know without a shadow of doubt that I am joyful when I am with you. I know that spending my life with you is exactly where I belong. I am not afraid of life. I am not afraid of challenges. Because in you I have reason to keep trying, to keep getting better.

'I am excited for the life we will be bringing into the world, and grateful to have someone like you to nurture the life I already have here. Masa and Leano are my life. They adore you. I know you adore them. And I struck gold with you. You have been nothing but incredible with them. You embrace them and you embrace me with them. I want to spend the rest of my life with you. I want to raise our family with you. I want to change the world with you.

'Mmapelo, can I send my people to your people?'

His brown eyes had an intense hue. It wasn't that he was afraid she would say no, but it was the acknowledgement of the blessing God had bestowed on him. Not many people can say they are lucky to find a true partner. He had been blessed. And he needed this blessing with him forever.

'Bušang Emmanuel Nkosi, I would be honoured. I love you too. And spending the rest of my life with you, creating, growing, and exploring life with you and with our family is a blessing I am happy to embrace wholeheartedly.

'You may send your people to my people.'

The Nkosis made it to the Mojapelos on a warm Saturday in April, a month before the baby's arrival. The whole neighbourhood was abuzz although they had done a good job to keep things on the down low. It was not every day that an eligible Nkosi bachelor came off the market. And thank God for the Nkosi's humility. The news of the gathering had not made it to Joburg's paparazzi. Such sacred meetings should not be sullied by gossipmongering.

Her dad was of course walking on cloud nine. He was the man! Mojapelo oa Bahlelerwa.

Many of their relatives had advised him to ask for ridiculous amounts of money for the lobola.

'The Nkosis are loaded,' they had said.

Her dad knew exactly what this was. A joining of families to bless and provide support for a couple taking on a journey of life partnership. This occasion would not be treated like a lottery win for the Mojapelos.

Her mother had been a subject of a few envious comments from some of the neighbours. 'What did Maserati do to land such a rich husband?'

Needless to say, they didn't make the invitation list and were watching the festivities from over their fences and walls.

Watching her parents interact with Ben's parents was beautiful. Her parents, while in awe of the Nkosis, were not intimidated by their presence. The Nkosis, despite their commanding presence and wealth, had the humility of a lamb. They were people before they were their money. It gave Maserati a warm fuzzy feeling knowing these were the support structures that she and Ben would be relying on as they established and built their own union, and their own family with their three children.

Maatla a Pula Nkosi – Power of the Rain – was born on a clear May day.

Life's opportunities seemed endless.

About the Author

Tshepiso Madihlaba was born and raised in South Africa, where she studied at the University of Cape Town (UCT) and qualified as a medical doctor. She currently works as a medical executive for a multinational pharmaceutical company in Chicago, USA.

Writing has been her passion since childhood and her high school stories – an instant hit with her school mates – were filled with teenage angst and the innocent fantasies of a life yet to be fully lived. Today, she brings a wealth of wisdom and life experience to her writing, and has crafted an engaging read for a contemporary audience.

Maserati is her first published novel.

Find her on:

www.iamtshepiso.com

Email: maseratialwf@gmail.com

———

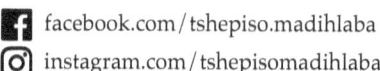

facebook.com/tshepiso.madihlaba
instagram.com/tshepisomadihlaba